Praise

BEL

'Sensual, empowered st

—Pu ers Weekly

'Don't miss a single one of Bella Andre's titles.'
—*Affaire de Coeur* magazine

'Bella Andre writes warm, sexy contemporary romance that always gives me a much needed pick-me-up. Reading one of her books is truly a pleasure.'
—*New York Times* bestselling author Maya Banks

'I am absolutely smitten with Chase, Chloe and the Sullivan family. I can't wait to read the rest of their stories.'
—*Guilty Pleasures Book Reviews* on *The Look of Love*

'*From This Moment On* is full of loveable characters, sizzling chemistry and poignant emotion.'
—Christie Ridgway, *USA TODAY* bestselling author

'If you are looking for something sweet and sexy, the Sullivan series by Bella Andre is absolutely perfect for you. Each novel in the series is unique, just like the siblings. However, there is one thing that all of the novels have in common: they are all amazing!'
—*Reading, Eating and Dreaming* blog

'I can't say how much I love this series without coming across as a gushing, babbling fool. This family rocks my world with awesome men and sisters, but also a closeness that only comes when a family truly cares for each other.'
—*DelightedReader.com*

'Wow… This is something to make us sigh and believe in love.'
—*Mrs Condit's Book Reviews* on *From This Moment On*

'I loved this book and I love this family. I love family series books and this is setting up to be one of the best.'
—*Smitten with Reading* blog on *From This Moment On*

Also by

BELLA ANDRE

The Sullivans

THE LOOK OF LOVE

FROM THIS MOMENT ON

CAN'T HELP FALLING IN LOVE

And coming soon

I ONLY HAVE EYES FOR YOU

IF YOU WERE MINE

BELLA ANDRE

Kissing Under the Mistletoe:
A Sullivan Christmas

Published in Great Britain 2013
Mills & Boon, an imprint of Harlequin (UK) Limited,
Eton House, 18-24 Paradise Road, Richmond, Surrey TW9 1SR

ISBN: 978 0 263 91031 5

28-1013

Harlequin (UK) policy is to use papers that are natural, renewable and recyclable products and made from wood grown in sustainable forests. The logging and manufacturing processes conform to the legal environmental regulations of the country of origin.

Printed and bound by
CPI Group (UK) Ltd, Croydon, CR0 4YY

Dear Reader,

As soon as I started writing about the Sullivan family with *The Look of Love, From This Moment On* and *Can't Help Falling In Love*, emails began to pour in about Mary and Jack Sullivan, parents of the eight Sullivan children who grew up to become the heroes and heroines in my series.

Was Jack as sexy and loving as his sons? Was Mary as feisty and sweet as her daughters? When did they meet? Was it love at first sight? Was their road to romance bumpy or smooth? And could I please tell their love story, too?

I've been asked many, many times about my favourite Sullivan. While I love them all for different reasons, as soon as I started writing *Kissing Under the Mistletoe: A Sullivan Christmas*, I was finally able to make my choice.

Mary and Jack Sullivan's love story is definitely one of my favourites that I've ever written. I hope that you love it, too.

Happy holidays,

Bella Andre

To all the 'Sullifans' around the world—I adore you.

To Sarah MacLean—your awesomeness is unparalleled.

To Mum and Dad—thank you for supporting my dream and helping to make it become an incredible reality.

And to my amazing husband, Paul—every single day you inspire me to write the kind of heroes I can't help but fall in love with. You've always been my forever.

Fall in love with The Sullivans

Prologue

Mary Sullivan looked forward to spending Christmas in Lake Tahoe with her family all year long. After seven decades of Christmas celebrations, she still felt the same wonder and joy for the winter holidays that she had as a child. Outside the large windows of the cozy log cabin on the shores of Lake Tahoe, the clear blue sky was quickly giving way to clouds. The thermometer hanging on the trunk of a nearby pine tree told her the temperature had dropped ten degrees since that morning. Mary had already lit a fire in the commanding rock fireplace that her husband, Jack, had built so many years ago with the help of his brothers.

The first snowfall of winter was always beautiful but,

tonight, sharing it with the people she loved most in the world would make it pure magic.

This year would be a truly special Sullivan Christmas, because her family—eight wonderful kids and their families, who had filled her life with so much love and joy—would be arriving by nightfall.

She couldn't wait to see them all, but before they all arrived and every room of the log cabin would erupt with constant chatter and laughter, she wanted to have a little quiet time with her precious memories.

Moving away from the window, Mary headed for the large storage room in the back of the house. Stepping inside, she spent a few minutes admiring the marks along the inside wall.

From toddlers to full-grown adults, she and Jack had measured each child's growth spurts over the years. How badly Smith and Chase had wanted to catch up to Marcus and when, at sixteen, Smith finally topped his older brother by half an inch you could have heard his bragging for miles. The twins, Sophie and Lori, had thankfully grown at exactly the same rate. Different in many ways, her girls had the most important thing in common: a big heart.

Jack and his brothers had built this log cabin nearly

forty years ago and she felt the love of the entire Sullivan clan on every shelf, every tile, every nail. Taking down the medium-size box from the middle shelf, she carried it back into the living room and placed it on a glossy wooden table near the bare Christmas tree.

Mary had several friends who put up elegant Christmas trees using only red-and-gold ornaments, or silver-and-white decorations. Their trees were holiday showpieces, so carefully put together that even Mary was nervous about knocking off one of the pristine ornaments. She always kept a good distance from these architectural wonders.

No one would ever call the Sullivans' big Christmas tree a showpiece or anything close to elegant, with its jumble of mismatched decorations…but Mary would never change a thing about it, even though her kids were all grown now. Every ornament on her tree had such a beautiful story behind it.

With a smile of anticipation, Mary reached into the box and pulled out a thin, flat, bubble-wrapped package. She carefully undid it to reveal a Popsicle-stick masterpiece. Six wooden sticks had been glued into the shape of a star. At the center of the star was a hand-drawn picture of the growing Sullivan family from more than thirty years ago.

Even as a little boy, family had meant so much to Marcus, her firstborn, who now owned the very successful Sullivan Winery in Napa Valley. Only four years old when he'd made this ornament, he'd drawn Smith as a toddler, dancing for their attention. Chase was crawling off in his diaper to discover a new adventure. Marcus stood between Jack and Mary, grinning as he held their hands. Already, Mary's eyes were slightly damp as she hung Marcus's ornament up on the tree.

The next bubble-wrapped package she chose was the heaviest one, which was how she knew it had to be Smith's. There had never been any doubt in Mary's mind that her second-oldest son had been born to be a star. She'd been applauding him with pride in every play, every musical and every smash hit movie he'd been in for more than three decades.

One day near the holidays when he was six years old, he'd pulled out a small bag of cement from the basement. After mixing it into the perfect consistency, he'd made his handprints in the cement, signing his name with a flourish beneath them.

Almost exactly two decades later, Mary had watched

Smith place his hands in wet cement again...only this time it was for his star on the Hollywood Walk of Fame. Finding an extra-strong branch to hang his cement handprints on, Mary placed Smith's ornament on the tree.

The next ornament came in its very own box, one that was as beautiful as the treasure it protected inside. When Chase, her third-oldest son, was eight years old, his third-grade teacher had sent a note home asking the kids to bring in family pictures for an art project. Rather than pulling photos from the albums Mary had put together over the years, Chase took the pictures himself, using the camera Jack had given him for his seventh birthday. Already, her talented son had been on his way to becoming a world-renowned photographer.

On the last day of school before Christmas break, he'd come home with this wonderful box, covered in a collage of the family photos he'd taken. In one photo, Marcus was swinging his youngest brother, Gabe, around in a circle as both boys laughed together. In another, Ryan was a blur as he ran after a ball. Zach was captured setting up a complicated toy race-car track in the basement and there was a shot of Smith as the star in a school play. In the photo beside that one, Mary and Jack were sitting side by side on the couch, each of them holding a baby girl. Chase had taken a picture of himself, too, in front of the mirror, half of his face covered by the large black camera.

Inside the box was a round plastic ornament with one big picture of the whole family together glued around it. A few years later, one of the kids got hold of the ornament and, with a black felt-tip pen, had drawn mustaches over everyone. Somehow, Mary thought with a grin as she hung it on the tree, she liked it even better with the funny faces.

After putting Chase's collaged box on the mantel for everyone to admire when they arrived later that evening, Mary dug back into the box of Christmas ornaments. When she drew out a long, thin ornament, her grin grew even wider.

Ryan, one of her two middle sons, had always been busy with constantly revolving seasons of soccer, basketball, baseball and football. Mary remembered realizing she wasn't going to get an ornament out of him unless she specifically asked him to make one. By then he was nine years old and believed he was too old to make Christmas ornaments, especially since his little twin sisters loved any excuse to be covered in glitter from their forays into Christmas ornament making.

More than one Christmas party guest over the years had been confused as to why Mary had hung a stick on her tree…at least until she told them to take a closer look.

Yes, the ornament he'd agreed to make was a stick. But it wasn't just any old stick. At her request, Ryan had walked out into their backyard, kicking a rock with each step, grumbling to himself since he would have much rather been in the park across the street kicking a soccer ball with his brothers. Mary surreptitiously watched him from the kitchen window, and when he stopped beneath the big oak tree and picked up the stick to bring inside along with a few pine needles, she wondered what he planned to do with it.

Ryan chose a pen from among the girls' coloring stash in the family room and, with his usual easy grace that extended from sports to everything else he did, he began to draw on the branch. When he was done making his illustrations, he stuck several pine needles into holes on either side of the stick.

A few minutes later Ryan walked back into the kitchen, where Mary was peeling potatoes for dinner, and showed her what he'd made. The reindeer was rather primitive looking, but it was unique. And fun. Just like her easy-going son. Most people never saw beyond Ryan's athletic talents, but Mary had always known he was bright and funny and quite artistic, as well. Now, as a grown man, he brought all of that to his career as a major-league baseball pitcher.

After making sure she hung his reindeer so that it wouldn't blend in with the rest of the branches on the tree, Mary reached back into the box and drew out the next ornament.

Her other middle son, Zach, had always been a practical joker. From birth he'd been such a shockingly beautiful boy that he could get away with anything simply by smiling. He had all the girls in his class under his spell, his teachers wound around his little finger and the other boys clamoring to be his friend. Now he ran a chain of auto repair shops throughout California and raced cars in his spare time.

One Christmas, Mary had just finished making a large tray of gingerbread cookies and had left them on the counter to go and help bandage one of the little ones who had fallen off their tricycle in the backyard. That was when one of the kids sneaked into the kitchen and took a bite out of each cookie.

How could she do anything but laugh when she returned to the kitchen? None of the kids would fess up to the Christmas crime but, come Christmas Eve, when Zach announced he had one more ornament for the tree, lo and behold, it was one of the gingerbread men with a bite taken out of him. Zach had coated the cookie in a thick layer of rubber cement so it wouldn't fall apart and had pushed a paper clip through the center of its forehead to use as a makeshift hanger.

Life with her kids had never been dull, that was for sure, she thought with a chuckle as she hung the fun ornament up on the tree. And she wouldn't have traded a minute of those crazy years when they were all together in the ranch house in Palo Alto for anything in the world.

The next set of ornaments was also in its very own box and Mary made sure to pull each one out with extreme care. Her youngest son, Gabe, had always been intrigued by fire, so it was fitting that he'd become a firefighter. He'd barely been four when Jack brought home a little Bunsen burner and suggested they try to blow some glass ornaments by hand. Mary had loved the way Jack had explained the history of the first-ever Christmas ornaments to the kids, explaining they had been made just like this.

Mary remembered the two of them, standing side by

side, focused intently on the job at hand. She recalled how Jack took absolute care to make sure his son didn't get hurt, just as he always had with all of his children and her, as well.

The resulting small glass ornaments were lopsided and imperfect...and utterly precious to her as she hung them up on the tree now and every year.

When Mary returned to the box and pulled out a large ball wrapped in pink paper that rattled in her hands, she knew exactly whose this was. Lori—aka "Naughty"—was one of her twin girls. Mary and Jack had already had six boys, who were more than enough to keep them busy from sunup to sundown, but that didn't stop both of them from longing for a girl.

She stopped unwrapping the ornament as she thought about that Saturday morning so long ago when Jack had realized Mary was pregnant again. The house was still quiet—an amazing and rare feat with so many rowdy kids. Jack woke her with his sinfully sweet lovemaking, and, oh, how she'd loved those sleepy moments in his arms, when pleasure would drift over and through her in gentle waves.

She had almost fallen asleep again in his arms when she heard Gabe call out from his bedroom down the hall. Only two years old, he was the earliest riser in the house, especially when he was hungry. And as a little firefighter in training, he was *always* hungry.

She was just climbing out of bed when Jack stopped her with a gentle arm around her waist. His dark eyes were full of so much love it stopped her breath.

"You're pregnant."

She had been so busy with her six boys that she suddenly realized she'd missed the signs this time around. Now she could see that her breasts were fuller, her waist slightly thicker.

Jack splayed his hands over her belly. "You've always glowed during pregnancy, but this time you're more beautiful than ever." He drew her close and whispered against her lips, with utter certainty, "We're finally going to have a girl." It was crazy, but she swore she felt it, too—the slightly different energy inside of her compared to the six boys she'd carried.

But there were more miracles to come when they found out they were having twins! And what lucky little girls Lori and Sophie were to have six older brothers to protect and care for them.

A gust of wind through the trees outside the cabin brought Mary back to the present. Realizing she was still holding Lori's wrapped ornament in her hands, she laughed with delight when she finished opening it.

Dozens of plastic goggle eyes stared out at her from the round ball. Only Lori would think to glue moving eyeballs all over an ornament. As a professional dancer and choreographer, Lori was always in motion—but, at the same time, she didn't miss a thing. More often than not, she was the one moving from one sibling to the other giving expert advice. Neither her twin sister nor her older brothers escaped her notice. Her intuitive comments were always delivered in her typically sassy way, of course.

Mary hung Lori's ornament on the tree, then moved back to the box to take out a small, white felt bag. Sophie—aka "Nice," as Chase had christened her so many years ago—had quite possibly put the most thought into her ornaments. Sophie was now a librarian, but even as a small child she'd tend to think things over for a long time before taking action. She was quiet enough that people sometimes made the mistake of discounting her. But Mary never had. Sophie was incredibly sweet, extremely wise, and she'd always had a gentle patience that Mary still worked hard to attain most days.

She remembered the day Sophie had asked to be taken

to the local sewing shop, right before Christmas. Mary had tried to teach all of her kids to sew, but the only two who had any interest in needles and thread had been Smith and Lori, probably because they were always putting together costumes for plays, musicals and dance recitals. Of all her kids, Sophie had had the least interest in sewing, so when Sophie made her request Mary wondered if her daughter could have had a sudden change of heart.

The minute they walked into the store, Sophie made a beeline for the button drawers. One by one, she carefully studied the buttons before making her choices.

Mary loved to sit back and watch her children's minds work. They never ceased to surprise and delight her. Keeping an eye on her daughter as she chose new fabric for bedroom curtains, Mary watched Sophie take her pile of buttons to the counter to pay. When the woman at the register asked what they were for, Sophie told her, "They're a Christmas surprise for my family."

Mary nearly laughed out loud at the confusion on the woman's face. Clearly, the woman believed Sophie would be giving out buttons for Christmas presents. Mary couldn't wait to discover Sophie's plans.

When they returned home, Sophie disappeared into

her bedroom with her bag of buttons and Mary's sewing kit. For the rest of the day, Mary was so busy baking treats and wrapping presents in preparation for Christmas Eve that she was surprised when Sophie stood up after dinner and announced, "I've made a special Christmas ornament for everyone in the family."

Reaching into a little bag she'd made out of white felt to hold the buttons, Sophie walked slowly around the table and placed one button on a string in each of her siblings' hands.

Marcus was the first to hold his up. The large black button with flecks from all the colors of the rainbow swung from a dark string Sophie had threaded through one of the holes. Smith's button ornament was a bright red and silver that caught the eye at every angle. Chase's was a simple yet masculine navy blue. Ryan grinned at the way his button had been painted to look like a baseball. Zach's button was sleek black, like one of the race cars he dreamed of driving. Gabe's button had flames etched onto the front of it. Lori's was the flashiest of all, covered in sparkles and glitter. The button Sophie had chosen for herself was a rectangle that looked like a miniature hardcover book.

"What a fantastic surprise," Mary said as she marveled at the way Sophie had managed to brilliantly capture each of her siblings' personalities with buttons, of all things. Each of the kids agreed as they headed over to the tree to hang up the ornaments.

Sophie slid onto Mary's lap. "This one's for you, Mommy."

Sophie had placed a heart-shaped button in Mary's palm. Her eyes were already full when Sophie took one more button out of the bag.

"I made one for Daddy, too." This final button was covered in brown corduroy and was warm and solid in Mary's hand. "Do you think he'd like it?"

Mary hadn't been able to prevent two tears from spilling down her cheeks. "He would have *loved* it."

As a burst of wind shook the tall pines outside the log cabin and Mary came back to the present, she realized she was standing in the middle of the living room holding the felt bag against her chest, over her heart. Moving back over to the tree, she carefully hung each of the buttons in a group on the thick green branches, then placed the bag back into the box.

Only two ornaments were left—the first ones that Mary and Jack had ever given each other as a young married couple. She lifted them out and went to sit in the chair by the fire. After unwrapping them carefully, she placed them side by side on her lap and ran her fingers over the familiar contours.

And as Mary closed her eyes to savor her memories of falling in love with Jack Sullivan, the first snowflakes of winter began to fall. . . .

One

Early December, nearly forty years ago…

Jack Sullivan needed a Christmas miracle.

"There's no question that the Pocket Planner is a great and cutting-edge product. That's why we agreed to manufacture thousands of units in anticipation of big Christmas orders," Allen Walter explained. The distinguished gray-haired man who had founded Walter Industries held Jack's invention in his hand. "Unfortunately," Allen said as he put it on the table and slid it a couple of inches away, "our sales reps have all reported in to let us know that their accounts are far more interested in ordering toys like the Pet Rock and posters of sex symbols such as Jacqueline Bisset for the holiday sales rush. My company has already lost a great deal of money on several great products this year. What we need to sell this Christmas is a sure thing, so we're going to have to cut our losses now. I'm afraid this is the end of the road for the Pocket Planner."

Ten years ago, Jack had just begun the PhD program in electrical engineering at Stanford University when he'd woken up in the middle of the night with a crystal clear vision of a portable electronic device that would help people keep track of their appointments and to-do lists. His colleagues had thought he was crazy at first, but he'd held on to that vision with unwavering focus. By the time he graduated with his doctorate, three of his fellow PhD candidates had joined his quest to develop the Pocket Planner.

In classic Silicon Valley style, Jack, Howie Miller, Larry Buelton and James Sperring had left the campus labs and set up shop in the garage of a house Jack was renting on a suburban Palo Alto street. James married a year later and left the group to take a steady job with a paycheck. But Larry and Howard had stuck with Jack through hundreds of cold slices of pizza and cups of coffee while they sweated it out over their computers and calculators. They'd had plenty of failures and had made endless mistakes over the years, but there'd been enough success—along with part-time engineering jobs to keep the bills paid—to continue moving forward with their plan.

This morning, when the three of them had put on suits and ties to come to this meeting with Allen Walter, they'd assumed he had great news to share with them about how things were shaping up for their big holiday product launch. Walter Industries had been one of the early investors in Hewlett-Packard and, as far as Jack was concerned, they were the only partner he would have trusted with his baby. It had been a thrill when Allen's company had signed on earlier in the year to manufacture and distribute the Pocket Planner to retailers this Christmas.

Jack had worked too long and hard to let Allen and Walter Industries pull the plug. Even if several other new products had underperformed this year, he knew his wouldn't. Fortunately, he'd done extensive research and he knew exactly what had underperformed and why.

"The Factomatic doesn't appeal to a broad enough market," Jack said. "And the Playerphone is too similar to the Stylophone. But our Pocket Planner isn't just a gadget for men to get their tech fix with. Women will love using it, too, because it will make their busy lives easier. Even kids can use it to keep track of homework and after-school games." Jack remembered how busy his mother had been raising four boys while putting in part-time hours at the school district office. She would have loved having his invention at her disposal to keep track of household purchases and school schedules. His father would have used it to track his favorite sports teams and investments.

"I don't doubt that you're right, Jack," Allen agreed. "The problem isn't whether or not people will enjoy using your invention. I'm sure they would. The issue is getting the retailers to stock it in the first place. Between rising inflation and slowing economic growth, we're finding it more and more difficult to get stores to give a new product a chance. They truly have to believe that people will want to part with their hard-earned dollars to buy it."

Jack could see his partners, Larry and Howie, deflating more and more with every word out of the chairman's mouth. But it would take a heck of a lot more than a couple of lukewarm sentences to make a Sullivan give up.

"We appreciate your concerns, Allen, and would like to come back in twenty-four hours with a marketing and publicity plan that will convince you that our invention can be extremely profitable for your retailers."

Howie shot Jack a look that he could read without needing to hear him speak aloud: *Why are you volunteering to come up with a marketing plan? We're engineers, not PR people.*

Larry's expression was even easier to read: *it's over.*

Allen shook his head. "I admire the work you've put into this, Jack, but times have changed—too fast, if you ask me. People aren't interested in wholesome or helpful anymore." He picked up the Pocket Planner again. "Tell you what—if you can figure out a way to give this device sex appeal we may be able to continue the conversation."

Jack could have easily proved its usefulness. And he could have definitely detailed its time-saving benefits.

But sex appeal?

Even Jack knew when he was staring straight into a dead end.

Still, he'd bought them twenty-four hours. Now it was time to use those hours to make absolutely sure he and his two partners came up with something big enough, reassuring enough, and "sexy" enough, that the retailers couldn't say no.

Careful not to let his doubts show, Jack stood up to

shake hands with Allen and the other board members. Then the clock began to tick.

In silence Jack and his two partners took the elevator down from the twentieth floor to the lobby. None of them said a word until they'd stepped out of the large glass doors and onto the sidewalk. Ten in the morning was a busy time of day in San Francisco's Financial District and they had to speak loudly to be heard over the noise of the traffic and the suited businessmen and women rushing around them.

"How are we supposed to give the Pocket Planner sex appeal?" Howie asked, clearly frustrated.

"If we could have gotten it out two years ago, before the economy started to tank, the retailers would have taken it on without blinking." Larry's mouth was turned down at the corners as he spoke. He was a genius, but more than once he'd reminded Jack of Eeyore, the morose donkey from the children's books his mother had read to him when he was a young boy. "But now? It will take a miracle to convince them to stock it."

Howie was the realist. Larry was the pessimist. And Jack was the energy that kept their inventive and brilliant motors running, no matter what.

"The three of us are going to grab a cup of coffee and start brainstorming."

They'd been planning to pop open champagne right now, not down more java. Jack pushed the thought away to focus on the problem at hand: making their device "sexy," not only for men, but for women, too.

Of all the problems Jack had faced over the past decade, worrying about sex hadn't been one of them. He had a great appreciation for women. He liked to watch them move, liked to feel them soft and warm beneath him and enjoyed the way their minds worked. And yet, just as eating and sleeping had always played second fiddle to his work, so had women and sex.

Larry sighed as they got off the trolley and rounded the corner into Union Square, which was fully decorated with lights in every store window and huge green wreaths hung from the lampposts. "If we can't convince the retailers to carry our product this Christmas, we'll officially be out of money. And I'm getting too old to keep living on the edge of completely broke like this, guys."

Howie gestured toward the center of Union Square, where there was a portable trailer on the corner. Several large lighting rigs had been set up around the area to shine down on the snow that had been brought in for the scene. Flakes of fresh snow fell from another rig positioned above the brightly lit stage.

"Imagine having the funds to put something like this together to sell our invention."

Their usual coffee place was just ahead but, instead of heading inside, Jack detoured toward the crosswalk.

"Where are you going?" Howie asked.

"To take a closer look."

Larry was right. They'd need a miracle in the next twenty-four hours to keep their dream alive. Jack knew it wouldn't be the end of the world if they didn't make this deal. He'd easily be able to get a job working for one of the high-tech companies in Silicon Valley. But he'd never wanted to work for anyone else. And just as this snowy scene in the middle of San Francisco had been some director's impossible vision, Jack wanted to see his own impossible vision come to life, too.

A sixth sense had him moving quickly toward the Union Square set. He didn't know exactly what he was going to learn by watching the filming of a movie or commercial. It was just that today he needed to witness fantasy become reality.

Turning up the collars of their suit jackets, and shoving

their hands deep into their pockets to try to keep warm against the strong Bay breeze that whipped between the tall buildings, the three men crossed at a busy corner. They had just stepped up onto the sidewalk when the door to the trailer opened.

And the most beautiful woman in the world stepped out.

Jack stopped so suddenly that Howie and Larry both barreled hard into his back and a car rounding the corner nearly knocked them down.

Glossy, straight dark brown hair moved over shoulders covered in red velvet. Soft fabric clung to a perfect hourglass figure and swirled seductively around an incredible pair of legs, made even sleeker by extremely high heels. Long, elegant fingers were painted red to match the dress and the full lips that were curving up into a smile.

The woman on the Union Square set wasn't only the most beautiful woman Jack had ever seen, she was also the most vibrant. As she took her place on set beneath the lights the photographer began taking pictures of her. Though Jack didn't know what it was she was selling, he wanted it anyway.

And *her*.

He wanted her, too.

"My girlfriend is never going to believe it when I tell her I saw Mary Ferrer live and in the flesh." Howie's expression was starstruck.

Larry's eyebrows went up. "You know her name?"

"She's on the covers of a bunch of magazines Layla has lying around in the living room. Hard to believe it, but Mary Ferrer is actually better looking in person."

Men, women and kids of all ages stopped what they were doing in the middle of downtown San Francisco to watch the beautiful model pose for pictures. As she smiled, flirted and laughed for the camera, she was sexy without being too sexy, sweet without being too sweet.

A little girl broke free from her mother's hand and barreled onto the set with a squeal of joy. The model scooped the girl up into her arms with a laugh and the two of them chatted cheerfully until her mother rushed up to take her daughter back. Jack couldn't hear what they were saying, but he could see that Mary was waving away the woman's apologies without a second thought.

That was when something inside Jack's chest twisted tight…and he immediately knew why.

"She's the answer to our problems."

But what he felt when he looked at the beautiful stranger didn't just come from thinking she could be the perfect spokesperson for their invention. Jack was a scientist who believed in what he could prove with numbers and calculations and wires and chips hooked together. At the same time, he'd been following a dream long enough to understand that passion lay beneath it all.

Suddenly he had to ask himself, was love at first sight actually possible?

Larry and Howie had turned to stare at him as if he'd lost his mind. "How on earth could that gorgeous creature have anything to do with our problems?"

"Our device needs sex appeal. She's got plenty of that. But we also need someone to represent it who will appeal to the broadest possible market." He could see it all so clearly, just as clear as his first vision had been ten years ago. They would need both still shots and live commercials of her holding the Pocket Planner. Because people wouldn't be able to take their eyes off her, they also wouldn't miss the product she was selling. He gestured at the large crowd of men and women, boys and girls of all ages. "Everyone is clearly mesmerized. Even two-year-olds can't resist her."

"Okay," Howie said slowly, "you're making some good points. But how are you going to convince Mary Ferrer to work with us? Especially since she has to be one of the most expensive models in the world and our budget at this point barely covers our coffee."

"Don't worry," Jack said. "I'll convince her."

Howie and Larry looked at each other with raised eyebrows, but neither of them expressed another doubt. Both of them knew that when Jack Sullivan decided to make something happen, it always did.

Two

Mary Ferrer could hardly believe this was her final photo shoot.

During a brief break when Gerry, the photographer, changed film and the hairstylist touched up her hair, she looked around at the set that had been created in Union Square for the shoot.

How many bright lights had she sat beneath in the past thirteen years? How many makeup artists and stylists had she worked with? How many high-fashion looks had she sold? How many beautiful pairs of shoes had she worn that had felt as if she'd been walking on nails? How many big cities had she flown to for fashion shows then departed from as soon as the curtain fell so that she could get to her next booking on time?

Though Mary never took her good fortune for granted, the truth was that she'd started to lose interest in all those fabulous trappings somewhere in her mid-twenties. She had been discovered at nineteen by a very well-dressed young modeling scout who had passed through Mary's small village looking for a cup of coffee while he was on vacation in Italy. The man had given Mary his card and had begged her to let him represent her as a model. She'd reached out for her big chance with both hands.

All her childhood friends had been either married or engaged by eighteen. Just like the other women in her village, Mary knew her girlfriends would have a handful of children by their mid-twenties…and they would stay in the same place their whole lives.

But Mary had always dreamed of more.

Of bigger.

And better.

She had always wanted to travel the world, had been filled with a deep need to see what else was out there. She'd read everything she could get her hands on in the library about other countries, from compelling travel journals to somewhat dry atlases. She'd also made sure to learn English so well that she could read it fluently by the time she'd graduated from school. Alone in her bedroom as a child, she would read her English language books out loud and try to mimic the tones of the actresses starring in the subtitled American movies at the theater in Rome.

Unfortunately, all Mary's mother had wanted was for her to settle down with a nice man who was up to the job of "taming" her wild urges and giving her babies. If Mary closed her eyes and blocked out the sounds and activity around her, she could still remember their final conversation as if it had happened yesterday.

"I will not allow you to leave," Lucia Ferrer had declared.

But Mary had not only inherited her mother's dark hair, flashing blue eyes and olive complexion, she'd inherited her stubbornness, as well.

"This is my chance to finally get out of this small town," she'd retorted in rapid-fire Italian. The two of them were so similar that the years since Mary had hit adolescence had been fraught with tension. Her father had done his best to try to smooth things out between mother and daughter, and she could see the alarm in his eyes at their exchange.

"That man you met at the coffee shop wants to take you to New York so that you can bare your skin to strangers in flashy clothes after they've painted your face with makeup like a tramp."

Terribly frustrated with the way her mother was automatically assuming the worst—and the fact that she wasn't giving Mary any credit at all for knowing right from wrong—she explained again. "Randy is a scout who works with a very successful agency. He says he can get me work as a model with famous designers in Paris and London and New York City." Lifting her chin, she declared, "There's nothing you can say or do that will stop me from going."

But her mother refused to see things Mary's way. "If you leave today, don't bother ever coming back. You will no longer be my daughter."

In that moment, one she'd never forget, Mary had let her mother's absolute refusal to see reason—and her own flaring temper—push her all the way out the door and away from their small country village.

But Mary had never believed her mother would stand by her threat.

She'd been wrong.

As Mary opened her eyes, she was glad of the chance to focus on the lights and excitement of downtown San Francisco at Christmastime rather than giving in to the gnawing pain in her heart that had grown bigger and bigger over the years that she'd been estranged from her parents.

But though she dearly wished she and her mother could have seen eye to eye over her career opportunities, Mary couldn't imagine giving up the experiences she'd had all over the world or having had the chance to work with so many talented and passionate people. The past thirteen years had been exciting, lucrative and challenging. Despite the long hours and working in conditions like today, when the winter wind blew straight through the thin velvet of her dress and chilled her from the inside out, she would never complain about her career.

Gerry, one of her favorite photographers, moved to where she was standing at the side of the set with an apologetic smile on his face. "Sorry for the delay, Mary. I know it's cold out here. Are you ready to get started again so we can finish up and then go get warm?"

Shaking off her thoughts of the past, she smiled back at him. "Absolutely."

But instead of picking up where they'd left off, he put his hand on her arm. "I still can't believe this is the last time I'll get to photograph you. Please tell me you've changed your mind."

Mary would have hugged him if it didn't mean sending all of the stylists into a panic and losing another fifteen minutes to more touch-ups to her hair and makeup and clothes.

She'd had an amazing career, and was still in high demand around the world for both print campaigns and runway shows, but after seeing what happened to models when they kept working past their prime, and how bitter they became when they were inevitably passed over for younger women, she'd made the decision to step into the next phase of her life.

"I've loved working with you, Gerry. Hopefully we'll work together again in a different way in the future."

"Have you decided what you're going to do next?"

As soon as she'd announced her retirement from modeling, Mary had been offered plenty of opportunities to consider: fashion editor for a major magazine, working with Randy at the agency, taking on an advisory role for a makeup company. As a teenager, she'd known becoming a fashion model was exactly the right choice. Now, after thirteen nonstop years, she knew she needed to take as much time as necessary to think through her next steps. And she would start by settling into the beautiful attached house she had rented last month on Nob Hill, just a few blocks from Union Square.

"As soon as I decide," she promised her friend, "you'll be one of the first to hear."

As she moved back onto the set, she turned her gaze to the side and saw an extremely handsome man who was watching the shoot. He was wearing a suit, but his dark hair was a little too long and his five-o'clock shadow looked as if it hadn't been touched for half a week, at least. His eyes were interested, like those of so many others. But something about the way he was looking at her was slightly different…as if he was looking deeper than men usually did.

Oh, my.

Mary had worked with the best-looking men in the world, but none of them had ever made her feel this shock of attraction. Especially not with just one look.

The suit, frankly, looked all wrong on him. And not just because it needed better quality fabric in the hands of a top-notch tailor. Something told her that well-worn jeans and a favorite long-sleeved shirt would have accented the man's rugged sensuality much better.

"That's perfect, Mary," Gerry called out to her. "Your

look of longing is exactly right. Hold steady with it while I get some shots from the other side."

She'd been so lost in the beautiful stranger's eyes that she hadn't realized Gerry had started shooting again.

It wasn't like her to be caught off guard while working. She was known for her focus and stamina. And, sometimes, if people were being disrespectful to her or the crew on a shoot, her Italian temper would be revealed. Since she always gave her best, she didn't think it was too much to ask others to do the same.

Longing. That was what Gerry called this feeling inside her chest. And perhaps he was right.

Mary had been a virgin when she left Italy at nineteen and, with her mother's voice continuing to ring loudly in the back of her head, she'd been careful not to let anyone take advantage of her innocence, either personally or professionally. At twenty-one, she'd truly believed she was in love with her first lover and that he felt the same about her. Too late, she'd realized he was simply in love with her glossy image. He was always gone before the morning light brought bed head and morning breath. Then, when she'd been hit with an awful flu and he wouldn't come anywhere near her, she'd had to finally accept the truth that he only appreciated her when she was the "perfect" version of Mary Ferrer.

She'd been more careful with her next boyfriend, and the one after that. She'd made certain they had plenty of occasions to see the real her. And yet, as each relationship progressed and then eventually fizzled, she couldn't help but feel that they had all expected so much more from her than from other women. She wondered if she would ever be able to live up to the idealized image men had of her from all her magazine and newspaper photos.

But it was her last relationship that had taught her the most. Romain Bollinger owned the finest watch company in the world. She had been hired to promote his important new line of Swiss watches, and though she'd always been careful not to mix business with pleasure, he was persistent—and charming—enough that she became his lover, as well. However, when the admen decided the next phase of advertising for the ultra-important brand would be better served in the future by a woman ten years Mary's junior, Romain agreed with them by replacing Mary not only in his ads...but in his bed, as well.

That was when she learned that he had wanted her not for herself, but for her value to his company, both in his campaign and on his arm at parties. When her value disappeared, so did any pretense of affection. She'd been determined to finish out her contract, and that final week of photo shoots with Romain hovering over her harshly critiquing every pose and expression had been excruciating.

As she'd walked out of Romain's Geneva penthouse for the very last time after finding him in bed with her young replacement, she'd sworn that she would never give up her freedom for anything but true love.

Now thirty-two, and still nowhere close to finding true love, Mary was all but certain her "freedom" would last forever.

But as the stranger's eyes remained locked on hers while she held his gaze so that Gerry could get the shot he wanted, a shiver went through her that had nothing to do with the cool December air rushing over her skin.

Mistaking the reason for her shiver, Gerry called out to one of the crew to turn up the portable heaters on set.

For the next couple of hours, she continued to pose. Strangers came and went all around Union Square, but the beautiful stranger remained exactly where he was. Perhaps she should have been wary from his interest, but he didn't look alarming in any way.

He simply looked like a man who was interested in a woman.

Maybe, she thought as Gerry finished shooting his final roll of film and the gorgeous stranger walked toward her, *today won't be an end, but the beginning of something new and amazing.*

Three

As the sun set behind the buildings in Union Square, the temperature immediately dropped by several degrees. Normally, once they called a wrap, Mary would have rushed back to her dressing-room trailer to warm up with a cup of tea but, despite her shivers, she headed toward the man to meet him as he walked directly toward her.

Instead of simply holding out his hand and introducing himself, he took off his jacket and draped it over her shoulders. If another man had done this it would have felt presumptuous, but Mary sensed that he was genuinely concerned for her having been out in the cold for so many hours.

His jacket, so big that it swamped her slim frame,

smelled like clean, warm male. She wanted to burrow deeper into it, but instead she held it closed across her chest with one chilled hand while holding the other out to him. "I'm Mary. Mary Ferrer."

"It's been a pleasure watching you work, Mary. I'm Jack Sullivan."

Despite having stood outside in the cold for the past several hours without any lights or portable heaters nearby, when his fingers closed over hers, they were warm. Even in her heels, she had to tilt her head to look up at his face and figured he was at least three inches above six feet. His shoulders were broad, his hips trim, and his hand over hers was large and strong.

"Could I take you for a cup of coffee or something to eat? You've been working so hard, I expect you're starved." He grinned and said, "I know a place not far from here that's got the best cherry pie you've ever tasted."

She couldn't have contained her pleasure even if she'd tried. "I love cherry pie." She gestured at her dress and heels. "I just need to get out of this outfit first and thank the photographer and his crew."

"Take your time. I'll wait here."

She started to take off his jacket, but he put his hands

over hers where she was holding the lapels. "Keep the jacket. You can give it back to me once you've changed."

Every time he touched her, she lost her breath. And as she moved to where Gerry and his crew were packing things up, her hands were still tingling from the brush of his fingers over hers.

Making sure not to rush her goodbyes, Mary hugged each member of the crew. "Thank you so much for making my last shoot one of my very best."

Hugs and kisses came from people she'd worked with countless times over the past thirteen years. What she'd miss most about modeling wasn't seeing her face on magazine covers; it would be not seeing the family of photographers and lighting technicians and stylists she'd grown to love so much.

Gerry held her the longest. "I know you're ready to move on, Mary, but I'm going to keep holding out hope that we're going to do this again. Soon."

Her eyes were damp when she finally stepped into her trailer to strip out of the red velvet dress and put it back on the soft hanger. By the time she'd slipped off the beautiful heels and pulled on her jeans, along with a turtleneck and a loose sweater that floated over her curves, excitement—and heady anticipation—was moving through her.

Okay, so it was just coffee and pie with a gorgeous man, but some of the greatest things started from something small, didn't they? And hadn't the last big change in her life—thirteen years ago—happened over a cup of coffee with Randy?

Mary didn't waste any more time checking her appearance before opening the trailer door and walking back toward Jack. She even liked the sound of his name.

Jack Sullivan.

His dark eyes were intense as he held her gaze, and she felt every inch of her skin come alive beneath his gaze.

"You've been standing in the cold for hours," she said as she held out his jacket. "You should really have this back now."

But instead of taking it, he asked, "Where's your coat?"

"It was surprisingly warm this morning when I came on set, and since I figured I'd be heading straight back home in a taxi after the shoot, I didn't bother to bring one."

He took his jacket from her, but only to slide it back over her shoulders again. "It looks better on you."

He put his hand on the small of her back, and even through all of the fabric she could feel how warm he was.

They didn't speak as they walked the couple of short blocks to the diner, but it wasn't an uncomfortable silence. On the contrary, Mary couldn't remember the last time she'd felt so immediately at ease with someone. And yet, at the same time, her skin felt just a little too sensitive, her lips fuller and tingly, her breath coming faster even though they were on one of the rare flat streets in the hilly city.

When Jack held open the door for her, Mary took note of the small gesture with pleasure. She was all for women's liberation, especially considering she'd been earning her own way for more than a decade, but she couldn't see why it had to mean the loss of common courtesy.

The gray-haired woman behind the counter greeted Jack like an old friend and eyed Mary with obvious interest. "Two pieces of cherry pie, warm, with big fat scoops of ice cream on top?"

Mary smiled at the woman, who reminded her of her mother's friends back in Italy. Everything that needed to be said could always be said with food. Warm pies, cold ices and fresh baked bread all spoke loudly of love as well as words ever could.

"That would be lovely, thank you," she said as she slid onto the shiny red seat in a corner booth. "And some coffee, as well, please."

"I'll take some java, too, Betty." Jack waited until Mary had taken off his jacket before saying, "I've never seen a model at work before. It was fascinating."

Long ago she'd learned how to accept a compliment graciously, something she thought was at least as important as knowing how to take constructive criticism. "Thank you. Gerry, the photographer, is wonderful to work with. He makes the process as easy as possible for all of us."

Betty brought over their slices of pie, the ice cream already melting down the edges of the thick crust and warm cherries. But it was the coffee that Mary went for first to warm her cold hands. She held on to it for a moment and enjoyed the heat against her palms before taking a sip.

"How long have you been modeling?"

At the beginning of her career, fame had been tremendously fun and heady for a young girl from a small Italian village. As the years went by, however, it had become more and more invasive. And surprisingly lonely, even with people constantly around her. It was rare that she met anyone who didn't know who she was.

"Ever since I left Italy when I was nineteen." She didn't see a point in hiding her age, so she added, "That was thirteen years ago."

His eyebrows raised in surprise. "We're the same age." He gave her one of his devastating grins that made her heart beat faster. "The years are another thing you wear better than I do."

"If you ask me," she murmured, "they look pretty good on you, too."

Mary couldn't remember the last time she'd flirted with a man. She was always so careful not to lead anyone on, just in case he thought she was feeling something she wasn't. But the attraction that had simmered between the two of them in Union Square was heating up with every moment they spent together.

"Where in Italy?"

"A little town nobody has ever heard of called Rosciano."

"I imagine your life over the past thirteen years has been very different from how you grew up."

"Well, I had hoped it would be." Feeling that had come out wrong, she clarified, "I had a great childhood, but I desperately wanted to see more of the world. San

Francisco is one of my favorite places, which is why I've decided to stay for a while. This city certainly isn't small, but it still reminds me of my old town in a lot of ways. The hills. The water nearby. How friendly the people are."

Mary had been interviewed dozens of times over the years, by some of the best journalists in the business. But none of them had ever looked at her with such honest interest. Because even when they'd been friendly with each other, she'd only been a job to them. Mary had worked so much during her adult years that she'd always met the men she dated on the job.

She was extremely glad that Jack had nothing whatsoever to do with her career. It made her feel even more convinced that something might actually be possible with him. She wasn't a product for him. She wasn't connected to his bottom line.

She was simply a woman getting to know him.

"Did your brothers or sisters leave the country, too?"

"Unlike most Italian families, I was an only child. My mother—" She paused and tried not to betray the emotion that always came over her when she spoke of her mother, but she could already hear the little bit of an Italian accent that always slipped into her voice when she spoke of home and her childhood. "She always longed for more children, but her prayers weren't answered."

"Yes, they were." His eyes were gentle as he said, "She had you."

It took Mary a few seconds to push away the emotion his simple words evoked. "Do you have any sisters?"

"Nope, three brothers." Her eyes widened at the thought of all that testosterone in one family as he asked, "Why do you ask?"

"Because if you had had sisters, you would have known that headstrong young girls and their mothers are rarely a conflict-free combination." Feeling that she'd already said too much, and knowing she should change the subject before her emotions got the best of her, she asked, "Did you and your brothers grow up here?"

"Born and raised. I went to college locally, too, and haven't really had much time to travel."

"That's another great thing about San Francisco," she said, pausing in her extremely enthusiastic bites of pie. "Between Chinatown, Japantown, the French Quarter, the Mission and North Beach, it's like having the world at your fingertips. The people, the traditions and especially the food." He was so easy to talk to that she realized she'd gotten off track again. "What about your family? Are they all close by?"

"I wish. My oldest brother is up in Seattle with his wife and toddler. Another brother has a house in San Francisco but he is usually in a skyscraper overseas concluding another major business deal. My youngest brother is probably locked in his studio back East painting a masterpiece, and my parents are happily wintering in Florida."

It amazed her how their conversation was so effortless and yet so totally full of sparks.

"What do you do?"

"I'm an engineer. I've been working on a product I invented for most of the past decade."

Sexy *and* smart. Now, that was a wonderful combination in a man, she thought as she took another bite of pie and ice cream. A cherry popped on her tongue and the combination of sweet and creamy, warm and cool sent a soft moan of pleasure falling from her lips.

"You were right," she said after she'd swallowed. "This was amazing cherry pie."

Jack's dark eyes were intense as they held hers and he agreed, "Amazing," though he'd hardly eaten any pie at all yet.

"Help Me," the hit single from Joni Mitchell, was playing from a portable radio set up in a corner of the diner. And with Mary's heart pounding hard for a man she barely knew but already wanted so badly to know better, she felt as if Joni were singing about her.

Because after only fifteen minutes with Jack, Mary could tell that she was already falling too fast…with hopes about the future and worries about the past circling inside her mind and heart at the same time.

What if she didn't let those worries imprison her this time? What if she trusted her instincts, the same way she had when she was a nineteen-year-old girl? And what if, for the very first time in a long, long while, she let herself believe that true love might actually be possible?

"A decade is a long time to work on one thing," she said softly. "You must have incredible focus."

"When I'm passionate about something and want it bad enough, I always make sure I get it."

Her breath caught in her throat at the pulsing sensuality behind his statement. An impulse to lean close and kiss him wound through her, and she might have given in to it had she not noticed out of the corner of her eye that some of the other diners were pointing at her.

Mary wanted her first kiss with Jack to be special. So

instead of a kiss, she simply leaned slightly forward to try to get closer to him across the bright yellow Formica table and said, "Tell me about your invention."

She could tell he was pleased by her interest in his engineering career. She wanted to know everything about him—his passions, his dreams and his fears, too. And if things worked out between them, maybe she'd tell him about her passions, dreams and fears, too…something she'd never done with any man before.

He pulled something out of his pocket and placed it on the table between them. "We call it the Pocket Planner. It's an electronic calendar and personal organizer. It even has reminders built in for the items on your to-do list. After a decade of trial and error, my two partners and I have finally not only got it working, but technology has made it small enough to be able to carry it around without a forklift." He was even more gorgeous with the look of pride on his face.

"May I?" When he nodded, she picked it up and ran her fingers over the very interesting machine. "I think it sounds fantastic. In fact, I can think of half-a-dozen ways I could have used something like this in the past few years."

He beamed at her. "I can't tell you how glad I am to

hear you feel that way." She smiled back and was about to ask him more questions when he added, "In fact, that's one of the things I wanted to talk to you about."

Mary felt her smile falter on her lips. Years of holding poses regardless of whether she was happy or under the weather was the reason she was able to keep it in place. "It is?"

Jack pushed his plate away in his excitement. "We're hoping to get it onto shelves this Christmas, and there are thousands of units waiting in a warehouse already but, though the retailers like the product, they're convinced we need to add some se—" he cut himself off "—mass appeal to it. As soon as I saw you in Union Square, I knew you would be the perfect person to represent our product."

Her lips flattened and the cherries that had tasted so good just minutes ago now felt like little round bricks in the pit of her stomach. She worked to keep her voice steady. "So that's why you asked me here for pie? To see if I would consider representing your product?"

His eyes searched her face for a long moment and she could see his sudden confusion at her cool reaction. She could almost read his mind, the way he was asking himself how he could have misplayed things with her already.

Especially when he clearly needed her to make his dreams come true…

"Mary?" Jack shook his head, the tips of his dark head of hair moving over his broad shoulders. "No." He shook his head again. "Yes, but it wasn't the only reason."

Of course he had to say that. With as much elegance and pride as she could still muster, considering she'd been gazing at him like a love-struck teenager when he'd simply been calculating his potential gains all the while, she carefully slid out of the booth. "Thank you for the pie and coffee."

Jack reached for her hand before she could take more than a step away from the table. She looked down and saw how tanned his skin was against hers, how large his hand was as he held hers.

"Please, Mary, don't go."

God, it was pathetic how much she wanted to stay, even now that she knew the real reason he'd wanted to meet her. It now seemed as if the idea that she could eventually convince him to want more than that was mere fantasy.

But that wasn't how love worked. She'd learned over and over throughout the years that there was no point in wishing for a miracle…even at Christmastime.

"Today was my last shoot. I'm not modeling anymore." She didn't owe him any explanations, but she hated to come across as a spoiled princess who was storming out because she hadn't gotten her way…or because he'd inadvertently hurt her too-delicate feelings. "I'm sure you'll find someone perfect to represent your product."

She waited for him to lift his hand from hers, but he only gripped her tighter. "I already have found somebody perfect, Mary." She couldn't help but lift her eyes to meet his as he said, "You're perfect."

It was what she'd fought so long—the false perception that she was perfect. "I'm not."

She steeled herself for his protests. The last thing she expected him to do was smile at her and say, "You're right. How could anyone be perfect with ice cream and cherry juice on her face?"

He brushed the corner of her mouth with the tip of his index finger, and so much warmth flooded her from the tiny touch that she was amazed all of the ice in the diner didn't melt into a puddle right then and there just from the heat being generated between the two of them. And then, in the most shockingly sexy way, he brought his finger to his own lips and ran his tongue over his fingertip to lick off the cherry juice and ice cream.

"Please, Mary, let me start over and get things out in the right order this time."

They'd been standing by the side of the table for long enough now that people were starting to stare. A few of them pointed to her and she heard her name in loud whispers. But none of that mattered.

Only this man standing before her did.

He'd had her at the surprisingly sweet comment about cherry juice and his gentle touch to her lips, but she would never forgive herself for folding that easily. "The right order?"

He nodded and moved closer, his body lean and muscled and warm against hers. "My invention isn't the only reason I wanted to take you for pie and coffee."

"It isn't?"

"You've got to understand, Angel, a man like me looks at a woman like you and it's inevitable that I'm going to screw things up."

He had no right to make up a nickname for her or to say it in such a warm and inviting voice. And she had no business enjoying both those things.

But, for all her vows to protect herself from men like him who only wanted her for the improvements she could make to their bottom line, instead of walking away from him, she found herself saying, "It is?" in a breathless voice that hardly seemed to belong to her.

He nodded, his eyes growing darker still as they dropped to her lips for a split second, then moved back to meet her gaze again.

"You've got class. Beauty. Intelligence." He gestured to himself. "All I've got is a degree that took me too many years to finish and a dream that I'm praying will finally become real one day."

If he had gotten down on one knee to praise her beauty, if he had rhapsodized about her "charms," she would have forced herself to slip her hand from his and walk away.

But talk of dreams?

Dreams were the one thing she'd always understood, how they could take hold of you and make you risk everything.

Besides, she thought as she studied him, she had a feeling that once Jack Sullivan made up his mind about something, he wouldn't take no for an answer. And the truth was that the reason she hadn't chosen a new direction for her career yet was because she wasn't terribly excited about any of the opportunities that had come her way.

Representing a new technology like this would be fresh. Exciting. Yes, it might fail, as models and technology had rarely been paired successfully. But Mary hadn't let herself step into a position to fail in a very long time.

Maybe, she thought, it was time to take a risk again.

The biggest question remaining was whether the risk would be strictly professional…or personal, too? Because when he'd called her *Angel,* the sweet endearment had warmed her in places she hadn't realized had grown so cold.

"Your ice cream is melting," she finally said. "Why don't we sit back down so that you can eat some of your pie before it drowns."

Relief flared in his eyes, but beneath it she thought she recognized the same desire she hadn't been able to push down within herself. Which was why, as he finally let her hand go and they both sat, she said, "Before you tell me more about your product, there's something you need to know about me. I don't mix business with pleasure."

Jack looked surprised, and she got a sense that women hadn't turned him down very many times in his thirty-two years. And why would they, she asked herself, when he was not only extraordinarily gorgeous, but he had a smile that could instantly make you feel as if you were the only woman in the world who mattered?

"So if you agree to represent my invention," he clarified, "you won't let me ask you out?"

Her stomach fluttered at the sheer thought of a proper date with Jack. One that would likely end in a kiss.

Or more…

"It makes things too complicated."

She still remembered the pain of having to continue working with a man she could barely stand to be in the same room with, of having to listen to Romain's endless critiques and demands. She'd been too much of a professional to tell him where he could stick it, and had had to make do with the vivid fantasies of what she'd wished she'd said to him.

Jack studied her for a few moments. "In that case, we'll have to take care of business first." But he reached across the table for her hand again and brushed his thumb across her palm. "And then we'll move on to pleasure."

It took every ounce of self-control for Mary to slide her hand away from his and to convince herself it was better this way. Instead of jumping into a sizzling-hot affair that could burn out just as quickly as it flared up, they'd get a chance to know each other better by working together first. And then, after they'd concluded their business affairs, if the sparks were still there between them, perhaps they could see about starting another kind of affair entirely.

Only, as Jack showed her how the Pocket Planner worked, instead of being able to keep her distance, she was increasingly seduced not only by how gorgeous he was—and she'd seen plenty of handsome men in her career—but also by his incredible intelligence.

And his passion.

Four

"Thank you so much for agreeing to work with us, Ms. Ferrer," Larry said as he pumped Mary's hand enthusiastically in the lobby of Walter Industries the following day.

"You're a lifesaver, Ms. Ferrer," Howie said as he reached for her hand the very second Larry let it go, nearly pulling her arm loose from her shoulder socket in his excitement. "My girlfriend wanted me to tell you that she's your biggest fan."

She smiled warmly at both of the men. "Please, call me Mary."

Jack had done his research after putting Mary into a cab in front of the diner last night. He'd quickly confirmed that he'd been having pie and coffee—and fumbling through every last second—with one of the most successful models in the world. No doubt she had men throwing themselves at her feet, men with a hell of a lot more to their name than a dream.

She'd been right to get up and start to walk out on him last night at the diner. He'd deserved worse than that for the way he'd gracelessly asked her to be the face of their product, without making it clear that business wasn't the only reason he wanted to spend time with her. It was just that as soon as they'd started talking about his invention, and she'd been clearly interested in it, he'd automatically fallen back into engineering mode, the same way he would have with Howie or Larry.

The hurt that had flashed across Mary's face when she'd thought he was only interested in her as a spokesmodel for an advertising campaign had kept him up half the night.

Jack had lived his life using intelligent calculations and analysis. Not only did a model and an engineer not make any sense as a couple, but a serious relationship had never factored into his plans or his life. What was more, it had been less than twenty-four hours since he'd met Mary. He should have been up all night planning for this meeting today with the board. If ever he needed to have perfect focus on his work, on making his long-held dream come true, it was right now.

But thoughts of Mary had remained front and center since the moment he'd set eyes on her.

Placing his hand gently on her lower back, he guided her away from his partners. She looked incredibly beautiful this morning in a long-sleeved navy wrap dress and high-heeled boots. There was a slim gold chain around her neck and another on her wrist. Her dark, glossy hair moved over her shoulders like silk and her complexion was so perfect he honestly couldn't tell if she was wearing any makeup. She was both naturally sensual and, at the same time, approachable and down-to-earth.

He wanted to tell her that he'd thought about her all night long, but he knew he needed to respect her request to keep business and pleasure separate.

"Do you have any questions for me about what's going to happen in the boardroom?"

"I don't think so. From what you explained to me last night, and the documents you couriered over early this morning, I think I have a good understanding of the selling points for the Pocket Planner."

When they'd first met yesterday in Union Square, she'd smiled so easily at him. Now her eyes were guarded.

Jack silently cursed himself for putting those shadows there. She must still believe he wanted her more for business than he wanted her as a woman.

She was wrong.

"You don't have to do this, Mary."

She blinked at him, confused. "I don't understand. I thought you needed me to help you."

"You're perfect for the job," he agreed, "and we do need your help, but if it's a choice between selling a million Pocket Planners this Christmas and getting the chance to be with you...?" Maybe it was out of line to reach up and stroke her cheek with the back of his hand, but he'd never been this drawn to a woman and he honestly didn't know how to stop himself. "I'll figure out some other way to get this product off the ground."

When she put her hand over his where it rested against the incredibly soft skin of her cheek, he could have sworn his heart actually expanded inside his chest.

"I've never done anything I didn't choose to do, Jack. Not when I was nineteen, and certainly not now at thirty-two. If I didn't want to be here with you, Howie and Larry, I wouldn't be. You've worked hard to create something great and you deserve this chance at the big time." Slowly, she lowered his hand from her face and slipped her fingers from his. "I'm just asking you to be patient so that we can see the business through first."

He had so many questions for her. What had happened in her past? Who had hurt her to make her so cautious, so wary of his motives? But before he had the right to ask for answers, he knew he needed her to trust him. Which meant he needed to be completely straightforward with her at all times, no matter what.

"I'm sure you have your reasons for wanting things to be that way, and I'm also sure they must be good ones, but I have to be honest with you, Mary." He was blown away by her beauty all over again as she waited for him to explain himself. "I've never been a patient man."

"You worked for ten years on your invention," she said softly. "I'd say that shows more patience than most people will ever have."

"It's one thing to wait ten years for chips and wires and motherboards to fire correctly. But I knew ten seconds after we first met that I wanted to kiss you, Angel."

Mary's skin flushed and her full lips opened on a soft gasp at his impulsive declaration just as the receptionist walked into the entryway and indicated it was time for them to head inside to the boardroom. The young woman's eyes widened when she saw Mary.

"Oh, my gosh, you're Mary Ferrer! You're even more beautiful in person." The girl grabbed a notepad and pen from a nearby table. "Could you sign this for me?"

Mary's cheeks remained flushed from what Jack had said to her as she took the pen and paper from the young woman. Jack couldn't tell if she was upset about what he'd just admitted.

Usually he calculated, figured, assessed—and then, only then, made a strategic plan toward his goal. But with Mary, all of the rationale he'd lived by his whole life had flown out the window…leaving him with just his instincts.

"That's a lovely dress you're wearing," Mary told the young woman. "The color is so flattering on you."

Jack didn't think he'd ever seen anyone as happy as the receptionist was at that moment. "Do you really think so? It's new and I wasn't sure if I could pull off the hemline."

"You definitely can," Mary assured her. "I'd love to know your name so that I can personalize my autograph."

"I'm Sarah, with an *h*." Just like Jack, the young woman couldn't take her eyes off Mary as she wrote a quick but charming note to Sarah.

"Here you go."

The young woman stood staring at Mary for a few more seconds before she remembered her job. "Please, follow me this way."

When Jack's partners stepped aside to let Mary precede them into the boardroom, she gave the three of them a wide smile. "Ready to knock their socks off?"

It was just the right thing to say to give them the jolt of confidence they needed to close the deal. Larry and Howie grinned back at her. "Ready!"

Jack held out his arm for her, and when she took it, he felt the sensation rock them both. He was a large man and, despite being a model, Mary wasn't particularly tall. Yet, they fit together perfectly.

Jack had figured Allen would be impatiently waiting to send them on their way so that he could get on to other, bigger money meetings, and the way the gray-haired man was standing in the boardroom with his arms crossed over his chest confirmed that. But when he caught sight of Mary, his eyes went as wide with surprise—and pleasure—as his receptionist's had.

Without so much as acknowledging Jack, Howie or Larry, he moved to greet her. "Hello. I'm Allen Walter. I've long been an admirer of yours from afar, Ms.

Ferrer, but I must say that you are even more exquisite in person."

"Mary, please," she said as she let the gray-haired man draw her into the room and introduce to her the other members of the board.

Jack guessed she must have played this role dozens of times in her career, meeting strangers and making them feel as if they were already friends.

Once the introductions were made, Allen said, "I'd love to know to what we owe this pleasure?"

Mary took a seat beside Jack and nodded for him to deliver their news to the chairman. "Mary has agreed to be the face of the Pocket Planner."

After three decades of running his large and powerful company, Jack doubted there was much that surprised Allen anymore. This news, however, clearly had. Despite being quite obviously impressed that Jack and his partners had managed to pull Mary into the project, he approached the situation as any good chairman of the board would: with questions.

"You have been associated with some of the most exclusive products in the world. May I ask why you would agree to work with a group of fledgling start-up engineers?"

Larry was yanking at his tie as if it had just grown three sizes too small and Howie was sweating. Clearly, they were waiting for Jack to jump in and salvage the situation before it could go too far off track. But Jack simply sat back in his leather seat. He had every faith that Mary could answer the chairman's question better than anyone else could.

"I met Jack yesterday in Union Square. I believe it was right after your meeting, when you indicated that the product needed more sex appeal."

Though his partners' eyes went wide at her honest response, Jack appreciated her candid reply. She was nobody's fool, and she didn't expect anyone to be hers, even when he himself had tried to change the words *sex appeal* to *mass appeal*.

Mary smiled at each of the powerful businessmen in the room, not in the least intimated. Even as a brand-new teenage model so many years ago, he guessed she must have been a force to be reckoned with, her strong will just as potent as her gorgeous face.

"I appreciate the advertising power of sensuality," she said in a voice as smooth as Glenlivet whiskey, "but sensuality is nothing without the smarts to know what to do with it. The Pocket Planner is a brilliant invention.

More than that, it's actually useful. I can literally think of a dozen men and women I could give it to as a Christmas gift this year. And I can guarantee they'd all love it simply because it would make their lives easier."

That was when Allen actually clapped his hands in glee, a sixtysomething man who Jack thought might have just fallen head over heels in love with the beautiful woman sitting before him.

But when the man at his left leaned over to whisper something into his ear, Allen frowned. "There's no question that you're perfect for the job, Mary. However, there may be one small problem. At this point in the fiscal year, our budget is rather low and I'm sure your fee is, justifiably, extraordinarily high."

Jack had already decided on a solution to this issue. "I'll split my royalty share with Mary."

Everyone turned to him with a shocked expression, including Mary. "Jack," she said as she put her hand on his arm, "you don't have to do this."

"And you don't have to, either," he said softly, "but you're here."

"In that case," Allen said before anyone could change their minds, "I believe we have ourselves a deal."

The four of them shook hands with the board, and

while Mary was chatting with one of the other men, Allen pulled Jack aside. "I don't know how you pulled this off. Mary Ferrer is one in a million. People will be tripping over themselves to find out why she's so excited about your invention."

Jack liked and respected Allen. It was one of the main reasons he wanted to work with the man and his company. But he had no intention of using Mary as if she was a product to be sold.

"We're very lucky that Mary has agreed to work with us," Jack said in a measured voice. "Very lucky," he repeated, before adding, "I expect everyone to treat her with the utmost respect at all times, all the way down the chain of command. And if someone should forget to do so and she feels she must leave the campaign as a result, it will be our fault. Not hers."

Allen's eyes narrowed at the clear warning, but Jack didn't care how many millions the man was worth. The two men stared at each other in silence for several moments before Allen finally nodded. "Agreed." He glanced at her again. "She is most definitely one in a million."

Five

"It's time to celebrate!"

Howie had used the receptionist's phone to call his girlfriend, Layla, with the good news. She left work early to meet them at the Gold Dust Lounge in Union Square.

After they got off the trolley, Jack and Mary walked down the sidewalk behind his partners. He was strong and steady at her side, just as he'd been in the boardroom.

The sharp winds from the previous day had blown out of the city, leaving behind bright blue skies and a surprisingly warm sun. It was one of the things Mary liked best about San Francisco—the weather could be so topsy-turvy, with cool, foggy summers and warm, sunny winters. And now Mary felt just as topsy-turvy over what Jack had said to her just before they'd gone into the meeting.

If it's a choice between selling a million Pocket Planners this Christmas and getting the chance to be with you, I'll figure out some other way to get this product off the ground.

When was the last time a man had put her first?

She honestly couldn't remember.

Though she was a naturally positive person, Mary had seen enough over the past thirteen years as an in-demand model to develop a necessary cynicism. As much as she would have liked to take everything people said and did at face value, she made herself ask the difficult question: Had Jack simply been trying to make her feel good by telling her what he thought she wanted to hear?

Or was she right to feel that every word he'd spoken had rung with sincerity?

She couldn't forget the shocking offer he'd made in the boardroom to give her half his royalty share. It was completely crazy, and she could never take him up on it. He'd worked on his invention for ten years, whereas she would only be promoting it for a short while. But, still, the gesture said a lot about him as a man.

At quitting time on a Friday night, the popular piano bar was just coming to life. Some things, Mary mused, were the same all over the world. The bars in her hometown in Italy would be full of friends and family members greeting each other with kisses on the cheek and sighs of relief that they had a weekend of relaxation ahead of them. The only difference was that the men in her hometown would be coming from ancient palazzos wearing work clothes rather than from high-rise buildings wearing three-piece suits. And the women would be nursing a glass of wine while keeping one eye on their children playing tag out by the fountain rather than sipping cosmopolitans before deciding where to go dancing for the evening.

A sudden pang of homesickness for all that she'd left behind twisted inside her as she thought about the old friends she hadn't seen in over a decade.

"Mary?" Jack's eyes were concerned. "Is everything all right?"

She forced her lips up into a smile. "Of course it is. We're here to celebrate, after all."

Before he could probe further, she followed his partners into the bar and slid onto an open stool. Howie's girlfriend, Layla, came in then, and after several minutes of nonstop gushing about how excited she was to meet a world-famous model, Mary was extremely grateful when Larry appeared with a bottle of champagne.

"To the fabulous, amazing, lifesaving woman who saved our business single-handedly!"

Mary laughed at his obvious hyperbole and held her glass up even higher. "To the three fabulous, amazing men who invented the Pocket Planner!"

The five of them clinked glasses and toasted to the hopes of continued success. Mary had always enjoyed champagne, but with Jack beside her, all of her senses were on especially high alert. The bubbles felt crisper, the wine sweeter, the effect of the fizzy liquor headier.

When she noticed that Larry had pulled out a pen and was making notes on a napkin, Jack leaned over and said, "His brain rarely shuts off. Even," Jack said pointedly, "when we're here to celebrate rather than work."

"That's one of the things I like about the three of you. You're all so committed to what you're doing. So passionate about it. And," she said as she looked at how comfortable they were with each other after so many years of working closely together, "you seem more like brothers than business partners."

Larry held up the list he'd made. "These are our highest-level action items." He pointed to the first one with the tip of his pen. "Do you think you'll be able to get that great photographer you worked with in Union Square to work on this campaign with us?"

"I hope so. I'm sure Gerry will be as excited about it as I am, and even if he's busy, I'll do my best to convince him to squeeze us in."

Continuing to ignore the warning looks Jack was shooting him across the table, Larry said, "If we're going to get the word out by Christmas, we need to shoot the first ad by Monday, so—"

"Don't worry," she promised him, "I'll make sure we either have Gerry or another top photographer scheduled by Monday morning." With Jack so near her like this, Mary decided it would be a very good idea to keep herself wholly focused on business rather than how good he smelled or how deep and dark brown his eyes were. "In fact, while we're here, why don't we do some brainstorming about how you'd like to set up the ads?"

For the next thirty minutes, she had a great time throwing out ideas from what she'd learned in her shoots over the past decade, most of which were very well received by Jack and his partners.

"I honestly don't know what we would have done without you," Howie said when they'd put together a fairly comprehensive starting plan. "You're not just a model who's going to make our device look a heck of a lot prettier—you're like a whole ad agency wrapped into one person."

Jack nodded his agreement. "Walter Industries has connected us with a couple of ad agencies during the past year, but nothing they came up with was anywhere near as fresh as this."

"We've got some brilliant ideas here," Larry murmured almost to himself as he made a few additional notes on his stack of napkins before shoving them into the front pocket of his jacket.

So many times during her career, Mary had been treated as if she couldn't possibly have anything between her pretty ears. And, since she'd started modeling in her late teens, she'd never had time to get any degrees to prove that she did, indeed, have brains. Clearly, these three men with their PhDs from Stanford University were geniuses. For them to call her ideas brilliant meant a great deal to Mary.

"Look," Layla suddenly said as she pointed up to the ceiling above Mary and Jack, "the two of you are sitting under the mistletoe."

Mary looked up and confirmed that there was a fresh

green sprig of mistletoe hanging directly over her and Jack. After a quick scan of the rest of the room, she realized it was the only one in the entire bar.

What were the odds that she and Jack would end up sitting under it?

Larry, Howie and Layla were already happily making their way through a second bottle of champagne. Clearly, the bubbly had gone to their heads, because when Layla said, "I've heard it's bad luck not to kiss under the mistletoe," in an earnest voice, Jack's two partners nodded their heads, eyes bright from success and the drink.

Mary's heart hammered and the stem of her glass slipped beneath her suddenly clammy fingers. Jack had said he wanted to kiss her, but she'd made it perfectly clear that he'd have to wait until the campaign had wrapped.

But, she asked herself now, what harm could there be in one teeny-tiny little kiss under the mistletoe in a downtown bar in front of his friends?

And wouldn't it almost be stranger if they didn't share a playful smooch?

"In that case," she said slowly as she shifted in her seat to face Jack, "hopefully it will be *good* luck if we do."

Any other man would have already claimed his kiss,

or at least pressured her to give him one. But Jack wasn't like any other man. Because, despite the obvious desire she could read in his eyes, he said, "Mary, you don't have to—"

Oh, but she *did.*

She leaned closer, but before she could press her lips to his, his mouth found hers.

Their kiss was gentle and sweeter than any she'd shared in recent memory, little more than a split-second brush of mouth against mouth. But, oh, from the sparks that lit off all through her system, it was much, much more than one simple kiss under the mistletoe. Jack's lips tasted like champagne and she wanted to reach up to thread her fingers through his dark hair and pull him closer so that she could get an even better taste.

Stunned by her strong feelings for a man she'd met less than twenty-four hours ago, Mary instinctively pulled back. In the span of one short kiss, she'd forgotten not only that his partners were sitting at the table with them but that they were in the middle of a crowded bar. As a public figure, she'd long ago learned to be aware of her behavior in public, especially as her fame had grown larger and larger. Over the years she would often find her name and picture in the papers after a night out.

More than a little worried that she was going to do something to embarrass herself soon, she scooted off her seat. "Thank you for the champagne." She tried to smile at everyone as though everything was fine, but her lips were still tingling from the sweet pressure of Jack's mouth against hers. "I'm sorry to have to leave already, but I'll be in touch with the photographer's information and location for Monday's shoot by Sunday night at the very latest."

Larry and Howie were loose enough from the drink now that they gave her one-armed hugs goodbye. Layla also hugged her and whispered, "Thank you again for saving the boys. I don't know what they would have done without you."

Jack had gotten up from his seat, too, but instead of saying goodbye, he said, "I'll take you home."

Mary was having enough trouble controlling herself around him in a crowded bar. She could only imagine how little self-control she'd be able to muster up if they went to a more private location. Besides, at this point she desperately needed a cool and breezy walk back to her place to help clear her mind, a walk that was long enough for her to systematically rewind through each of the reasons why getting involved with Jack now—

when their promotional campaign had barely begun—was a bad idea.

"You should stay to celebrate, Jack."

But he was already slipping her jacket on over her shoulders. "I'll call you both tomorrow morning to coordinate our schedules for next week," he told Larry and Howie as he reached for his coat. After kissing Layla on the cheek, he put his hand on the small of Mary's back and walked to the entrance with her.

Despite his presence behind her, she felt unsteady in her heels for the first time since being a teenager on her first catwalk. Not because of the champagne, which she'd barely sipped, but because Jack's nearness affected her so powerfully.

Out on the curb he started to hail a cab, but Mary put her hand on his arm. "I'd much rather walk, if you don't mind."

He covered her hand with his to keep them connected. "Which way?"

She nodded in the direction of the Bay. "Nob Hill."

"That's a half-dozen blocks." He looked down at the heels on her boots. "You can walk that far in those?"

It had been a long time since she'd been with someone who didn't know the ins and outs of her world. Despite all of her warnings to herself to stop being charmed by every little thing Jack said and did, she found it really refreshing.

"When I'm working, I spend all day in heels, most higher than these. The first few months," she admitted, "I would hobble home at night from a shoot or runway show and soak my feet in an ice bath." And cry for her mother, who she knew would have called her crazy for sticking with a career that tore her feet to shreds like that. "Eventually, I got used to the pain." From the shoes, anyway.

"Well, if they do start to hurt, you should know I give a mean piggyback ride," he said with an adorable grin. "At least, according to my little nephew Ian."

Sexy she could deal with. Kind and intelligent certainly upped the ante and tested her mettle in a serious way.

But adorable?

How was she supposed to resist adorable?

Just then, a teenage girl waiting for the traffic light to change asked her for an autograph. Mary signed it and, after they'd crossed the street, Jack said, "If I had known you were this famous, I'm not sure I'd have gotten up the nerve to talk to you yesterday."

She raised an eyebrow. "You don't strike me as a man who lets nerves or doubts rule him."

"I never have before," he said, "but you're making me feel a lot of things I've never felt before."

Mary was used to men who practically rented out an orchestral hall and filled it from floor to ceiling with roses to set the stage for declaring themselves to her. Jack, on the other hand, simply said the most shockingly delicious things without any fanfare at all.

"Does it ever bother you to have people constantly looking at you? The way they all want to talk to you and ask for autographs?"

"Ninety-nine percent of the strangers who approach me for an autograph are lovely, polite people. Honestly, the only thing that bothers me about any of it is that I haven't done anything extraordinary enough for them to be so starstruck."

The sidewalk was crowded, but Jack didn't seem to care as he turned her to face him in the middle of it. "You were born with incredible blue eyes. Your mouth drives a guy crazy just looking at it. And you have a figure that Michelangelo could have spent a lifetime trying to set into stone and never done justice to it. But I've seen how hard you work during photo shoots and

I've just heard you come up with a half-dozen fantastic ideas for the ads we're going to shoot together. I'm certain that there are plenty of beautiful women who couldn't do what you do anywhere near as well, or make it seem as effortless."

"I know I'm good at my job," she agreed, "but I'm not a doctor curing cancer. I'm not an activist changing history. I'm not a mother with children who need me, either." She'd rarely voiced these doubts aloud, but for some reason, with Jack she couldn't stop them all from pouring out.

He reached over to gently stroke his fingers across her cheek, the heat of his touch in sharp contrast to the coolness of her skin. "You make people happy, Mary, and that's an extraordinary thing."

Jack's words warmed her, just as his touch—and his kiss—had. So when they began to walk again and a damp wind whipped up around them, she let herself hold his arm a little more tightly and move just a little bit closer, too.

Jack had never had any problems with the opposite sex. Girls and then women had always seemed to like his looks, and he'd never been nervous or fumbling around them. But with Mary?

He could barely think a straight thought…especially after that kiss under the mistletoe.

The kiss had been two sets of lips barely touching. They hadn't even held hands. And yet, she'd completely knocked his socks off to the point where his heart was still pounding hard and his veins were still buzzing with desire as they walked down the crowded street.

Had Mary been affected by their kiss in the same way?

And was there any way he could have felt that much if she hadn't felt it, too?

The first drops of rain came from out of nowhere. Within seconds, they were falling hard and fast. Jack was searching for an overhanging awning when he realized Mary was staring up at the sky as the rain poured down on her. And there was a big smile on her stunning face.

"I was eleven years old when *Singin' in the Rain* made it to Italy," she said as she let go of his arm to reach for a lamppost and swing around it, humming the title tune from the film. "It's still one of my favorite movies."

Jack had seen Mary as a supermodel, he'd seen her as a businesswoman, and now he saw her as she must have been as a young girl. Full of wonder from something as simple as an unexpected rainstorm, her long, dark hair wet and slicked back, drops of water falling from her eyelashes to her cheeks, her full lips catching drops of rain just moments before she licked them off with the tip of her tongue.

Once upon a time he'd loved to play in the rain but, over the years, as he'd focused more and more on his invention—with only the occasional break for a fast car or a pretty woman—he'd lost sight of those pleasures.

After everyone else ran for cover, Jack and Mary were the only two people left on the sidewalk. It felt, for a moment, as if the city was entirely theirs.

He reached out his hand for her again. "Dance with me."

She immediately turned into his arms as if she'd been waiting for him to ask. They might not be Gene Kelly and Debbie Reynolds, but neither of them cared as they danced. No other woman had felt so right in his arms, and none had laughed with such joy in them, either.

"No one has ever danced with me in the rain before." Mary had the same look of soft surprise in her eyes as she had after their kiss under the mistletoe.

"'This California dew is just a little heavier than usual tonight.'"

"You've seen the movie?" She looked delighted by the discovery that he knew it well enough to quote from the scene right before Don Lockwood went out to sing and dance in the rain.

"My mother was a big fan." And boy, was he glad that she'd taken him to the theater as a ten-year-old boy and made him watch it. In retrospect, the dance lessons hadn't been a bad idea, either.

Jack had meant it when he'd told her he was going to try to respect Mary's wishes to keep things professional between them until they were done working together. But as they stood together in the rain, kissing her again was inevitable. They were both leaning in toward each other when the rain abruptly stopped falling and dozens of people suddenly emerged from the overhangs and bumped the two of them apart.

"I'm just around the corner." Mary pointed to a building a few yards away. When they got to the bottom step, she immediately offered, "Why don't you come in and warm up with a cup of coffee?"

Jack badly wanted to spend more time with her, but he couldn't live with himself if he wasn't completely honest with her. "There's nothing I'd like more, Mary. But you have to know, I can't stop thinking about that kiss in the bar...or how much I want another one."

He wouldn't have been surprised if she'd taken back her invitation at that point. Instead, her gaze dropped to his lips and he knew she was being just as honest when she said, "Me, too." Tearing her eyes from his mouth, she shook her head. "Coffee. We're just going to have coffee." She softened the blow with a smile, then led them up the stairs.

Both of them were wet from the rain and he had a sudden flash of making love with her in a warm rain, skin slick from the heat of their bodies, her damp hand sliding into his, that beautiful smile on her face as he kissed every inch of her until she was begging for him to take her.

Jack was surprised to hear several young female voices when Mary opened the door and stepped aside to let him in. She explained in a low voice, "I'm an informal den mother to several young models while they're working in San Francisco. It's a very exciting and sometimes scary lifestyle to be thrown into, especially for girls who may never have left home before now. Basically, I promise their mothers that I'll make sure they eat enough, don't date indiscriminately and put on something warm when they go out."

He'd seen how much she'd loved holding the toddler who had rushed onto the set the previous afternoon. With an amused shake of her head, he watched her pick up a stray scarf and hat belonging to one of her modeling charges. She would, he thought now, be an amazing mother one day. Loving, but without holding on too tightly. Strict, but fair.

Jack's brother Max had a toddler with another on the way, but Jack had never thought about becoming a parent himself. Not, he was stunned to realize, until this very moment.

Six

"Mary, you're soaked!" Janeen was a beautiful twenty-year-old blonde model with legs that went on forever. Her eyes widened even further when she saw Jack standing behind Mary. "Well, hello there." The girl's voice had immediately dropped into a husky register as she slunk forward and thrust her hand into Jack's. "I'm Janeen."

More than a little disgusted with herself for feeling any jealousy at all where Jack and the girls were concerned, Mary went to grab a couple of dry towels from the linen closet while her housemates finished introducing themselves. By the time she returned to the large open-plan living and kitchen area, they had Jack in a captive circle of their youth and beauty.

In her experience, even the nicest man couldn't resist

three pretty girls fawning over him, so it wouldn't have been fair for Mary to expect Jack to not look at them with some appreciation, at the very least. But when she said, "Why don't I trade you this towel for your coat?" and Yvette boldly stepped forward to help him peel it off, Mary couldn't see even one trace of lust on his face for the stunning redhead. Only laughter when the wet fabric caught on his watch clasp.

At least until he turned his gaze back to Mary and took the towel she was offering. She'd also taken off her jacket and was standing in front of him in her wet wrap dress. Just that quickly, the desire in his eyes was back.

But only for *her.*

"Jack is the engineer and inventor I was telling you girls about last night," Mary explained.

"Mary is *so* lucky to get to work with you," Susan said with a seductive toss of her curly black hair.

"My partners and I are the lucky ones." He wiped his hair and face with the towel. In unison, the three young models all sighed over his gorgeously rumpled good looks.

Well, Mary thought as she barely held back her own sigh of appreciation, could she blame them? Jack really was that gorgeous, especially with his button-down shirt and slacks damp and clinging to his well-developed muscles. Clearly, he must not spend all of his time working.

People always asked Mary about her life because she was a celebrity, but she was just as interested in theirs. Journalist, waitress, mother, photographer, bus driver—they all had interesting stories to tell. What, she wondered, was the rest of Jack's story? She guessed he was close to his family from what he'd told her at the diner, and she knew he was devoted to his work. But neither of those things explained the slight air of danger—and risk—that he wore so easily. He hadn't been at all intimidated by the bigwigs in the boardroom.

"If you need any other models for your campaign," Yvette offered with her most alluring smile, "you know where to find us."

Feeling as if she'd accidentally dropped Jack straight into a shark tank, Mary stepped into the fray by gesturing to the three sets of sparkly heels on the wood-planked floor. "Looks like you have a big Friday night out planned?"

Janeen nodded, then looked back at Jack with a hopeful expression. "It's a new club Yvette heard about from the photographer on her shoot today. You two should come with us."

"I'm all danced out," Jack said with a grin for Mary that brought back every wonderful moment of their impromptu dance in the rain, "but thank you."

Mary watched Susan shoot the other girls a pointed glance. When Janeen and Yvette didn't immediately understand, Susan did the world's most obvious pantomime of Jack and Mary being a couple that included a heart drawn in the air and kissy motions with her lips.

"Oh," Yvette said as she looked between them. "Of course, you two don't want to go dancing with us."

Janeen chimed in with, "We should probably let you two be alone now, shouldn't we?"

What could Mary do but laugh as she turned on the kitchen tap. "I'm making coffee if you want some before you head out on the town."

But the girls were now a blur as they strapped on their shoes, grabbed their coats and sparkly purses and headed for the door. "Thanks, Mary, but our dates have already been waiting for us for a while."

Dates?

Mary followed them to the front door and caught them as they flitted down the front steps. "Be careful, and call me if you need anything. It doesn't matter how late, I'll come and bring you home." Reminding herself that they were young, but that each of them had a good head on her shoulders, she added, "And have fun."

A taxi immediately skidded to a stop for the three long-legged beauties and they blew her kisses as they got inside. "You, too!" Yvette called out before tucking her feet into the cab and closing the door.

Jack was laying both of their jackets over the radiator when Mary returned. She'd chosen the house not only for its views, but because she loved how big and open the rooms felt. Even with four people living in it, she never felt cramped. In fact, on nights like this, when the girls went out, rather than appreciate the quiet, she often found herself counting the minutes until they returned with their noise and laughter and exuberance.

She'd made it sound to Jack as if she was looking after them, but the truth was they looked after her, too.

"Sorry about all of that. It can be a bit of a circus around here sometimes, especially on Friday nights."

Jack was the first man she'd invited inside her house since moving in a month earlier. Seeing him looking so *right* in the midst of all the feminine disarray sent her thoughts into a different kind of disarray. What had she been doing before she'd rushed to see the girls off?

Thankfully, the half-filled boiler of her moka pot beside the sink provided a clue.

Still feeling flustered as she went back to filling the boiler and then setting it on low heat on the stovetop, she decided to face the situation head-on. "I hope they didn't make you uncomfortable. Especially," she added with a small laugh, "with all their flirting."

He laughed as he pulled up a seat at the bar. "They were charming, although I can see that they could certainly be a handful. I sometimes had trouble keeping a class of engineering undergrads from rioting in the middle of a lecture when I was a teaching assistant. My hat is off to you for taking on three energetic young women."

She was still amazed that he hadn't drooled over them the way men always did, especially when they'd been practically throwing themselves into his big, strong arms.

"Oh, we've had a riot or two around here in the past month," Mary informed him as she inserted the funnel in the boiler, then filled it with espresso beans she had ground that morning. "Especially the night they were all fighting over the same worthless guy. I ended up banning all social activities for the rest of the week." As she spoke she continued with the coffee preparations by screwing on the top container and watching as the coffee began to appear. “Of course, the girls are also a tremendous amount of fun.” Seeing that half the coffee had brewed already, she turned off the heat.

“I’ve never seen that kind of coffeepot. Is it from Italy?”

She nodded. “It’s called a moka pot.” She spelled out the word for him.

“Whenever you speak about Italy, your accent comes through.” His eyes were warm as he said to her, “Tell me about the country you were born in so I can hear it some more.”

She was a grown woman of thirty-two, not a naive teenage girl anymore. So how did Jack manage to make her blush so easily and so often?

“Much like the United States, Italy is a place with many different colors and textures. The golden ruins of Rome. The checkered duomo of Florence. The canals and opulence of Venice.”

“It sounds wonderful.”

“It is,” she agreed. “And if you’re not careful,” she added with a laugh, “I’ll end up regaling you with stories of Italy like a travel agent all night long.”

“I’d like that,” he said, and then, “Especially if they’re stories about your hometown.”

As always, just thinking about Rosciano sent feelings of conflict moving through her. On the one hand, she loved it like no other place on earth.

On the other, it was where her heart had been broken for the very first time by the person who had mattered most to her.

"On warm summer evenings, the teenage girls flirt with the boys out by the fountain in the middle of the square." She smiled as she told Jack, "Girls learn early in my town how to walk in heels on cobblestone streets without tripping. And once that flirting turns into something more, every couple in town ends up married in our church. As a little girl I would watch the beautiful women in their handmade wedding gowns. My mother made those gowns and I used to help her even though I wasn't nearly as good a seamstress as she was." Making herself focus on the other memories that were coming at her one after the other, she told him, "I used to love to watch the mustard grass bloom in the spring, the grapes growing plump in the summer, the vineyards turning color in the autumn. And Christmas was a time for celebration like none I've ever seen anywhere else."

Realizing she was rambling, Mary stopped herself with a laugh that was a little bit hollow from speaking about her mother. "See, here I go acting like a travel agent, just like I said I would."

"I could never tire of hearing you talk about something that you love."

He was right, she realized. Regardless of what had happened between her and her mother, Mary only ever looked back on her childhood, and the people who had made it so special, with love.

Just as she had when she'd been speaking of home in the diner the night before, and emotion had threatened to overwhelm her, she tried to dismiss it with a joke. "Next thing you know, I'll have you on a plane to Italy with an itinerary of the best secret spots that no other tourist knows about."

"I'd like that," he said, and she could suddenly see it so clearly, the two of them holding hands as they flew across the Atlantic. She'd never taken a lover to her country, had never stolen a kiss with someone in a shadowed alley that had been there since medieval times while the bells of the church chimed above them.

"Has your hometown changed much from when you were nineteen?"

Mary slowly stirred their espresso with a spoon in the

pot before pouring it into two espresso cups. Coming to sit beside Jack on a bar stool, she said, "I don't know."

He stopped with the cup halfway to his lips. "You don't?"

"No, I haven't been back."

She had never spoken about her family situation with anyone outside her closest circle of friends and confidants. A voice in the back of her head reminded her that it wasn't wise to reveal so much to Jack when they had met only twenty-four hours before. Still, when she looked down and realized he'd lowered his cup and had reached for her hands, his touch warmed her better than any cup of coffee could have.

"I truly loved my family, my friends, my town, but I always knew I was different. Because when everyone else was dreaming of wedding rings and babies, I was dreaming of adventures and airplanes. My father understood, and he would tell me about the places he'd seen in the war. But my mother—"

When she grew silent, Jack gently ran the pads of his thumbs over the backs of her hands. As always, there was a deep sensuality to his touch, but tonight she was more aware of the empathy in the gesture.

"Your mother wanted you to stay."

Mary nodded. "I was all she had, her only child. And she was afraid for me, afraid that I'd be hurt. I understand it better now that I'm watching over girls who are the same age I was when I told her I'd met an agent who wanted to make me a big star in New York City. I was so naive," she said with a laugh. "And very lucky that Randy—the talent scout—was honest and legitimate."

"That's why you look out for the girls when you could be living the high life in a penthouse. You want to make sure they make it home to their mothers safe and sound."

"Yes, and I'm not much for penthouse heights, either," she confessed. Though he smiled, she knew he hadn't missed the fact that she'd left out part of her explanation. "My mother was angry with me for being headstrong and foolish. I was angry with her for being stubborn and determined. We both said things we didn't mean." Mary swallowed hard. "When I called home the night I arrived in New York City, she refused to come to the phone. My father made excuses, but I knew. I *knew.* She'd meant it when she said I was no longer her daughter."

Mary couldn't stop her tears from falling as she wept for the mother who had never understood her daughter's need to open her wings and fly, if only to see how things looked from new skies and not because she wanted to fly away forever.

"But she's always been my mother. And I long for her every single day."

Jack drew her against him, his arms warm and comforting as he stroked her back. He didn't speak, didn't try to make everything better for her with simple platitudes. He simply held her and let her cry out the tears she'd held back for too long.

It wasn't until she'd drained her well of emotion dry that she realized he'd pressed his lips to her forehead in the kind of kiss one friend gave to another.

No man had ever kissed her that way before. As a friend.

And she'd never before slipped so easily into a man's arms, as if she'd finally found the place she was supposed to be.

Taking a shaky breath, Mary pulled back slightly and brushed a hand over the broad shoulder that she'd just cried on. "Just when you were starting to dry off, I got you all wet again." It would have been easier to stand, to fiddle with reheating their coffee, to talk about the ad campaign. Anything but remain in Jack's arms and meet his concerned gaze. "Thank you for listening," she said as she looked up into his eyes and was immediately caught up in desire. Just that quickly.

Again, that voice in the back of her head scolded her with reminders of caution. Maybe, she found herself thinking as she reached up to stroke her fingertips over the dark shadow across Jack's jaw, she was still the same foolish and headstrong girl now that she'd been at nineteen.

"You've already gone above and beyond tonight, dancing with me in the rain, holding me while I cried. I know I shouldn't ask for more, but—"

Before she could say anything more, or ask for all the things she shouldn't allow herself to desire, his mouth covered hers, hard and hungry.

Moments ago Jack had kissed her as a friend.

Now he kissed her as a lover.

One hand threaded into her hair, the other cupped her hip as he slid her from the seat to pull her against his body. My God, he felt good. Hard and strong, his caresses just wicked enough to make every nerve ending spike to life inside her.

His tongue slid across her lips once, then once again as if he hadn't gotten nearly enough from the first taste. And then, a moment later, she knew for sure that he hadn't because he was sucking her lower lip into his mouth and making her moan with pleasure as he scored it gently with his teeth.

Their first kiss had been a shockingly sweet press of lips that had sent pleasure humming through her. But this kiss—and the sharp, hot, deep rush of being so close to him—was setting off an entire fireworks show inside of her.

Both of them were breathing hard when he finally drew back an inch. "I've never tasted anything as good as you. Not even close."

He dipped his mouth down for another taste that had her toes curling in her boots, but too soon he pulled back again. She could feel the tight rein he was trying to keep on himself.

"I'm trying to be patient, Angel. I swear I am. I should go before I forget everything except how much I want you."

She'd asked him to see their business relationship through before asking for more. But that was when she'd assumed she could hold on to her own control when being around him.

"Please," she found herself begging him now, "before you go, give me one more kiss."

She expected him to draw her close again, to thread his hands roughly into her hair and devour her once more. But Jack Sullivan had surprised her from the start, and though his gaze ran hot with desire, the light brush of his fingertips over her lips was so gentle, so sweet, that she was stunned by the force of emotion that rocked through her as he touched her. She could feel herself melting into him and knew that if he kissed her again tonight, it wouldn't end there.

"I think we've tested our restraint enough for one night."

She wanted to argue with him, wanted to wrap herself around him and convince him with more kisses. She longed for bare skin against bare skin, and to forget the rules she'd laid down.

But Mary sensed Jack wasn't the kind of man who second-guessed himself once he made up his mind. And she knew he was putting on the brakes not because he didn't want her, but because he respected her too much to let a moment of heady passion destroy the friendship growing between them.

A friendship that might, if treated with the proper care, become the foundation for something much, much bigger.

As a model, she'd learned how to exercise a great deal of control over her body so she could hold difficult poses for hours on end, sometimes in brutal heat, other times in biting cold. It was that control she called upon now. She forced herself to slip out of Jack's arms and pick up his jacket from the radiator across the room.

"Next time I invite you in," she said with a small smile as she gave him his coat and walked him to the front door, "I'll let you drink your coffee."

He was standing on her front step when he said, "Next time you invite me in, I'm going to make love to you."

He covered her gasp of surprise with that last kiss she'd begged for. Before she had a chance to catch her reeling heart, he was gone.

She didn't know how long she stood at the front door, staring out at the people walking on the sidewalk below and watching the cars and taxis and buses move slowly through the Friday-night traffic. Jack Sullivan was everything she'd ever looked for in a man. Smart. Sexy. And with a heart full of so much warmth it stunned her.

And yet, she realized as she finally closed her front door with a soft click, instead of being calmed by that realization, she was more frightened than she'd ever been before.

Frightened and utterly enthralled.

Her heart still pounding hard, she headed for the phone. "Gerry, it's Mary. You know how you were saying you were hoping to work together again? Is there any chance you might be able to squeeze in a last-minute shoot this Monday for a really interesting ad campaign?"

Seven

On Monday morning, Jack walked onto the set where Mary would be shooting their first print ad. When he caught sight of her dark hair swinging over her shoulders and her long, toned legs that seemed to go on forever, for the very first time in his life, Jack could not figure out how to remain rational. In all honesty he couldn't remember why he should even keep trying.

The speed with which his heart was racing made him feel as if he were on a racetrack in one of the stock cars he'd retooled over the years. Race cars, he'd discovered back in high school, were the perfect antidote for the slow pace of invention and engineering development. Jack's experience on the track had taught him how to embrace not only the rush and the thrill…but the danger, as well. If you weren't risking on the track, you had no business being out there.

The risks he took on the racetrack seemed a hell of a lot more dangerous than the ones he took in the garage working on his computers but, the truth was, it was the other way around. Those risks were minuscule by comparison considering that he'd already given up ten years of his life for a risky dream.

And yet, as Mary's laughter moved through him, Jack finally understood that the stakes had never been this high.

Not only was his dream on the line…but it seemed his heart was, too.

Jack had done some serious thinking over the weekend. Thinking, after all, was what he'd always done best. He should have been thinking about the launch of the Pocket Planner. He should have been hunkered down over manufacturing schedules with Larry. He should have been going over distribution and sales outlets with Howie. He should have been approving final ad-campaign plans.

The very last thing that Jack should have been focusing on when they were in the final lap of a dream that had been ten years in the making was a woman.

He had always had to fit women and relationships into

the few spare slots of time and attention he had available. He'd never even come close to thinking about "forever" or love. He'd treated the women he'd taken out well, but work had always come first.

But Mary was no ordinary woman.

Of course it was perfectly natural to look at a woman like her and want her. But was it natural to *only* be able to think of her? To remember every flavor of sugar and spice on her lips as he'd kissed her? To keep feeling the silky softness of her skin as he stroked her cheek? To hear continued echoes of the sweet sound of pleasure she'd made when he'd taken their kiss deeper?

What was more, when she'd told him about her severed relationship with her mother, he'd thought of his own mother and how much she meant to him. He wished he could do something to help Mary gain back what she was so sure she'd lost.

As if she could hear his impassioned thoughts, Mary suddenly looked over her shoulder and saw him. He saw her eyes flare and her skin flush with what he hoped was a desire that matched his own.

Jack hadn't been able to forget the yearning in Mary's eyes when she'd asked him for one more kiss. Lord, all he'd wanted was to lift her into his arms and take her back to her bedroom and make love to her all night long. But she'd been so earnest in the diner when she'd asked him to be patient, and he intended to respect that which was so clearly important to her. Still, that hadn't stopped him from stealing one more kiss before he made himself leave.

Now Jack badly wanted to steal another kiss. He wished they could forget all about business. He longed to pull her into his arms and bury his hands in her hair as he drank in her scent, her softness and the sweet sounds she made when she melted against him.

But just as he'd been trying to remind himself all weekend, this was neither the time nor the place for wooing her.

"Gerry," she said to the photographer, "come meet Jack Sullivan."

Mary looked perfectly poised, but he didn't think he'd imagined the slight hitch in her voice as she'd said his name. Maybe he hadn't been the only one tied up in knots this weekend....

He held out his hand to the slim man with the bright green eyes. "Thank you so much for agreeing to work with us on such short notice, Gerry."

The photographer sized Jack up as they shook hands. “I’ve never been able to say no to Mary.”

Jack knew exactly how he felt. There were a dozen questions he should have asked Gerry about the shoot. Instead, he turned back to Mary. “Did the girls get home all right on Friday night?”

“It was closer to Saturday morning,” she said with a little shake of her head, “but apart from leaving a string of broken hearts throughout San Francisco, they came back safe and sound.”

Gerry was looking between Jack and Mary with raised eyebrows when the studio door burst open and Howie and Larry came in with Allen on their heels.

“You’re more gorgeous than ever,” Allen said as he kissed Mary once on each cheek. “I’m afraid I can’t stay, but I wanted to wish you luck, my dear, and thank you again for being a part of our product launch.”

Mary introduced everyone to Gerry, then excused herself from the group to go and take care of putting the finishing touches on her hair and makeup.

Jack and his partners were sitting on the folding chairs at the back of the set when Mary walked back out fifteen minutes later. Jack’s heart nearly stopped beating in his chest as he drank her in. She was dressed in casual black slacks and a soft red sweater that skimmed over her curves. She had put on just enough makeup to highlight her features in a beautifully elegant and simple way.

The campaign they'd decided on was simple and direct. Mary was not going to play a role for the camera. Rather, she was going to let the buying public know, via both still shots and a live-action commercial that they'd be shooting later that week, that she used the Pocket Planner and loved it. The set today looked a great deal like her actual living room and kitchen, and Jack realized it was because she'd brought in some things from home. A pretty blue-and-white vase of flowers. A sculpture of a dancing girl. A bowl of fresh fruit.

As she displayed their invention for the camera, Jack was impressed all over again. She worked nonstop for hours, not just in front of the camera but behind it, as well, as she assisted Gerry with his lighting and props. When Larry and Howie started grumbling about food and drink, Jack suggested they head out to pick up something for everyone. At the same time, Jack could see the faint lines of fatigue beginning to appear at the corners of Mary's eyes and mouth while Gerry changed cameras.

Standing up and walking onto the set, Jack said, "Time for a break."

Gerry sighed in clear relief as he put his camera down. "I'm going to run across the street for a triple espresso. Should I bring back one for everyone?"

Jack shook his head. The last thing he needed right now was more adrenaline coursing through him.

"Thanks, but I'm fine, too," Mary murmured, reaching around to rub a kink out of her neck. "I think I'll just get off my feet for a few minutes."

After Mary had left the set for her small dressing room, Gerry told Jack, "No other model of her caliber and fame would even consider assisting with lights and makeup like this. There isn't another woman like her in the world."

"You've got that right," Jack agreed.

"I was extremely surprised when Mary called me about your campaign. She was dead set on leaving modeling and no one could get her to change her mind. Not until you came along."

"I'm a very lucky man."

Gerry assessed Jack again with his cool green eyes before nodding once. "Don't ever forget it."

Jack headed over to the small room at the side of the set that Mary had disappeared into. At first he only saw the table where Mary had set up a mirror, and her makeup and hair kit. Just as Gerry had pointed out, she normally had a whole crew of people working on her photo shoots. Moving deeper into the room, he saw that she was sitting on a soft chair rubbing her neck and shoulders as if they ached.

She turned her head toward him when she heard his footsteps. "Jack, do you need something?" She immediately moved to stand, but when he replaced her hands with his own on her shoulders and began to massage the tight muscles, she sank back down into the chair.

Mary knew she shouldn't let Jack touch her like this—especially while they were working together—but when it felt so good how could she possibly muster up the strength to tell him to stop?

But she had to stop it. Jack's strong, warm hands on her would likely lead to more wonderful, deliciously sensual things.

The kind of *more* that she had specifically told him they couldn't do again while they were working together.

Oh, but what a struggle it was to make herself slide out from beneath his hands to stand. When she felt she'd removed all desire from her expression, she turned to face him.

"Friday night, I know the boundaries of our relationship got a little fuzzy—" particularly when she'd been begging him for one more kiss "—but you were right to leave when you did."

"It was a hell of a weekend without you," he said in his disarmingly direct way. "The only consolation was that I knew I'd get to work with you today." He shook his head, his eyes dark and intense again. "I wish just working with you would be enough."

Lord, the things this man did to her with nothing but a look and a few simple words. She was tingling head to toe, inside and out, as she made herself take a step away from him.

"It has to be enough, at least until the campaign is over."

"Tell me why we have to wait. Make me understand why I can't kiss you again right now when we both know how good it will be?"

She went to take another step back from him, before looking up into his eyes and realizing she had done the exact opposite. Instead of moving farther away, she'd gotten closer.

"I made a mistake a few years ago. A big one." A chill moved over her just thinking about Romain. "And what I learned from my mistake is that we should wait until our relationship isn't wrapped up in the ad campaign, or tracking how many units are being ordered. Then we'll both be able to think clearly about things."

Seeing her shiver, he slid his hands over her arms to warm her. "What I'm feeling for you has absolutely nothing to do with units or ad campaigns."

She wanted so badly to believe him, especially since her own feelings for him were growing at an exponential rate. His hands on her felt so good, so comforting and arousing at the same time that her body instinctively shifted closer yet again.

"You've worked toward fulfilling your dream for ten years," she reminded him. "You shouldn't even consider putting anything or anyone else first right now."

"Whoever it was that hurt you," he said in a low voice that rumbled through her, "was an idiot."

They were just inches apart as she agreed, "Yes, he was."

"Rumor has it," he said with a small smile that drew her in closer for the kiss she was trying not to give him, "that my IQ is quite high."

How could she possibly fight her feelings for him when he didn't just make her burn but made her laugh, too?

"Is that so?"

"One hundred sixty, and my mother still has the test results to prove it," he said with a grin. "Although I'll confess that sometimes I get an idea in the shower and forget to shave because I'm hurrying to get it down on paper."

She almost sighed out loud at how sweet and cute and sexy it was that his brain worked so fast he could hardly keep on top of normal, everyday things like shaving. Did his socks match? she wondered. But worse even than mulling about his socks was the fact that she wanted to nuzzle against the dark bristles he'd forgotten to shave away that morning.

Trying to keep things light between them—even if she knew she was only delaying the inevitable—she dropped her gaze to his beard-in-the-making. "You look good scruffy."

"Now that I know you think that, I'll never shave again."

She laughed again. "Remind me to look you up in two years to see how long your beard is."

"All you'll have to do is roll over in our bed to see that."

She'd never been with a man this confident—so sure they were meant to be together. And she'd never wanted to kiss anyone this much, either.

In order to distract her lips from the kiss they were dying for, she said his name instead, meaning it as a warning. "Jack."

He distracted her right back, not with her name, but by saying, "Angel."

It was an endearment that made her knees wobble every single time.

So when he slid one hand into her hair and another around the curve of her hip to pull her closer, she didn't have the strength of will to keep fighting this kiss any longer. All it took was the press of his lips against hers to dissolve the fierce reminders of how she'd been hurt before. All her intelligent thoughts vanished, as well.

"Mary, I know you said you were cutting back on caffeine, but I brought you—"

Gerry was halfway into the room by the time he realized she was wrapped around Jack like a teenage girl stealing a kiss from her secret boyfriend when she thought no one was looking.

"Sorry about that, folks," he said in his easy, seen-it-all way. "I'll just go take care of that film that needs changing."

The second Mary heard Gerry's voice, she should have jumped out of Jack's arms. Especially given that she shouldn't have been in them in the first place. But his kiss had made her limbs feel too loose and rubbery to do anything but stay right where she was.

Finally, she gathered up enough self-control to make herself shift away, one inch at a time until Jack had no choice but to let her go. "I can't believe we were doing that...and that Gerry caught us. Thank God it was him and not your partners."

"What if they had seen us? We're not hurting anyone, or anything, by kissing each other."

But what if you do end up hurting me?

Mixed into her fear of being hurt again by someone she worked with was the lingering memory of how humiliated she'd been by the knowledge that everyone in their circle knew just how foolishly she'd given her heart...and then been tossed aside. She couldn't stand for that to happen again, not when she was supposed to be older and wiser.

"Have you told them about Friday night, about what happened between us at my house?"

Jack looked more than a little insulted by her question. "Of course I haven't. I don't kiss and tell, Mary. What happens between us is private."

A moment later, Howie and Larry poked their heads into the room. "Hey, Jack, Mary, we brought back a sandwich for you both."

She could easily read the frustration on Jack's handsome face as she told them she'd join everyone in the common area in a couple of minutes. They all left the room and her hands were trembling as she sat down at her mirror and picked up her hairbrush. A moment later Gerry walked in and closed the door behind him.

"I thought something was going on between the two of you." Gerry grinned at her in the mirror. "Now, before we start shooting again, tell me *everything* about that gorgeous man who can't keep his hands off you."

In order to keep expenses down, Mary was taking care of her own hair and makeup and wearing clothes from her own closet. Now, as she ran a straightening iron over a lock of hair to get ready for their second set of shots, she had to work to keep her hand steady so she didn't burn herself.

With another photographer she might have tried to hide what she was feeling. But, with the man who had known her for her entire adult life, there was no point in pretending Jack's touch had been innocent. Besides, there was a reason Gerry was such a great photographer—he saw things other people didn't.

"Jack is different from any other man I've known," she admitted.

She knew she shouldn't say anything more, but she was dying to talk to someone about Jack. She couldn't possibly have discussed him with the young models she was looking after, not when she was trying to set a good example for them. But Gerry had watched her grow up. First, from behind a camera lens, and then later when they became friends. He'd held her hand and let her cry when her various romances hadn't ended in happily ever after. If anyone would understand how confused she was right now, he would.

"The men I've been around have always been so self-aware, so conscious of everything they did and said, and especially how they looked. But Jack's brain is working so fast all the time—he's so different. He told me that sometimes he doesn't even remember to shave."

"Adorable," Gerry said, echoing her own thoughts.

She sighed. "Agreed, but I still shouldn't have kissed him just now."

His eyebrows went up. "Why the hell not?"

"Because we've agreed to keep things strictly professional between us for now. As I'm sure you recall, last time I mixed business with pleasure things went horribly awry."

Gerry frowned. "Romain Bollinger was a worthless piece of scum. I thought you were over him."

"Of course I am," she insisted, horrified that anyone would think she was still pining for that horrible excuse for a man. "I'm just trying to be careful."

"If that was a careful kiss, I would love to see what a dangerous one looks like," he teased.

So would I, she thought, despite knowing better. *So would I.*

Between the kiss Jack had given her this afternoon and the one from Friday night, Mary knew he had made his intentions abundantly clear. If she couldn't resist temptation, then she'd just have to make sure not to put herself in its path. She was not a young, naive girl anymore who would melt into a puddle at a few sexy words from a good-looking man. If anything, her experiences with love had hardened her to the point that sexy words were far more likely to put her on her guard.

And yet, all weekend—and then all day today during the shoot—she'd been replaying his sinfully sexy words: *next time you invite me in, I'm going to make love to you.*

She didn't think he had said it to shock her or even to turn her on.

He'd simply said what he was feeling…and what he clearly believed would happen the next time they were alone together in her house.

When she and Gerry finally wrapped the shoot, Howie and Larry got up out of their chairs and showered her with compliments. She tried to be gracious as she thanked them but, at the same time, she wondered where Jack was. Would they think it was strange if she asked about him?

Fortunately, before she could make a lovesick fool out of herself, Howie said, "Jack had to take care of some urgent business back at the garage." He turned red as he realized what he'd just admitted to her about where they worked. "I mean, our office. But he said for you to call him if you need anything at all."

Despite the fact that Mary had been reminding herself again and again all afternoon that she and Jack needed to keep their distance, disappointment came swift and strong.

"We're going to help Gerry get his equipment loaded into his van," Larry said. "Can we give you a lift anywhere after that?"

She shook her head. "Thanks, but I've got some errands to run. I'll see you both at the commercial shoot in a few days."

After kissing Gerry goodbye on the cheek, she wound her scarf tightly around her neck and shoved on her hat. Yesterday she'd needed a brisk walk through the city to try to walk off her attraction to Jack. Today, she needed to try to burn through her irritation with herself...and to keep herself away from the phone so that she wouldn't give in to the temptation to take him up on his offer to call if she needed anything.

Because, Lord help her, she needed *him*.

By the time Mary arrived home her feet were killing her and all she wanted to do was collapse into a bubble bath with a glass of wine and a good book.

So what if kissing Jack again sounded a thousand times better than the bath-wine-book combo? She'd just have to get over it.

It was incredibly comforting to come home to a house full of voices. She was going to miss the girls a great deal when they headed to their respective homes for the holidays.

The scent in the air was one that always reminded her of Italy at Christmas. "You bought a tree," she exclaimed as she walked into the living room.

Yvette grinned down at her from her perch on top of the ladder. "Surprise!"

Janeen put on a Christmas record and pulled Mary into an impromptu jig that made her momentarily forget that she wished she were somewhere else, with someone else.

"We've got cookies and eggnog, too," Susan said from the kitchen.

After Mary went into her room to put down her things and take off her heels, Susan handed her a glass so that they could toast each other. "To you, Mary, for taking all of us in and giving us a home away from home."

Mary hadn't spent Christmas with her family for the past thirteen years, but tonight she felt as if she was finally part of a family again. As they clinked their glasses together, she was afraid she would spoil the moment by crying, but then Yvette said, "We're dying to find out how your shoot went today with the gorgeous Mr. Sullivan."

"It went fine," she said in her primmest voice.

"Ooh," Janeen said, not fooled in the least, "you're blushing."

Mary lifted her free hand to her face and felt how hot it was. "We're just business associates," she protested.

"From the way the two of you look at each other," Susan noted, "it sure seems like more than just business."

Mary hadn't realized they'd been that obvious when she'd invited him inside the other night. But she had just finished dancing with him in the rain, and it had been so wonderful, how could she not have stars in her eyes?

"He kissed me."

Everyone's eyes grew big—including Mary's—at what she'd just admitted.

She was supposed to be setting a good example for the young models, which meant teaching them that it was a bad idea to get involved with a business associate. But her long walk home through the city hadn't done a darn thing to push away the memory of how it felt to have Jack's hands in her hair, his hard heat against her, his delicious mouth pressing against hers.

"I'll bet he's a great kisser, isn't he?" Yvette said with a dreamy look on her pretty face.

This was Mary's chance to explain to them what a mistake the kisses she'd shared with Jack had been. Instead, she nodded and said, "The best."

As a group, the girls spontaneously hugged her. "When are you going to see him again?"

"I'll be shooting a TV commercial for his new invention in a few days. I'm sure he'll be there." She hoped her voice sounded more nonchalant than she felt. How on earth was she going to make it through a handful of days without seeing Jack? Especially when he was all she could think about....

"Or you could call him now and invite him over tonight," Janeen suggested. "We wouldn't mind having a gorgeous man in our midst, would we, girls?"

Needing to do something with her hands so that she didn't pick up the phone and call him right that very second, Mary lifted a sparkly ornament and walked over to the tree to hang it on a branch. "We've agreed to keep things professional between us until the campaign wraps up."

Susan gave her a very knowing look for a nineteen-year-old. "Stolen kisses are the best kind, aren't they?"

"They weren't—" she began, before admitting, "Okay, they *were* stolen." And Susan was right—his kisses were the very best of Mary's life. "But they were the very last ones I'm going to let him steal until after we wrap up the campaign."

From the doubtful looks on their faces, Mary knew she looked even less convincing than she sounded.

"Personally," Yvette said as she lifted her drink to her lips, "I prefer forbidden kisses."

Mary had been intent on letting the conversation peter out, but now she turned from the tree and pinned Yvette with a laser-sharp gaze. "Who are you having forbidden kisses with?"

Yvette reached into the box of ornaments so that Mary couldn't see her face as she muttered, "No one," but it hadn't been *that* long since she was nineteen, and Mary knew better than most about being headstrong and foolish. Maybe, she thought, she should tell them about her mistakes. But with the Christmas carols playing and their laughter ringing out, she didn't want to ruin the evening with what would surely sound like a lecture.

Not for the first time since the three models had moved in with her, Mary realized what her mother must have gone through. How did you give advice to someone you cared about without ruining your relationship? And what could you possibly say to get a young woman with the entire world at her feet to listen to your advice without storming out in a huff?

Hopefully, one day when Mary had children of her own, she'd have some of the answers.

Eight

Over the course of the next few days, Mary not only gave dozens of radio, print and TV interviews about the Pocket Planner, but she and Gerry traveled all through San Francisco taking pictures of her using it in different parts of the city. After the handful of kisses Jack had stolen from her—and especially given how quickly her resistance had fallen both times—Mary knew she should be glad for this break from seeing him to regain her sanity. Before Jack Sullivan had walked into her life, she'd been perfectly fine. Content. Comfortable.

Mary frowned. Was that what her supposedly glamorous, jet-setting life had turned into? *Fine, content, comfortable?* If that was all she had to show for her adventurous life, had it really been worth turning her back on her old life? After all, she could have stayed in Italy and gotten married to the first boy who proposed and ended up with *fine, content* and *comfortable.*

She was so lost in her turbulent thoughts that she walked right into Gerry's studio and opened the door to his darkroom without paying attention to the red light above the door.

"Shut the door!"

Some photographers were yellers, but not Gerry. In fact, she couldn't ever remember him raising his voice... until now. Mary slammed the door shut behind her, but Gerry was already swearing over the print he'd lost because of her stupid mistake.

"I'm so sorry," she said, even though her apology couldn't fix a thing. "I don't know what I was thinking."

But she knew perfectly well what she'd been thinking. She'd been trying to convince herself that not being tempted by Jack was a good thing. Yet she had as little restraint when it came to thinking about him as she did to kissing him.

The harder she tried to push him from her mind, the deeper he stuck.

Dropping the ruined photo into the trash, Gerry turned to face her. "I take it Jack hasn't called?"

The room was dark, but not dark enough that her friend couldn't see the truth in her eyes. "He's just doing what I asked him to do."

"I've known you for more than a decade and I've never seen you like this." Gerry cocked his head and pinned her with his deep photographer's gaze. "That's why you agreed to take on this campaign, isn't it, and why you're working so hard on it? You've fallen for the brilliant—and gorgeous—engineer."

Allen had commented before one of her interviews that she was going to be very glad she'd given up her fee in favor of a portion of the profits. Of course, she didn't tell the chairman that it was all for Jack, that on their first night together in the diner she'd fallen head over heels for him before realizing he wanted more from her than pie and conversation. Gerry, on the other hand, had seen right through her.

"I've tried so hard to keep my head on my shoulders around Jack, but..."

She found it extremely difficult to put into words what she was feeling. If it were simply attraction, it would be easy. But the emotion rolling through her was something much deeper than that.

She knew better than to want this much or feel so

strongly when every time she'd given her heart to someone, they'd tossed it aside without a care. And yet, she hadn't been able to stop herself where Jack was concerned.

"I've never known anyone so driven by a dream, or so passionate about making it become reality."

"I have," Gerry said. "You."

Mary couldn't contain her surprise. "Me?"

"I'll never forget that first day you walked into my studio. You were as green and inexperienced as they came, but Randy had promised me there was something special about you, something that went beyond your outward beauty. You stepped in front of my camera and even though you weren't polished, or had any clue whatsoever about what you were doing, I saw exactly what Randy had been talking about. Your passion for life, and all those dreams you wanted to make real, was right there in your eyes." He put his hand on her arm. "I know the business hasn't always been easy on you and that you've been through tough times with your family and with men who didn't deserve you, but can't you see it's only made you stronger?"

From the line above his head he pulled a few prints that had dried and slipped them into an envelope. "Jack and his partners need to see these tonight so that they can pull their favorites to present to the board. I've got to leave right now for another meeting. Their address is on the front of the envelope."

Jack followed the Realtor through the large building on Page Mill Road with Howie and Larry. Now that Mary was working to support the Pocket Planner, retailers were starting to come on board in big numbers. Allen wanted to make sure they had their offices ready and new employees in place immediately after the Christmas boom so they could begin R & D on new products. The past few days had gone at warp speed and Jack shouldn't have had a spare moment for anything but the production demands and planning the future of his company.

But as Jack worked to focus on what the Realtor was saying about manufacturing floors and office space, all he could think about was how Mary had felt in his arms. How soft her skin was beneath his fingertips. The sweet taste of her lips. The surprise in her eyes when he'd talked about waking up next to her in two years. And how he'd barely been able to stop himself from calling her or, worse, showing up on her doorstep.

"How does that sound to you, Jack?"

Howie's question knocked Jack back into the present. "Sorry, what was the question?"

"We're supposed to meet Gerry back at the garage in a few minutes to look over the pictures he and Mary have taken over the past few days. You've got the best eye for the ads anyway, so we were thinking we'd finish up here and let you take that meeting."

Knowing he wasn't being any help here anyway, Jack quickly agreed. During the drive back to their soon-to-be-closed office in his garage, he thought up another dozen excuses for calling Mary and meeting with her. But, damn it, no matter how badly he wanted to see her, he knew better.

Jack and his brothers had been raised to honor and respect everyone, especially women. And yet, the few times he and Mary had been together, he'd had a hell of a time trying to respect her wishes by not letting their kisses spiral off into more.

He was just pulling up the driveway when he realized he'd have to figure out how to get a grip on himself, and fast. Because Gerry wasn't there waiting for him with the photos for the campaign.

Instead, the most beautiful woman in the world was standing right there.

★★★

Mary had expected to see Howie and Larry with Jack but, obviously, something had held up the other two men. She couldn't ever remember being this nervous around a man, not even when she'd been a young teenager with her first school crush.

Jack's eyes were darker, even more intense, than she remembered them being as he walked toward her. She worked to keep her legs from trembling, or from running straight into his arms.

It didn't help one bit when Jack said, "I've missed you, Mary."

Her breath caught in her throat at how much she wanted him at that moment. Oh, God, why had she agreed to let Gerry maneuver her into coming here? She knew he thought he was doing what was best for her, probably thinking she'd been playing it safe for too long, but surely that didn't mean she should dive headfirst into the most dangerous waters she'd ever known. Did it?

Trying to break through the heated moment, she said, "I can't wait to finally see where the magic happens."

"I'm afraid there's far more dust and a mess of wires than magic," he said as he reached down to unlock the garage door.

The muscles in his arms and back flexed beneath his cotton shirt as he pulled the door open, and though she knew it was rude to stare, she couldn't have stopped herself for the world. Especially when she knew firsthand just how good those hard muscles felt pressed against her.

She caught her breath for a different reason when he motioned for her to come inside. He was right about the dust and wires, but what really made an impact on her was the wonder of creation in every spare inch of the room.

"It's amazing, Jack." She had no idea how any of it worked, but she wanted to. She pointed to a screen with a bunch of knobs all around it. "What's this for?"

"It's an oscilloscope, which is a type of electronic test instrument for looking at wave signals."

She walked over to a group of similar smaller boxes. "And what about this?"

"This is a voltage generator. It's what we use to power up the prototype motherboards."

She put her hand on his arm. "It really is magic, isn't it?"

A muscle jumped in his jaw as he stared down at her. "I think you'd better show me the pictures you brought."

Suddenly realizing how close she was standing to him,

she took a step back. "I'm sorry. I shouldn't be wasting your time—"

"You don't have a damn thing to be sorry for," he said, cutting her off before she could finish her apology. "But I will be sorry in a moment if I don't figure out how to gain some self-control around you."

She'd always thought she was a fair person, and a strong one, too. But how could either of those things be true when she was desperate for Jack to lose control and kiss her again so that she could get lost in his arms and not have to make any tough decisions at all?

He deserved her honesty at the very least, if she couldn't give him fairness or strength. "I missed you these past few days, too. There's no point in trying to pretend I didn't."

But even that wasn't nearly honest enough. She needed to finally tell him why she was trying so hard to keep things professional between them during the campaign.

"Remember how I told you about the mistake I made a few years ago? His name was Romain. He owns a big Swiss-watch company and I was the model they chose for a crucial campaign. He was very charming, very persuasive and attentive, and we began dating soon after I started working for his company. We were seen everywhere together. He made sure of it so that his profits would soar even higher. Until he decided profits would be even higher without me." She sighed, thinking how young, how foolish she'd been. "He was about to inform me of my future replacement on the day I decided to surprise him at his penthouse." She laughed, but there was no humor in it. "All three of us were surprised."

"Three?"

"Me, Romain and the model in his bed. She was quite a bit younger than me, one of the up-and-coming girls who was as naive as I used to be when I first started in the business. Clearly, she'd been just as easily charmed by him as I was. I broke things off with him, of course, but I had signed a contract, and I knew I couldn't live with myself if I broke my promise to his board and the investors. Those last few photo shoots were horribly painful."

"You would have been perfectly within your rights to break a business promise, since he had done far worse by breaking his personal promise with you."

"No. I couldn't let him know how badly he'd hurt me, or admit to the world what a fool I'd been. I was just as foolish as my mother accused me of being all those years ago." She took a breath to try to shake it all off and come back to Jack and his garage full of magic. "Since then, I've always been careful not to blend my work life with my personal life."

"I would tell you I'm not like him, but you already know that, don't you?"

"I do, but—"

How could she explain that it wasn't Jack she didn't trust, but herself? The biggest mistakes she'd made in her life had been about giving and losing love.

"Every day I had to work with him shattered another little piece of me. It's taken a long time to heal those cracks."

He reached for her hands and threaded their fingers together. "I promised to try to be patient, and I couldn't live with myself if I broke my promise to you."

She'd never met anyone like Jack. He had such respect for the meaning of a promise...not to mention such respect for her as the model that so many people had discounted over the years as nothing more than just a pretty face.

"You know what you want and what you need to do to get it," she said softly, "but you never compromise your values—or your word—to get there. How do you do it?"

"I could ask you the same question. You're so beautiful that you could have anything you want, but you earn everything through hard work."

"You make me sound better than I am. Especially when I know it's not fair to want so badly to kiss you after I've just laid down the rules again…but I can't figure out a way to stop myself from asking."

"Nobody's perfect," he said with a smile that didn't do a thing to mask his desire.

It was just the right thing to say after the pressures she'd faced while building a career based on perfection. "In that case, I hope that means you'll forgive me for what I'm about to ask." She moved closer again, putting her hands on his chest and slowly sliding them up to wind around his neck.

"Ask me anything, Angel."

Her insides turned to liquid heat at his endearment. "Kiss me, Jack."

She was still saying his name when his mouth covered hers in a kiss that stole her breath away entirely. Both of them fed greedily from each other's lips, their days apart having fueled their hunger for each other and bringing it to new heights.

Mary had been kissed at the top of the Eiffel Tower. She'd been kissed in a horse-drawn carriage in the middle of Prague. She'd been kissed on the Copacabana Beach in Rio de Janeiro. But this kiss with Jack, in his garage surrounded by cables and machines and stale cups of coffee, was the most romantic, most thrilling kiss she'd ever shared...and one she knew she'd remember forever, regardless of how things turned out between them.

He backed her up into one of the tables, and the next thing she knew, he'd lifted her up onto it so that she could wrap her legs around his waist. Again, she felt like a naughty teenager making out with her off-limits boyfriend as she locked her ankles together behind his hips and pulled him even closer.

The fireworks sparking off inside her were on the opposite scale from *fine,* from *content.* On the contrary, she felt as if she wasn't just on the edge of Jack's worktable, but teetering on the edge of something deliciously dangerous. Shockingly wicked.

And absolutely *wonderful.*

For all of her protests that they needed to keep business strictly business, yet again it was Jack who retained enough sense to lift his mouth from hers. Not once had she been the one to stop their kisses. If he had been any other man, they would already be stripping off each other's clothes, promises be damned.

But as desperate as she was physically to take things to the next level, Mary knew in her heart of hearts that though her body was ready, her heart wasn't.

Forehead to forehead, they each worked to catch their breath. As a new rush of longing swept through her, Mary closed her eyes tight. Reminding herself that his partners could walk in at any moment, she took a deep breath, then lifted her lids to find Jack's dark gaze on her.

His eyes were extraordinarily beautiful, a deep brown with flecks of green and blue throughout. He also had naturally thick eyelashes, the kind that women spent too much time and money trying to replicate with makeup. Up close like this, finally letting herself look her fill, she realized he had a small scar just at the top of his left cheekbone, and his nose looked as if it had been broken a long time ago.

As he'd said, no one was perfect, and his imperfections only made him more beautiful to her. He had the dangerous good looks of a heartbreaker, but the more time she spent with him, the less she believed that he could ever break anything, let alone someone's heart.

Mary had told Jack the truth about Romain, but what she hadn't admitted was that she'd been trying to put the pieces of her broken heart back together ever since the day her mother had disowned her.

When, she wanted to know, would she be ready to let the broken pieces go so that she could finally start over and be whole again?

As Jack gently helped her down from his worktable, he said, "There's something I need to tell you."

Not sure she could yet trust her voice, she simply nodded for him to continue.

"I like you." He brushed a lock of hair away from her cheek, tucking it gently behind her ear. "More than I've ever liked anyone else. Much, much more."

Many times over the years men had declared their love for her, but Jack's simple statement that he *liked* her was a million times sweeter.

When they'd been kissing on his desk, she'd felt like a naughty teenager. Her parents had been protective enough that she'd been an untouched virgin when she left Italy. Being with Jack made her feel giddy, as if she were having her first truly important crush with a boy she couldn't stop thinking about.

Smiling, she said, "I like you, too." Needing to touch him again, she gently ran her fingertip over his left cheekbone. "Where did you get this scar?"

"My brother Max and I were playing hockey. He ended up switching to tennis after this."

"Is he the one who broke your nose, too?"

On a laugh that easily could have warmed her on the coldest night, he shook his head. "That was all me. You have to promise me you won't laugh before I tell you how it happened."

She made a cross over her heart. "I promise."

"I walked into a wall."

She had to bite her lip to stop the laughter from bubbling out. When she was fairly sure she could speak without giggling, she asked, "How?"

One eyebrow raised, humor in his eyes, he said, "I was in college and had my first breakthrough with understanding how the Shockley Diode worked. I'd been up all night, and when I went to brag to Howie about my amazing accomplishment, I somehow missed the doorway."

It was either laugh or kiss him, and since she'd made a promise not to do the first, she happily gave in to the second. But before their kiss could turn to more, she made herself take a step back.

"Pictures." The word came out of Mary's mouth slightly high-pitched and breathless. "I should show you the photos. Especially since Howie and Larry will probably be here soon, and I—" oh, how she hated the way the words would sound, even though she knew she had to say them "—I wouldn't want them to catch us kissing the way Gerry did."

When, she asked herself again, would all those broken pieces inside her finally begin to heal?

She also hated seeing the flash of hurt that moved across Jack's face before he quickly erased it and said, "Right, we should look at the pictures. How do you feel about pepperoni and black olives on your pizza?"

Her stomach growled before she'd so much as opened her mouth to tell him she'd love that. Larry and Howie pulled up outside a few minutes later, and as the four of them ate pizza and drank beer straight from the bottle, they began making decisions about which pictures to use in the ad campaign. With Jack's passionate kisses tingling on her lips all the while, Mary didn't envy the three of them their easy camaraderie…because they made her feel she was one of them.

And she loved every second of being part of their team.

Nine

Jack had nearly walked into half-a-dozen walls after Mary left his house last night. He'd simply been too preoccupied thinking about her to pay attention to anything around him. The kiss they'd shared in his garage had blown his mind, but so had the cute way she'd valiantly tried not to laugh at him when he'd confessed how his nose had been broken. And then she'd amazed him all over again when she'd settled into pizza and beer with his partners as if she'd been hanging out with them since college.

At the same time, his chest ached a little bit when he thought about the way she was so intent on hiding their budding relationship. He understood why she was still wary of being with him, especially publicly, and why she continued to ask him to be patient with her. But all that didn't stop him wishing for more.

Today they were back in the studio to film a TV commercial for the campaign. The moment he walked in the door, Jack did a quick scan of the studio looking for Mary and saw her in conversation with a tall woman wearing all black, with thick, black-framed glasses.

My God, Mary was beautiful in the casual jeans and green sweater they'd all agreed she'd wear for the shoot, but not in any kind of artificial way. Her hair was loose and glossy, her mouth was the same shade of rose as when he'd kissed her, and her laughter could have easily fueled him through another week of sleepless nights.

Mary moved to go to her dressing room, and that was when she saw him. She paused at the doorway and blinked hard several times, as if she was working to get her bearings again. Jack was glad to know he wasn't the only one who got knocked off balance simply from being in the same room. Giving him a slightly flustered smile, she disappeared into her dressing room.

Although he wanted to go straight to Mary, Jack headed toward the director to introduce himself. "Thanks so much for working with us." He held out his hand.

"I'm Jack Sullivan, one of the engineers who created the Pocket Planner."

"Georgina Callem." The director had a firm handshake and a serious face as she took her time studying him. "I've known Mary for almost a decade. I would do anything for her."

Jack didn't check himself before saying, "So would I."

The woman's stern mouth cracked just the slightest bit. "Good. Now stay out of my way today and I think we'll get along just fine."

No wonder Mary appreciated Georgina so much. He imagined that as a very successful model, she would have quickly grown tired of having people pandering to her. Clearly, she liked straight shooters.

Finally, Jack went to see the woman he couldn't stop thinking about. "Good morning."

She was standing in the middle of the room looking as if she'd forgotten why she'd come in here in the first place. But the light in her eyes as she turned to face him told him that she was as happy to see him as he was to see her.

"Good morning."

The air around her shimmered differently today, and as he searched her face for clues his heart leaped as he realized what it was: much of the wariness she sometimes had around him seemed to be gone.

"Did you sleep all right after you got home last night?"

She seemed to war with herself before shaking her head. "No."

"Neither did I."

"The girls have all gone home for the holidays. It was too quiet." Then, as her pretty skin flushed, she added, "But that wasn't the real reason I couldn't sleep." Honest desire reflected in her eyes. "You are."

Lord, he'd never wanted anything as badly as he wanted to pull her into his arms to kiss the fresh lipstick off her gorgeous mouth.

In a low voice, he said, "The only reason I'm not kissing you right now is because Georgina will skin me alive if I mess you up in any way. I'm not too proud to admit that she scares me."

Mary's lips curved up as she took a step closer anyway and reached behind him to close the dressing-room door. "I'm really good with makeup. I can fix it."

He would have had to be superhuman to resist that invitation and, since Jack was just a flesh-and-blood man, a split second later she was in his arms and he was kissing her senseless.

Sweeter every time he tasted her, her scent and the feel of her soft curves in his arms had him nearly forgetting where they were as he spun them around so that she was pressed up against the door and her hands were in his on either side of her head.

Dragging his mouth from hers, he looked into her eyes to see they were soft and fuzzy with pleasure. "One of my brothers called this morning. Ethan is unexpectedly back in town for the weekend, and it turns out my brother Max and his wife and son will be here from Seattle, too. Unfortunately, William can't make it in from the East Coast due to other commitments. Come with me after the shoot. I want you to meet them."

"That's very sweet of you to ask." Her lips curved up into a smile that didn't quite reach her eyes. "But you've already been spending so much time with me. I'll be fine on my own tonight."

His hands reflexively tightened over hers as she tried to let go. "There could never be enough time with you."

Her eyes widened and he silently cursed himself for saying too much too soon when the depth of his feelings was bound to scare her off instead of bringing her closer. Somehow, he managed to slip his fingers from hers and take a step back to give her some personal space.

"It's just that I wouldn't want them to get the wrong impression," she said softly, "or to think that I was leading you on, especially since I keep telling you we should keep our distance for the rest of the campaign. And then, at the same time, I can't seem to stop asking you to kiss me." Guilt flickered in her eyes.

"You've been completely honest with me from the first moment we met," he reminded her. "And I've been honest with you, too." He ran a rough hand through his hair. "So let's be honest one more time, okay?" When she nodded he said, "I'm not going to deny that I'd love to be able to tell them you're my girlfriend. I hope to do that in the very near future. But, for tonight, I'm asking you to come meet my family as my friend. My very, very good friend whom I love to steal kisses from."

This time when her lips curved up, her smile was entirely real. "I would love to meet your family."

They were interrupted by a hard knock on the door that had them both jumping away from it a split second before it flew open. Georgina shot both of them an irritated look.

"You," she said, pointing to Mary, "had better fix your hair and makeup, or people are going to think we're shooting a love story rather than an electronics campaign. And you—" Jack was instantly reduced to feeling like a naughty little boy as the woman pointed out the door "—need to do a better job of staying out of my way today."

Barely resisting the urge to salute, Jack caught Mary's eye as the director stalked out, and he was glad to see her gaze filled with barely repressed laughter.

Later that evening as they stood on Jack's brother's doorstep, Mary couldn't wait to meet Jack's family so that she could find out where a man like him came from. He wasn't only intelligent and sexy and wonderfully straightforward, he was also a gentleman who walked her home and noticed when she was getting tired in front of the camera. She had been invited to a half-dozen glitzy entertainment-industry Christmas parties and she hadn't wanted to go to them, so Jack's invitation was perfect in so many ways.

Ethan Sullivan opened the door to his tricked-out bachelor pad with a grin. He shook Jack's hand and Mary loved the easy way it automatically turned into a hug.

"Ethan, I'd like you to meet Mary."

Just like Jack, Ethan was an extremely good-looking man. Tall, dark and handsome obviously ran strong in the Sullivan gene pool. But where she was sure most women's hearts probably beat a little faster for the wealthy man in the sharp, tailored suit, Mary felt nothing more than healthy female appreciation.

"It's lovely to meet you, Ethan."

"Same here. Come on in. Max and Claudia will be here soon with their little guy. They would have been here earlier, but they called and said something about a diaper emergency."

"How long are you home this time?" Jack asked his brother while he poured drinks for them at the bar in the corner of the living room.

"Depends on how the deal I'm working on shakes out over the next couple of days." Ethan handed Mary a glass of white wine. "You must do a lot of traveling."

"I do. Or rather," she amended, "I have in the past."

He raised an eyebrow in question, his gaze moving between Mary and his brother. "Have you made a change of plans recently?"

"I've been planning to move away from being in front of the camera for a while now," she explained. "San Francisco seems like the perfect place to set down some roots and explore a few new directions."

She didn't say that when she'd been looking at her

options, she'd never for a moment thought that a man might factor into them. Because in the space of one short week, Jack Sullivan—and his incredible kisses—had started to change everything....

The sound of a laughing child came from outside Ethan's front door. "I'll get it," Jack offered.

Again, the two brothers hugged and when they came into the living room, Jack was holding an adorable toddler. "Mary, this is Ian the Incredible."

Her heart melted as she looked at the gorgeous, dark-haired toddler. No question about it, Ian Sullivan was going to be a heartbreaker when he grew up.

"Hi, Mr. Incredible. It's nice to meet you."

He looked at her with his big brown eyes and reached out to touch her hair. "You're pretty."

Mary was blushing at his very sweet comment when Jack said, "You got that right, little guy."

"I'm Claudia." The petite blonde who held out her hand was pregnant and glowing. "And this is my husband, Max."

Taking in the third specimen of Sullivan male perfection, Mary couldn't help but think how her agent, Randy, would salivate if he could see the brothers all together. As she shook everyone's hand, Ian wriggled down out of Jack's arms.

"We're so glad you could be here with Jack tonight," Claudia told her. "All this testosterone in one room can be a little overwhelming sometimes—even if," she added in a lower voice, "it is nice to look at."

Mary couldn't hold back her laughter. This was all so normal, and she loved that Claudia wasn't gushing over her fame as a model. Instead, she was treating her just as she would any other woman her brother-in-law might bring with him to a family gathering.

Relaxing, Mary said, "When are you due?"

Claudia put her hand over her stomach. "Four mon—" Before she could finish answering, she was shooting off across the room to pick Ian up again before he knocked over a vase. Seeing this near miss, Max told Ethan, "I'm going to put a few things away before they end up in pieces on the floor."

"Sorry about running off in the middle of a sentence," Claudia said to Mary when she came back holding her son. "Look," she told Ian as she put a soft blue bag down on the carpet, "Daddy brought in your toys."

He gave Mary a blindingly cute smile. "Play?"

Clearly, thought Mary as she grinned back at him, the

straightforward Sullivan gene had passed through to the next generation, along with the good looks.

"I thought you'd never ask, Mr. Incredible."

Glad that she was wearing pants instead of a dress tonight, she sat down cross-legged on the floor with the toddler. He grabbed a puffy plastic book that she guessed did double duty for teething and baths and climbed onto her lap.

"Read this."

He smelled so good she wanted to bury her face in his soft hair. Instead, she read the title. *"The Sunshine Princess and the Stinky Dog."*

The little boy in her lap held his nose and made a face. "He's smelly."

Mary's heart turned over inside her chest. She'd never wanted to be one of those girls in her village who married in their teens and were pregnant nine months later. And yet, for all her amazing experiences traveling the world, she'd never had this.

She opened the book up and began to read. "One day the Sunshine Princess was sitting in her bedroom looking out the window at the gray and gloomy day." For the next few minutes, while adult conversation went on around them, she and Ian got lost in the adventures of the stinky dog hiding from the princess who needed to give him a bath. On every page, Ian would point to something that made him laugh, and she was amazed by how much he noticed about the illustrations and the story.

The moment the story ended, he scrambled out of her lap, grabbed a cracker off the table and shoved it into his mouth in one bite. Mary was just starting to get up when Claudia gave her a hand.

"Thanks for reading to him. He really likes you."

"It was my pleasure. And I really like him, too."

"Ian is easy to like," Claudia agreed. "Even being pregnant with him was easy. This pregnancy is, too, actually. I guess I'm one of those lucky ones, between Max, Ian and baby-on-the-way." She flushed. "I have a tendency to gush."

"If I were you, I'd be gushing, too."

They watched Ian repeatedly jump up to try to reach a signed baseball Ethan had on display on a shelf, his face a picture of concentration. "He really takes after his father," Claudia said with a laugh. "Easygoing until he decides he wants something. And then there's no changing his mind."

"That sounds familiar," Mary murmured.

"Does it?" Claudia looked extremely pleased by that

piece of information, but before she could say anything more, she was dashing across the room again to stop Ian from trying to climb up Ethan's bookshelf as though it were a ladder.

Mary turned to pick up her glass of wine from the coffee table and found Jack looking at her. She'd seen desire on his face. She'd seen admiration and respect in his eyes. But until this moment, she'd never seen such warmth.

So much warmth that, if she didn't know better, she would have said it looked like love.

Ten

"I never thought I'd see one of the world's most beautiful fashion models sitting on the floor letting a kid drool all over her." Ethan shot Jack an incredulous look. "How'd *you* meet her again?"

"Pure luck." Jack still marveled over it. "Somewhere along the line, I must have done something right."

"That's just how I felt about the day I met Claudia," Max said, looking across the room at his wife with love in his eyes. "And I've felt that every day since."

Jack had never tried to fight what he felt for Mary, not when it had been so strong and clear from that first moment they'd met in Union Square. But when he realized she was becoming more important to him than the work that had held his focus for over a decade, he thought he should at least try to apply to the two of them the same arguments and calculations that he had always lived by.

But it had taken him less than ten seconds of watching her read to his little nephew to realize that all the brilliant analysis in the world didn't mean a damn thing when it came to love.

People had often called Jack Sullivan a genius. Now he'd finally prove they were right by being smart enough to listen to what was in his heart.

Jack wanted Mary as more than another business colleague. He wanted her as more than a stunningly beautiful woman who made his blood simmer.

He wanted *her.*

He wanted the woman who laughed so easily with a toddler. He wanted the woman whose skin was so soft, whose arms were so strong even as he tried to turn them to rubber with a kiss. He wanted the woman who possessed so much intelligence behind her shockingly beautiful face. He wanted the woman who took care of three young models so that their mothers would know they were safe.

Claudia put Ian into his arms. "It's your turn to keep him out of trouble while I make good on my promise to put together something for us all to eat tonight."

Mary ran a hand over Ian's soft, dark hair, then followed Claudia into the kitchen.

Mary drew Jack like a magnet, so he turned to Ian and asked, "Want to follow the pretty ladies to see what they have for us to munch on before dinner?"

Ian grinned at him, four sparkling white teeth in a mouthful of gums. "Want candy."

Jack laughed and gave the little boy a kiss on his forehead. "Let's see what goodies we can find hiding in Uncle Ethan's kitchen."

Maybe he should have been surprised to find Mary with her hands in flour and eggs at the kitchen counter while Claudia sat with her feet up on a chair, but he wasn't. Yes, she was a gorgeous, successful model. But first and foremost, she was a woman who clearly enjoyed children and food.

"Mary offered to make fresh pasta," Claudia told him as she sipped a club soda and relaxed deeper into her seat. "I assumed it would be too difficult to make at home, so I've always bought pasta at the store. Where did you learn to make it, Mary?"

Mary deftly brought the flour and eggs into a ball, then began to knead it on the kitchen counter. "I was barely older than Ian when my grandmother showed me how. Homemade pasta is a tradition in Italy."

"Is that where you're from? I thought I heard the slightest hint of an accent."

"You should have seen how hard I worked to get rid of it when I moved to New York City." She laughed at herself. "I was so desperate to look and sound like everyone else back then."

"Are you kidding? I would have loved to have had an exotic accent like yours. I'm sure if I had," Claudia joked, "the men would have been lining up around the block for me."

"You're beautiful," Mary said in her unaffected manner. "I'm sure the men were already lining up."

"Have I mentioned how much I like you yet?" Claudia shot a meaningful glance at Jack, one that he could see clearly asked, *Have you convinced her to be yours yet?*

He shot his sister-in-law back his own clear message: *trust me, I'm working on it.*

"I'd love to know how you and Max met, Claudia."

"I was dating Max's best friend, actually. It was all very scandalous and we both tried to fight what we felt for each other for a long time, because we didn't want to hurt anyone. But eventually, neither of us could fight what was meant to be. Even if it meant hurting someone we both cared about."

As Max and Ethan came into the kitchen, Claudia told them, "I was just telling Mary how we met."

"Have you gotten to the stolen-kisses part yet?" Max asked as he leaned down to give her one.

"I love hearing tales of true love," Mary said with a small smile. "My mother and father are like that. There's nothing they wouldn't do for each other. Nothing they wouldn't support each other in."

The longing on her face had Jack nearly moving to pull her into his arms and kiss her, too, in front of everyone. And he might have if Ian hadn't poked at his cheek and said, "Thirsty." Knowing that kissing Jack in public—especially in front of his family—was the last thing Mary would want to do, Jack knew it was something he had to resist...for now.

Meanwhile, Ethan was leaning against the doorjamb looking extremely cynical about the scene in front of him. His divorce had been finalized last year and, since then, he had been burning even more midnight oil on the road looking after his business.

"Too bad William isn't here tonight," Ethan said. "He and I could raise a toast to the happily single."

The implication was clear: everyone thought Jack and Mary were dating. Her eyes met his and, instead of clarifying things with his family, her mouth curved up just the slightest bit at the corners. The air was knocked straight out of Jack's lungs.

Did this mean she was finally ready to be more than friends who stole kisses from each other at every possible opportunity? And if so, what had changed her mind?

Mary changed the subject as deftly as she rolled out the dough. "The four of you must have been quite a handful for your mother."

Max grinned. "Mom looked so delicate and pretty, but she never let us get away with a damned thing."

"I got away with plenty," Ethan countered. Although, a moment later he rubbed his right ear and admitted, "I still get phantom pains sometimes from the way she would drag me to my room."

"What about you?" Mary asked Jack.

He gave her an innocent look. "I was an angel."

Her blue eyes flared with heat for a split second at his use of the endearment that always spilled from his lips when he was kissing her, but then she shook her head and said, "I doubt that."

"You've got this joker figured out," Ethan said with

a laugh as he sat down at the table with his brother and sister-in-law. "How many times did you nearly burn the house down with one of your inventions gone wrong, Jack? The way I remember it, the fire trucks used to patrol our street on a regular basis, just in case."

Ian looked up at his uncle, his voice solemn as he informed Jack, "Fire trucks are red."

He kissed his nephew on the nose. "They sure are. And what do you want to bet that's the same color your shirt's going to be after we eat spaghetti tonight?"

Spending time with Ian when he could during these past eighteen months had made Jack realize how much he liked kids. But it wasn't until he'd met Mary that he'd begun to wonder what it would be like to have his own children.

"Spaghetti!" Ian bounced in Jack's arms as he shouted out the word and all of them chuckled, the boy's happiness contagious.

A short while later, Mary cut the pasta she'd rolled out into thin slices and dropped them into the water already boiling on the stove. Max sat down to give his wife a foot massage. Even though she looked as if she was in heaven, Claudia said, "Are you sure you don't need any help with dinner, Mary?"

"I love to cook. It's one of those things I didn't get to do enough of, bouncing around from hotel room to hotel room over the years."

Mary started on the sauce by quickly cutting up the fresh tomatoes Claudia had brought over. Jack's sister-in-law asked, "Do you have any exciting projects lined up after your campaign with Jack comes to an end?"

"Actually," Mary said as she lifted her gaze to Jack's, "I'm trying to figure that out as we speak. I've been on the move for so long that I'd like to set down some roots for a while."

"The exotic destinations. The clothes. The shoes." Claudia sighed with just the slightest bit of envy. "It sounds so glamorous."

"Yes, I have been really lucky to have seen the world, and to have worked with some truly amazing photographers and designers and makeup artists. It was what I always wanted."

Jack could see that Mary didn't want to disappoint Claudia with the truth that he saw more of every time he watched her work. The hours were long, the lights were bright and hot, and she had to be beautiful on command every single day, without fail, regardless of what was going on in the rest of her life. So while her job had more glitz and glamour than most, that didn't mean it wasn't hard work.

Knowing she'd never say any of that, he told his family, "Mary is so good at what she does that she makes it look deceptively easy." Never having been in a TV studio before, Jack had been fascinated by the process, the machines and the people who ran them, and he explained what he'd seen to his family.

Blushing from his compliment, Mary turned her attention to the sauce simmering on the stovetop. Jack could tell that his siblings were blown away by her. Not only because of her stunning beauty—he still lost his breath every time he looked at her and had come to realize he always would—but also because she was as comfortable in couture as she was playing with a child and making dinner for a group of people she'd only just met.

Even more amazing, she didn't seem to notice the effect she had on people. There was no vanity. No efforts to impress. She was simply being herself.

And he was in love with her.

Jack squeezed Ian a little too tightly as the realization hit him hard in the solar plexus. The little boy tugged on his hair to get his attention.

"Uncle Jack-Jack okay?"

He pressed a kiss to the little boy's cheek, then shifted his gaze to Mary, who had looked over at them when Ian asked his question. "I've never felt better."

"Hey, Jack," Ethan said as he got up from the kitchen table, "come help me set the table in the dining room."

Jack passed Ian to Max, and when they were in the dining room with the door closed, Ethan handed him a stack of plates. "I'm still trying to work out how my engineer brother who's had his head stuck to a motherboard his whole life has landed one of the foxiest models on the planet."

Jack shot his brother a warning look, his fingers curling hard around the edges of the plates. "Mary is a hell of a lot more than just a foxy model."

"Sure she is," Ethan quickly agreed, "but the fact is, she's way out of your league. You might have gotten lucky catching her eye, but you're going to have to count on more than luck to keep her."

Nothing like family to rub in the truth, was there? "Nice to know you're on my side," Jack muttered.

When he looked up, Ethan was grinning at him. "Does she have any sisters?"

"No." Thinking of the young models living with

Mary, he added, "And before you ask, I'm not going to introduce you to any of her friends, either."

"Times like this make me wonder why I ever bothered to cover for you with Mom when we were kids," Ethan said as he dropped silverware beside the plates Jack had laid out on the table.

But even as they continued to razz each other, Jack could read the subtext of their conversation loud and clear: even if Ethan couldn't understand how the engineer and the model could fit so well together, his brother was happy Jack had found Mary...and he hoped things would work out for the two of them.

Spending time with his family had always been Jack's favorite pastime, especially when, as adults, his brothers' jobs and moves around the country meant they didn't get to see each other nearly enough. But tonight, while he'd enjoyed catching up with everyone, Jack realized he was looking for excuses to leave so that he and Mary could be alone. And when she tried to hide a yawn behind her hand and he realized how beat she must be from her long day in front of the TV camera, not to mention making dinner for all of them, he pushed back from the table.

"Time to call it a night, folks."

Ethan looked around at his once-pristine home in dismay. Between the meal and Ian's fort made out of the cushions on his couch, his place was a mess.

"What am I supposed to do with all of these dirty pots and pans and dishes? My cleaning lady won't be back for another few days."

Max grinned at him. "We'll stack them real neat by the sink for you."

A while earlier, Claudia had tucked Ian into the middle of Ethan's big king bed with pillows propped up on each side of him so that he couldn't roll off and hurt himself. Claudia began to slowly stand to go get him, but when Mary offered to rouse him instead Claudia nodded sleepily and tucked herself in tighter against Max.

From where Jack was standing in the living room, he could see Mary get to the master-bedroom doorway then stop in her tracks. Wondering what had her halting, he moved down the hall.

"Mary?"

She held her finger to her lips, then pointed to the bed. Ian was sprawled on his back, three of his four chubby little limbs spread wide. His thumb had found its way into his mouth and his cheeks were pink from drying spaghetti sauce and the exertions of sleep.

Jack had been careful all night long to keep what was between them private. He hadn't touched Mary. Hadn't dragged her against him for a kiss. Now he threaded his fingers through hers and lifted her hand to his lips.

She stared into his eyes and what he saw in hers made his chest tighten with love again, even tighter, even stronger this time. "Claudia and Max are waiting for me to bring him out."

Reluctantly, Jack let her hand go and watched her sit gently on the bed beside Ian. She stroked his hair back with a soft touch so that the little boy wouldn't wake too quickly, and Jack wasn't surprised when the first thing his nephew said after finally opening his eyes was "Pretty."

Mary smiled down at him. "Your mommy and daddy miss you. Can I take you to them?"

When the little boy held out his arms and Mary lifted him up and buried her face against his warm, soft body, Jack's heart skipped more than just one beat.

Eleven

The night was so clear that the stars seemed to be putting on a show in celebration of the beautiful San Francisco winter weather. Mary couldn't remember the last time she'd enjoyed an evening so much, and she didn't want it to be over yet.

After saying goodbye to his family, Mary turned to Jack with a smile. "What do you say we walk off some of that pasta?"

She'd never felt so comfortable—or so completely alive—with anyone else. It was just as natural to laugh and talk with Jack as it was to enjoy the quiet night as they made their way down the city sidewalk.

"Your family is wonderful," she said as she linked her fingers with his.

"They obviously feel the same way about you. Claudia was clearly thrilled about no longer being the odd woman out with all of us boys. And she'll never forget that you made dinner so that she could put her feet up for a little while."

"Your brother and his wife seem so happy together."

"They definitely are now, although like Claudia said, it was a pretty big mess at first. Max was a basket case, falling in love with her while she was engaged to his best friend. He was pretty badly torn up about it. I spent more than a few nights closing down the bars with him back then."

While all of the Sullivan men had the same rugged good looks, each of the brothers she'd met tonight had very different personalities. Max had been the easygoing one. Ethan was sharper, darker somehow. And Jack, well, not only was he brilliant and focused, but he was also the only one who made her heart beat hard and her lips tingle with pleasure even before he'd pressed his mouth to hers.

She'd loved seeing how close Jack was to his brothers. And despite the differences and the disagreements four brothers that close in age must have had over the years, it was clear that they'd do anything for one another. What was more, tonight she'd felt as if he'd welcomed her into his family without any reservations whatsoever...whereas she'd been so afraid to let him do more than kiss her.

"They're all so proud of you." Every time his invention had come up during dinner, his family had been extremely supportive and excited.

"My brothers have all been really successful with their careers, but they never tried to get me to leave my dusty garage. I guess they figured if my vision didn't end up working out, they knew I could come to them for help."

"That's why you never needed to," she marveled, "because you really did know they'd always be there for you. No matter what."

"Always."

"When I was a little girl I thought that, too, about my own family. But—" Not wanting to ruin a perfect evening with self-pity, she tried to brush away her comment. "Listen to me, sounding like I'm still that little girl when it's been long enough for me to have gotten over it by now."

Jack squeezed her hand. "We all want our families to approve of us and the dreams we're chasing."

"Why aren't you married already, Jack?"

Mary gave a slightly embarrassed laugh. She hadn't

meant to blurt that out, but when he kept saying such sweet things, she simply couldn't understand why he wasn't already snapped up.

"That didn't come out quite right. I just meant that not only have you got two great examples of happy marriages between your parents and your brother, but, at this point, most men would be running away as fast as they could from their weepy dinner date who can't seem to get over something that happened when she was a teenager."

"Even though I can see that my brother Max is happy, and that my parents have something really special with each other, it never occurred to me to look for a wife or to start a family. Not when work always came first."

"That makes sense," she agreed. "The timing has to be right—otherwise you could end up losing the woman you're supposed to be with, like Max almost did."

"You know what?" Jack stroked his thumb over her palm, sending shivers through her that had nothing to do with the cool night air. "I don't think bad timing is the entire answer anymore."

Her senses came completely alive as she asked, "It isn't?"

"Now I know that when I meet the right woman, I

won't have any problem at all making time for her. In fact," he said as his gaze locked on hers, "it will be the most natural, easy thing in the world to put her first."

Her heart fluttered in her chest as she realized they were standing at the base of her front steps. And as she drank in Jack's rugged beauty in the winter moonlight, Mary couldn't stop thinking about what Claudia had said: *"We both tried to fight what we felt for each other for a long time. But eventually, neither of us could fight what was meant to be."*

Why, she had to ask herself, was she still fighting so hard against what she'd felt for Jack Sullivan from the first moment she'd set eyes on him?

What if we are meant to be?

"I don't want to say good-night yet," she whispered.

"Neither do I."

Jack put his arms around her and pulled her in tight to him so that his face was buried in her hair and her cheek was pressed to his broad chest. She could have stood in the circle of his strong arms until sunrise.

But she wanted more.

Which meant that she would finally have to be brave enough to risk not only her body...but her heart, too.

Lifting her face from his chest, she remembered what

he'd said to her the first and last time he'd been to her home: *"Next time you invite me in, I'm going to make love to you."* A shiver of need ran through her as she looked up at him.

"Come inside, Jack."

His dark eyes flared with heat and so much desire it took her breath away. But he didn't make a move for the door.

"The campaign isn't over yet and I made you a promise."

"I love that you're willing to stick by the promise you made to me, no matter how hard it is to do that. But I don't need that promise tonight, Jack. I just need you." She'd made the rules and now she was the one tossing them away, at least for one night.

Despite how much he obviously wanted to come inside and make love to her, he didn't move from the step he was standing on. "Be sure, Angel, because once I come inside and your front door is closed, there's going to be no turning back tonight." His hands tightened on her. "Not for either of us."

She could have tried to lie to herself by believing this was all just about sex, that she and Jack were simply going to take the night to let their attraction come to its inevitable conclusion. But Mary had never been a convincing liar…and deep inside, a voice that had been silent for far too long told her that making love with Jack would, instead of being an ending, be the beginning of something so much better, sweeter and more amazing than she'd ever dreamed.

"After watching you with Ian—" Emotion swept through her again as she thought about how sweet Jack had been as he'd held and played with the toddler. "You were so good with him and he obviously trusts and loves you so much."

"Watching you with my family had me feeling the exact same things. Wanting you, needing you has kept me up every night since we met." She could nearly taste his lips on hers, but instead of kissing her, he said, "But you need to know that I'm going to want more than just one night."

Yet again, he was the most honest, straightforward man she'd ever known. Instead of sweet-talking her into rushing to open her front door so that they could fall into bed, he was giving her every reason to push him away again by asking for too much, too fast.

"Let's start here," she said softly. "With tonight. Please, Jack, come inside."

She held her breath as she waited for him to decide if what she was offering was enough for him.

Finally, he lifted her hands to his lips and kissed them. "Let's go in."

Nerves fought with heady anticipation as she led him up the steps. He might spend all day working on computers in a dusty garage, but Mary knew just how dominant, how alpha Jack could be. She'd felt it in every stolen kiss, in the hard press of his body against hers when she'd sworn that getting tangled up with him wasn't what she wanted. But tonight she sensed he wanted her to lead him only as far as she was comfortable going...even if it was a distance she honestly couldn't yet calculate.

Her house was so quiet she wondered if he could hear how hard and fast her heart was beating. He helped her off with her coat, and even though she was still fully dressed, she felt as if she was already standing naked before him in her foyer.

"When will the girls be back?" His warm breath heated the bare curve of her neck as he remained behind her with her coat in his hands.

"They all went home for the holidays." Mary took both her coat and his from him and hung them up before turning back and saying, "We have the place entirely to ourselves."

"I've never wanted anyone the way I want you, Mary. I didn't think it was possible to want like this."

He hadn't yet reached for her, hadn't yet pulled her in for a kiss. But when he spoke, heat rolled across her skin as if he'd done that and more.

And yet, though she knew Jack was different from the other men she'd been with, the hard lessons she'd learned over the years had her wondering if it was just her face, just her body, he wanted so badly.

"I'm sure you've been with plenty of beautiful women before." And, Lord, she prayed she could measure up to them.

"Don't you dare try to act like that's what this is about." There was a fierceness in him now. "Yes, you're beautiful. And yes, your stunning face, your gorgeous body might have been what first drew me to you, but that's not why I'm going to make love to you tonight."

"Then why?"

"You could be at a glittering Christmas party full of movie stars and moguls. You could snap your fingers and a dozen of the world's most eligible bachelors would come running to give you everything you desired and more. Instead, you spent the night with my family and even made us dinner. You laughed with my brothers. You put my sister-in-law at ease and you played on the floor with my nephew."

Ever since Mary had become famous, the men she met assumed she craved the glitz. The spotlights and flash-bulbs. Only Jack had ever seen the truth—that she'd take spending time with a loving family over all of the fame and flash.

Just like that, her nerves fell away, and she reached for him. He'd remembered to shave that morning, but his jaw was already dark with an evening shadow. Gently, she ran her fingertips over his face as he slid his hands around the curve of her hips.

"It's my turn to steal a kiss from you tonight," she whispered as she ran her thumb across his lower lip. He was so tall that she had to go on her tiptoes in her heels and thread her fingers into his dark hair to pull his mouth down to hers.

And as she kissed him, the breath Mary realized she'd been holding since the moment she'd met Jack Sullivan escaped her lips in a happy sigh.

Twelve

Mary's lips were so soft, her breath a whisper of warmth across Jack's mouth. Every kiss they'd shared had been spectacular, but nothing could have prepared him for this. He'd been stealing passion from her before, but now she was giving him her boundless sensuality freely… and so damned sweetly that his hands were shaking as he cradled her hips.

She drew back just far enough to murmur, "You taste so good, like lemons and sugar and *you,*" and then she was kissing him again, slicking her tongue over his lower lip. Meeting her halfway, his tongue found hers and she gave up a gasp of pleasure.

The small tastes of her that he'd had this past week had made him ravenous for more than just a few fleeting moments of heaven. He wanted to learn every inch of the incredible woman in his arms. What made her pant. What made her plead. What made her eyes flutter closed as she came apart in his arms.

Slowly, he slid his hands up her curves, from her hips to her back and shoulders. She was trembling by the time he threaded his fingers into her silky hair, and as he took their kiss deeper, her hands clasped his shoulders as if she needed to hold on to him to keep her balance.

Tilting her head back farther, he began to rain kisses over her jaw. Drawn like a magnet to the rapidly beating pulse at the side of her neck, he covered it with his mouth. Her skin was even softer here and she shuddered when the bristles from his evening shadow brushed over her. When she arched back, he licked once into the hollow at the base of her throat, before moving down to press his lips over the bare skin of her collarbone where her sweater had pulled away.

In the heat of their passion, they'd moved so that he was pressing her back against the front door, and as he cupped her face to kiss her again, she lifted one leg around his hips to try to pull him even closer.

Sliding his hand from her hair back down her body, he realized he'd never lost control this fast. He could barely focus on anything but how sweet her lips were, how soft her skin was, how good her hair smelled, how much he loved her soft moans of pleasure as she kissed him back with a desire that matched his. He knew that if they didn't get into her bedroom soon, he was bound to take her their first time right here against her front door. He gave her one last, hot kiss, then swept her up into his arms.

He should have known she wouldn't miss a beat as she drew his mouth back down to hers. Somehow he made it through the living room and down the hall to the door at the end of the hall without just dropping with her to the floor like a wild animal. Pushing her bedroom door open with his foot, he carefully walked through with Mary in his arms and laid her gently on top of her coverlet.

Wanting to remember every moment of their first night together, he took a step back from the bed and gazed down at the beauty before him. Mary's long, dark hair was spread out across the pillows, and her dark green sweater and gorgeous flushed skin were utterly enticing as she lay atop the red velvet bedcover.

"Come be with me, Jack." She shifted up on the bed to reach out for him. "Please, I need you."

As he went back to her, he made a silent vow to give her everything she deserved—not only more pleasure than she'd ever known before, but also the love he'd been keeping deep inside just waiting for the moment when she appeared in his life.

Mary's lips curved with joy as she pulled him down over her on the bed. He didn't know how long they kissed, rolling over with each other on the soft velvet, hands stroking, mouths devouring in their hunger for each other. Her passion matched his, and he found himself wondering if a lifetime could possibly be long enough to fill such a deep well of need.

And then her hands were moving to the buttons of his shirt, and he didn't stop kissing her as he captured them with his. Holding her captive against him, he gave a final nip to her lower lip before lifting his head to stare down at her.

Already a stunning woman, with her cheeks flushed and her eyes heavy with arousal, there wasn't any painting, any vista, any wonder in the world that could match her beauty as she lay in bed beneath him.

Jack's breath caught in his chest as he looked down at her. "What did I ever do right to deserve you?"

"Everything. Everything you do is exactly right."

Shifting over her, he found the pulse point at the side of her neck again and let his teeth scrape gently over her sensitive skin. The way she arched against him put the silent vow he'd made to go slowly their first time almost out of reach.

Sliding his hands beneath her back, he found the hem of her sweater and carefully lifted it. Her breath came quickly, her chest rising and falling fast beneath the soft green wool as she shifted her shoulders so that he could slide the fabric up to reveal the swell of her breasts above her lacy bra.

"Beautiful."

Forgetting all about stripping her sweater the rest of the way off, he reached out and brushed his fingertips over her soft flesh.

"Jack."

His name shook on her lips as he lowered his head to trace over her skin with his mouth. Her scent made his head spin, her soft sounds of pleasure sending his heart racing faster than it ever had before.

When he'd been stealing kisses from her, he'd always been gentle. But now, as he gripped the softness of her sweater in his fists, Jack couldn't stop himself from roughly dragging it all the way off. Excitement glittered in her eyes as she stripped away her slacks from her legs so that they landed on the colorful rug beside her bed.

If he'd been stunned by the flash of lace at her breasts, the lace at her hips knocked every last bit of oxygen from his lungs.

For a long moment he couldn't think, couldn't move, couldn't do anything but marvel. Lost in the wonder of her, he didn't realize Mary had taken his hands in hers until she lifted them to her lips. One quick kiss to his knuckles and then she was slowly opening his hands to slide them down over her jaw, her neck, her collarbones, and then—sweet Lord, he wasn't sure he'd manage to make it through tonight in one piece—she placed them over her breasts.

As she let him feel the hard beat of her heart, then lifted her hands from his so that he was the only one still touching her, Jack knew she wasn't just silently telling him she wanted him to make love to her...she was also saying she trusted him enough, for tonight at least, to put her heart in his hands.

Notorious for his steady hands as he soldered the wires on a circuit board, Jack couldn't keep his fingers from shaking as he moved to slide the straps of her bra down off her shoulders. She trembled beneath him, just as unsteady but with him all the way as he finally uncovered one perfect breast and then another.

It was pure instinct to cup Mary's soft flesh with his hands and lower his head to take first one peak and then the other into his mouth. She tasted even better than she looked, and as he drew on her with lips and tongue, she arched into his hands and mouth to let him have even more of her.

Reaching behind her, he flipped open the latch on her bra and tossed it to the floor to join her clothes. Her skin was rosy and damp from where he'd been kissing her, and when he brushed his jaw across her aroused nipples, her hips came up against him in a silent plea for more. Her stomach muscles quivered beneath his lips as he ran kisses down the center of her body. When bare skin was replaced with lace, he drove both of them crazy by tracing the edges of her panties with both his fingertips and tongue. She was even softer here, her scent spinning through him.

Lace scratched against his tongue as he covered her with his mouth, and then he was being just as rough with her panties as he'd been with her sweater in his desperation to have her completely bare and open to him.

Again, his name fell from her lips in a whisper of

breath and need, and he answered the sweet plea with a slow brush of his tongue over her. A moment later, his fingers found her hot and slick, and when she shuddered and cried out his name, Jack was so lost in the pure sensuality of the way she moved beneath him that he nearly fell over the edge with her even though he was still fully clothed.

Slowly, he kissed his way down her legs, from the incredibly soft skin of her inner thighs to the sensitive spot behind her knees, then over her toned calf muscles, until he was pressing soft kisses to the arches of both feet. With his hands, he massaged her muscles, making her moan from the pleasure of his touch. He could have spent all night working his way back up her body with hands and mouth, finding all of the spots he'd missed on the way down, but when she took his hands in hers, he let her pull him back up over her.

Her kisses made him dizzy enough that she easily rolled them over so that he was on his back and she was gorgeously naked over him. Silently, and with intense focus, she began to work open the rest of the buttons on his shirt. When she had the fabric completely open, instead of moving it off his shoulders, she leaned in and pressed a soft kiss over his heart.

Jack had never known a woman as beautiful, as intelligent, as gracious as Mary. And he'd never known lovemaking like this before, either. Because with every kiss, with every touch he and Mary gave each other, heart was as important as heat.

That kiss over his breastbone was the first in a sweet path of damp heat she made across his chest, neck and jaw, until she'd made it high enough to cup his face in her hands. When she rocked into him and they moaned into each other's mouths, he was too greedy for another one of her beautiful climaxes to even think about taking things further.

"Again," he urged, following his words with caresses that had her eyes closing as she levered up over him again to rock closer, faster, harder against him. And as her breath hitched and her hands gripped at his forearms, she was so heartbreakingly beautiful that he knew she really was an angel.

His angel.

Jack could have listened to the sweet sounds of her releases all night long and might have done just that had she not reached for his belt buckle. The light brush of her fingertips over his abdomen was almost too much to handle by that point, and he had to tense every muscle in his body to keep from losing control as she finally pulled the leather open and slid down the zipper.

She didn't tease him as she stripped the rest of his clothes and his shoes and socks away, but when her elegant hand came around him a beat later, a hard hiss of air whistled out from between his clenched teeth.

Jack wanted their lovemaking to be as much an equal adventure as everything else they did together, but he was too close to the edge to let her keep touching him like that tonight. In one quick move, she was back beneath him, her hands in his on either side of her head as he kissed her.

For a week, Mary had clearly believed she needed to fight what was meant to be, and Jack had worked to hold on to his rapidly disintegrating patience until she felt that she could give herself to him without reservations. But now the time for waiting was long past. And yet, even as she whispered to him that she was protected and she lifted her hips to welcome him into her, in the moment that he moved between her legs, Jack wanted to stop everything so that he could tell her how much she'd already come to mean to him.

But for tonight Jack knew he'd have to use his body to tell her everything he felt in his heart instead.

The pleasure built with every stroke, with every thrust, with every kiss. Damp skin against damp skin, heated breath over aroused flesh, they were perfect partners in passion.

And as they moved together, with desire driving them higher and higher, Jack knew that every breath, every dream, every prayer had led him here, to the warmth of Mary's arms around him.

The velvet coverlet and sheets lay tangled around their bodies as they held tightly to each other, still breathing hard, Mary's head cradled in the crook of Jack's arm. Outside her bedroom window the rest of the city was sleeping. Warm and safe in her bed with the most wonderful man she'd ever known, sleep should have finally come to claim Mary, too. But so much had happened tonight, much more than just lovemaking that had left her breathless. It would be a long time before she could settle down enough to get some badly needed rest.

Tonight she'd trusted Jack with her body, but though that might have been enough for another man, she knew Jack wanted much, much more.

He wanted her to trust him with her heart, too.

Not just for one night but forever.

For a few hours, she'd been able to drop her guard and allow desire to take the place of decisions. Jack's touch, his kisses, had brought her fully to life in a way that no other man's had before him.

Come morning, she'd have to decide if she could let what was between them continue to grow…and risk letting herself fall in love with him.

She'd known from their very first kiss that making love with Jack would be wonderful. But nothing could have prepared her for the extraordinary sensations of his mouth moving across her skin, the sensuality of his hands caressing her…or the perfection of coming together with him until she lost hold of where she ended and he began.

Nothing could have prepared her for the wonder of feeling as though he was her very first, her only.

And nothing could possibly have prepared her for the way the heart she'd been so careful with had opened wide with reckless abandon.

Fortunately, looking at their entwined fingers resting over his chest helped to calm her racing heart. As if he could read her mind, he lifted their hands to his lips and softly, slowly, kissed each of her fingers.

Raising her gaze to meet his, she was hit with yet another shock: Jack wasn't hiding a single emotion from her. And—*oh, God*—what she saw in his eyes echoed what she felt in the deep, secret part of her heart she thought she had locked down, sure it was the only way to prevent ever being hurt again.

Through the haze of her post-pleasure brain, Mary couldn't lie to herself: From that very first moment he'd spoken to her, from the very first press of his lips against hers under the mistletoe, had she ever had a choice about falling for Jack Sullivan?

Suddenly finding it difficult to breathe, Mary tried to move from his arms, but he wouldn't let her go.

"I promised you I'd be patient," he reminded her softly. "I'm not going to break my promise."

Didn't he see that just because he hadn't said the word *love* aloud, it didn't mean his body, his expression, his heart beating steadily and hard against hers, weren't saying it to her even now?

Mary had been on her own for all of her adult life and had carved out a successful career in a supremely difficult field. Yet, as Jack held her on her bed, she finally had to face her own weaknesses...and accept just how far and deep her fears ran. Fears that had plagued her since the day she'd walked away from everything she'd known as a teenager.

One night. Couldn't she have one night to take a break from the confusion, from the doubts?

Maybe it wasn't fair to ask Jack to give her that when he was already giving her everything else, but Mary had never felt this safe, this cherished, with anyone else.

Letting the sheets fall away, she put her hand on his chest, his pectoral muscles jumping beneath her palm and fingertips as she slid them up to caress the beautifully masculine planes of his jaw and chin. Desire had been sated just minutes ago and, still, as she leaned forward to press her mouth to his, the sparks flew again, even hotter and higher this time.

Because she now knew exactly how good making love with Jack was, it sent her hunger for him spiking once more. But even as she tried to focus on the physical, she knew there was one important reason she so desperately needed to make love with him again.

Mary had been called beautiful a thousand times in her life, but no one had ever actually treated her as if she was special *and* beautiful. With every brush of his skin against hers, with the heat from his dark eyes that watched her so carefully every single moment to make sure she was happy, Jack only cared about her.

And she knew in her heart of hearts that he would

never do anything to hurt her. Both of them rose to their knees on the bed, and as he moved his hands to her hips to pull her flush against him, she loved how hard every inch of him was. Already, she was addicted to the delicious scratch of hair from his chest and legs against her smooth skin, the burn from the dark shadow on his jaw as he ran kisses all across her face and neck and shoulders and breasts.

She'd been amazed by the way he'd held on to his patience as he'd stripped her earlier, taking her from peak to peak while keeping the reins on his own needs. She'd never, ever forget the beauty he'd shown her, how gentle he'd been even as he drove her toward utter madness.

But as renewed passion wrapped around them like a velvet ribbon tying them together, the ravenous need that grew bigger and stronger with every moment they spent in each other's arms took the place of patience and self-control. And as they fell back onto the bed, tangled in each other, Mary didn't have a prayer of keeping up with Jack's hands, with his mouth, with the demands he made of her pleasure.

Breathless as he found her sweetest spots again, needing to give him just as much, they tumbled so that she could rove her own hands and mouth across his hard, heated body.

And then he was gripping her by the waist and pulling her up over him, coming into her again in one hard thrust. Capturing her mouth with his, with low growls of pleasure rumbling from his chest to hers, from one heartbeat to the next, they drove each other higher.

Giving. Taking. Sharing.

Loving.

And as Mary shattered into a thousand beautiful pieces in Jack's arms, everything she'd tried to trap inside for so long, all of the emotions she'd been so afraid to feel, finally burst free.

Thirteen

Mary woke to the warmth of sunlight streaming over her skin. Surprisingly bright winters were one of the things she loved about San Francisco, especially when she could easily find snow within hours of the city by heading to the mountains surrounding Lake Tahoe.

This morning, however, the sunlight wasn't the only reason she was warm. Jack was wrapped around her, his front pressed to her back, his legs curled into hers.

A sudden flash of terror at just how much of herself she'd given him the night before threatened to send her heart racing. And yet, nothing felt the slightest bit wrong about the way she was holding one of Jack's hands to her chest, his other hand tangled in her hair, while the warmth of his breath tickled the sensitive skin on the back of her neck. In fact, it was true that nothing had ever felt so right as waking up in bed wrapped in Jack's arms as if she were a precious gift he couldn't bear to part with.

His breathing remained even, but his fingers began to slide, feather-light, over her skin. Had he been waiting for her to wake so that they could continue their sensual adventure into a new day?

He'd been completely straightforward on her doorstep in telling her that one night wouldn't be enough for him, and maybe it was sending the wrong message to let one night turn so quickly into more.

But how could any woman on the planet resist Jack Sullivan?

The lightest flick of his tongue over her neck sent a shiver running through her, head to toe. As her brain warred with her heart over what the right thing to do might be, her body gave the answer by arching just enough so that he could more easily nip the skin he'd kissed.

Shuddering with need just that quickly when he shifted their hands on her chest so that they were both cupping one breast together, as his name fell from her lips she was shocked to find her throat slightly raw.

A dozen sensual visions from the night before came at her then. She'd never been one of those women who felt they had to put on a show in bed, but with Jack, she hadn't been able to stop herself from calling out his name.

He was hot and hard against her bottom and all it would have taken was the slightest shift of his legs and her hips for him to be inside her again. But where they'd rushed to have each other in the darkness the night before, this morning he was torturing her with slow, sweet caresses, as if he wanted to commit every inch of her to memory.

From breast to waist, then waist to hip, then hip to thigh, then front to back before starting all over again, Mary didn't know whether to praise or curse Jack's boundless patience as he lazily stroked her naked skin and curves. No man had ever taken so much time, so much care with her before. As she reveled in his caresses, her hunger for him was so strong that she had to turn and slide her hands into his hair for a deep, heated kiss.

Oh, but there was something wonderful about a man who knew when to give a woman what she wanted… and when to give her what she actually needed. Hard and fast would have been amazing, but as she realized he wouldn't be rushed—and that all she could do was relax into the stroke of his hands, the kisses from his lips, the gentle scratch of his teeth against her skin—Mary finally stopped trying to fight, to lead…or to worry.

Gasps of pleasure were followed by moans of delight as he discovered her secret pleasures inch by inch. Kisses landed like butterflies across her skin until he was fluttering them across her lips again. Joy rose up inside her, bigger and brighter than any happiness she'd known before Jack.

And when he finally moved his fingers between her legs and Mary tumbled into ecstasy with his name on her lips, even then he didn't rush to finish what he'd started. Instead, he rolled her onto her back and slid his hands over hers to keep her steady as he came into her so slowly and sweetly that her arousal heightened all over again from the delicious weight of his body over hers.

Jack's heart beat hard against hers, his eyes dark and full of emotion as he loved her. And in that moment—when all of her walls fell down and she gave herself to him completely—Mary knew she loved him right back.

In the minutes that followed the most extraordinary lovemaking of her life, Jack remained levered over her, his dark gaze not wavering as he stared into her eyes. What, she wondered, was he thinking as he looked at her the way he was now?

As if he was seeing her anew...

Reaching instinctively to smooth her hair, she realized it was knotted behind her head. She'd loved it when he slid his hands into her hair and tangled his fingers in it as he'd made wild love to her. But in the aftermath of that wildness, she knew she didn't look anywhere near her best.

"I should probably go clean up. And then," she said with an attempt at an easy smile, "I'll make us some breakfast. Do you like eggs?"

"Breakfast can wait." Jack draped an arm and a leg over her and held her where she was beneath him. "I'm not done looking yet."

Mary tried not to grimace. "I'm sure I look like a mess."

As if to confirm her statement, he reached out to run a finger through her hair and it got caught on a tangle as he rolled the lock up around his finger. "You've always looked so perfect," he murmured. "I've never seen you like this, rumpled, with lines from the pillow on your cheek."

Her heart sank to her stomach as she realized her mistake. She'd been so comfortable with Jack, so head over heels for him and his kisses, that she'd forgotten to keep up the mystique of being *Mary Ferrer.*

Before Jack, she would have worked to glide over it with a laugh and a witty comment. But after the sweet intimacy of lovemaking, her emotions were close enough to the surface that she said, "It's a good thing, then, that I have a big bag of model's tricks to make myself *perfect* again."

Surprise jumped into Jack's eyes at her defensive tone. "What's wrong? What did I say?"

Her looks had been her ticket to adventures all over the world and a glittering career that had exceeded any expectations she'd had as a girl full of dreams. Even so, sometimes she hated the fact that keeping that ticket valid meant she had to spend so much time on keeping up her appearance. She'd never owned a pair of sweatpants. She'd never gone out for a cup of coffee without at least some mascara and lipstick.

She would never take what she had for granted, but if she had known the price it would come with—not just losing her mother's love but this endless focus on perfection—she might have walked more slowly through that childhood door into her adult life.

Despite everything they'd shared since last night, did Jack only want to see the perfect version of her? Mary had to close her eyes against a bolt of pain that hit her at the thought.

A moment later she felt Jack's gentle caress on her cheek.

"Don't shut me out, Angel. Not now."

She'd been brave enough to give him her body. Knowing she should have the courage to answer his questions now, she made herself meet his gaze head-on.

"You're right that almost no one has ever seen me looking like this, or as anything less than the perfect model they're expecting to see."

"Then that makes me the luckiest man in the world. Which," he added with a sexy grin that made her heart skip a beat in her chest, "I already knew."

But wait—what had he just said?

"Lucky?" she repeated. "But my hair is knotted and my makeup has rubbed off all over the pillowcase."

"Every time you've been in front of a camera, I've been stunned by your beauty and by how well you do your job. But getting to see you now, a little messy, all of your stunning features a little out of focus while you're still catching your breath from making love with me—" He picked up one of her hands and put it over his breastbone. "It does something to me. Right here."

Feeling his heart beat strong and steady against her palm steadied hers, too.

"You'll always be beautiful to me, Mary. Especially now."

His sweet words meant more to her than any jewel, than any expensive gift, than any poetic words possibly could have.

No one but Jack had ever truly wanted her the way she really was.

"You're right," she murmured as she wrapped her naked limbs around his. "Breakfast can wait."

Unlike most models, Mary ate a healthy diet. Part of staying slim enough for the camera was good genetics; the other part was that she loved being in motion. Walking, swimming, dancing…making love. Besides, she loved eating too much to ever consider giving up delicious food.

But as she sat at her breakfast table across from Jack an hour later, she couldn't manage even the tiniest bite of the eggs, crisp bacon and toast he'd just whipped up for them while she spoke briefly with Janeen on the telephone. Mary supposed it stood to reason that a bachelor in his early thirties would have to know how to cook or else he might starve, but this was a breakfast that under other circumstances she would have wolfed down.

She'd loved every second in Jack's arms. He'd made her feel cherished and safe while giving her pleasure she'd never known before. She'd never been with a man like Jack, one who held nothing back and gave even when he couldn't guarantee getting anything in return for himself.

And yet, somehow, she still wasn't sure what her next step should be…and she hated herself for it.

But just because she was horribly afraid he was going to hate her, too, that was no excuse for ignoring the two-thousand-pound elephant in the room. She'd never been a coward and she wouldn't start now, not when she had far too much respect for Jack to willfully hurt him.

"You mean so much to me," she began in a soft voice as she twisted the napkin on her lap, "and last night was incredible."

Her breakfast table was small enough that he could easily reach for her hand. "Being with you made it the best night of my life," he told her, his voice gentle and sincere. "But that doesn't mean I've forgotten what you said about taking it one day, and one night, at a time. Or about keeping what's between us just for us to know about."

In her experience, men heard what they wanted to hear, regardless of what she actually said to them. She'd been pretty sure by now that Jack was different, but after what they'd just shared, what man wouldn't have assumed she'd changed her mind about going slow and not mixing up business with pleasure if they could help it?

"I haven't forgotten what you said, either, about wanting more than one night." Even though he didn't look at all angry with her, she felt terrible about taking what he offered when she herself had given him so little in return. "I don't know what's wrong with me, why I—"

"There's nothing wrong with you." He tugged her onto his lap and said, "You make me happy. Happier than I've ever been."

His sweet acceptance of her just the way she was made her heartbeat settle and the knot in her stomach uncoil. Framing his face in her hands, she told him the one thing she knew for sure.

"You make me happy, too."

Fourteen

The next few days followed in a blur of meetings and promotional activities, while the nights were a dazzling rush of sweet and sinful lovemaking. Somehow, Jack managed to keep his promise to Mary, not only about keeping their relationship a secret but by holding back the one small but very meaningful word that was burning a hole inside of him.

Love, his mother had once told him, might not always be easy, but whatever struggles or pain that might come with it, true love was always worth it.

Jack had seen the truth of that in his parents' marriage. And now he understood that for all these years he'd been waiting for Mary. She was his destiny. And, whether or not she was ready to accept it yet, he was hers.

But just because they were meant to be together, he knew better than to think he could simply sit back and let things take their natural course. He wanted to give her everything—not just pleasure but romance, too. Apart from that first evening in the diner, he'd never taken her out on a date. And though they'd been extremely busy working on the campaign, that was a poor excuse.

Tonight, no matter what, he'd give her not only flowers but memories of more than passion and heat, too.

When Mary let him in that evening, she was so beautiful and she tasted so good that he nearly forgot his plans for the evening. Her eyes widened at the red poinsettia plant in the green-painted pot that he was holding out to her.

"You bought me flowers," she said, slightly stunned.

They'd shared the ultimate intimacy, yet he found he was nervous as he held out the flowers. "I was going to get you roses, but when I saw these, I immediately thought of you."

She took the pot from him and admired the large flowers. "When I was a little girl, there were hundreds of these plants all over town at Christmastime." She lifted her gaze to his again, wonder in her eyes as she asked, "How do you always know me so well?"

He prayed that she already knew the answer...even if he'd promised not to speak those words of love aloud until she was ready to hear them.

"I should find a good spot for this," she said. But instead of moving into the living room, she simply put the pot down on the floor, then pulled him toward her and pushed the door closed behind him. Her lips found his and then she was raining kisses from his mouth to his jaw, before nipping seductively at his earlobe. "I missed you today," she told him between kisses. "So much."

He'd made plans to give her romance, and Jack Sullivan always followed through on his plans...but how could he possibly keep his hands from roving down her curves?

"I don't just want you for your body," he told her as he tried to keep hold of the reins long enough to take her out for some long-overdue wooing. "I want to give you a romantic evening tonight."

Her eyes flared with surprise, and obvious pleasure at his intention, but when she lifted one leg and wrapped it around his thighs and kissed him again, Jack realized that for the next few minutes he had no choice but to completely give up the tenuous control he had over himself.

His hands dived into her hair as he crushed her mouth

beneath his. Together they moved just far enough inside to sink down onto the soft rug in front of her Christmas tree. She pulled off his sweater and he untied the sash around the waist of her dress. His belt buckle opened at the same time silk slid from her shoulders. He got the clasp of her bra to come free just as she gave up on the final buttons of his shirt and yanked it open.

They rolled together on the rug with Mary on top, straddling his hips as she pressed hot kisses all across his chest. But moments later he was the one moving over her, his hands stroking her body so that she was crying out with pleasure. There was no rhythm to their love-making tonight, no plan, no goal as both of them followed their wild—and loving—instincts.

They were lying side by side on the rug, her hand in his, when he told her again, "I had plans for us tonight." He was still trying to catch the breath she'd stolen from him.

Post-climax, her eyes were hazy but still filled with wickedness as she informed him, "So did I."

He grinned back at her. "Clearly." But when he was helping her back onto her feet, he couldn't stop his eyebrows from going up in shock. "Ruining your dress wasn't in my plans. Forgive me?"

She seemed stunned when she looked down at the state of her outfit. The bodice of her elegant silk dress was down around her waist and the delicate fabric was badly wrinkled from where he'd grabbed it in his fist to drag it up by the hem as he'd moved between her legs to take her. One stocking was still in place around her thigh, but the other was a couple of feet away, tossed onto a corner of the rug in the midst of their passion. But Mary seemed most stunned by what she'd done to his button-down shirt—one sleeve ripped, half of the buttons strewn across the rug.

"I did that?" Alongside the surprise on her face was a hint of sensual pride that heated him up all over again.

"I'll bet that's how you open Christmas presents, isn't it?" he teased.

"I would if I ever had a Christmas present as good as you," she teased back.

They were already behind schedule, but if he couldn't tell her he loved her, he needed to say it with a kiss instead. Her lips were still heated from his earlier kisses and sensitive now from their wild lovemaking. Quickly, the kiss began to spiral into something more, but Jack carefully drew back from her.

His voice gruff with emotion—and desire that grew from moment to moment—he said, "Go put some new clothes on so I can take you out for a special date."

"Jack, it's really sweet that you want to do something romantic for me tonight, but don't you know you've been wooing and romancing me every single second since I've known you?"

"Pie and ice cream isn't wooing. Dinner with my family isn't romance."

Her blue eyes were clear and full of emotion as she told him, "It is when I'm with you."

My God, he loved her. So damned much the word was right there on the tip of his tongue.

"Hurry, or we're going to be too late."

He thought he saw disappointment in her eyes before she turned away and moved down the hall to her bedroom to change. It was almost as if she'd secretly hoped he'd break his promise and confess his love for her.

Mary didn't recognize the address Jack gave the taxi driver, but she knew his romantic surprise would be amazing. Just as she'd told him earlier, he really did know her.

And yet, instead of being able to completely enjoy it, she felt twisted up inside.

She'd never had a secret relationship before. As a teenager she'd been a good girl, too focused on her dreams to waste time on the local boys at school. She knew some people found having a secret affair exciting, but Mary hated not being able to put her hand in Jack's in the back of the taxi without worrying that the driver would see them, then recognize her and end up telling someone.

Why, she asked herself for the millionth time, was she still being so careful, so wary? What would it hurt if people knew that she and Jack were falling for each other? Heck, if being careful was her main goal in life, she'd still be in her childhood town, with babies and children playing at her feet while she helped her mother sew wedding dresses for the other women.

But Mary knew that worrying about other people's reactions wasn't the main reason she wasn't ready to give up the secrecy. The real reason was much more complicated.

Jack was wonderful…so wonderful that a part of her was absolutely terrified.

What if he realized one day soon that he'd had his fill of her and decided to move on?

Or what if the product launch ended up going badly and he couldn't separate the success of his business from her role in it?

Or what if she screwed up and made a rash decision that he couldn't forgive her for…just as her mother once had?

The happier Mary was every moment they were together, the more she worried when they were apart, simply because Jack mattered to her—more than any other man ever had.

As the secrecy continued to eat away at her, she had to wonder if never publicly acknowledging their relationship would make losing him any easier.

The taxi pulled up to the curb, and when she looked out the window, she realized they were in front of a beautiful old movie theater. The words in lights on the marquee made her heart skip a beat.

"They're playing *Singin' in the Rain?*" She turned to Jack in surprise. "How did you find this?"

"Some things," Jack said softly, "are meant to be."

He extended his hand to help her out of the cab, holding it a few moments longer than a friend would have but not long enough that strangers would wonder…unless they happened to notice the way the two of them were looking at each other and noticed the flush of heat spreading across Mary's cheeks.

The fog off the Bay was thick tonight and she pulled her coat closer around her as she looked at the long line of couples waiting to get their tickets. But just as people began turning to take a second glance to see if she was who they thought she was, Jack gently propelled her toward the entrance and handed their tickets to the young man at the door.

"Follow the stairs to the left all the way up and you'll find your seats."

Instead of heading for the stairs, Jack led her over to the concession counter. "I hope you like your popcorn dripping with butter."

"Only if it's doused with salt, too," she told him with a smile she couldn't possibly contain. Mary hadn't been on many movie-and-popcorn dates in the past thirteen years. She felt, for a moment, like any girl out on a long-awaited date with the boy she couldn't stop daydreaming about.

A few minutes later, when their arms were laden with candy and soda and an absolutely enormous tub of popcorn, they climbed up the narrow stairs to the balcony. Mary stopped at the top of the stairs in surprise.

"There are only two seats up here."

Jack looked incredibly pleased with himself. "I know."

She hadn't needed romance or wooing to fall for Jack Sullivan. But now that he was giving them to her on a silver platter filled with popcorn and malt balls and ice-cold Coke, Mary wasn't sure how she could ever have thought she'd be able to resist him.

In their private seats high above the rest of the theater, as the lights went down and her favorite old film began to play, Mary not only didn't have to worry about secrecy, but she realized she could stop worrying entirely for two hours.

Snuggling into Jack, loving the feel of his arm over her shoulders, she reached into the tub of popcorn and knew she was the luckiest girl in the world.

A little less than two hours later, Mary was startled when the houselights came up. She'd been utterly lost in the fantasy of being Jack's girl and in the incredible sensuality of his fingers brushing over her shoulder, his thigh pressed against hers, his breath warm as he whispered into her ear during his favorite parts of the movie.

She hadn't dated much as a teenager, and as an adult the men who asked her out wouldn't have dreamed of taking her to see an old movie while munching on popcorn and candy. Just as none of them would have bought her pie and ice cream in a diner.

Jack had been careful to buy tickets ahead of time so that they could walk inside the theater quickly, and had also thought ahead about reserving the private balcony to make sure their relationship stayed under wraps the way she'd insisted. Which also meant that they would have to wait until the seats below emptied so that they could sneak back out unnoticed.

Mary thought about the end of *Singin' in the Rain,* when Debbie Reynolds's character, Kathy, had stood hidden behind a curtain as she sang...and how wrong it had been for her to hide herself away like that.

Wasn't that exactly what Mary was making the two of them do by forcing them to keep their true feelings hidden, not just from strangers in a movie theater but also from the people with whom they were working?

Her stomach twisted as she forced herself to face the truth.

No! She didn't want to let go of Jack's hand when they

went back downstairs. And she definitely didn't want to pretend that he hadn't come to mean everything to her.

It was time to come clean, not just with the rest of the world, but with Jack...and with herself, too.

To hell with caution. Mary wanted everyone to know she was his.

"I was wrong, Jack."

She had felt the warmth of his gaze on her as soon as the lights went up. Now he took her hands in his and gently asked, "*Singin' in the Rain* isn't one of your favorite movies, after all?"

She'd been focusing so hard on her guilt and trying to be brave. Only Jack could have made her smile in a moment like this.

"Not about the movie—I still love it, and seeing it with you has made it even more special. What I meant was that I was wrong about hiding our relationship."

Even though she knew he didn't want them to continue as a secret, he said, "I didn't bring you here tonight to try to make you change your mind, or to make your reasons seem less valid."

"You could have never done that, Jack." It was why she'd come to care about him so strongly, so quickly. Working to ignore the flutter in her belly that proved she wasn't nearly as brave as she was trying to appear, she declared, "I'm tired of letting the past rule my present. And my future."

The way he was looking at her, Mary swore he could see right down into her soul.

"I'll wait as long as you need me to wait," he vowed in a low voice.

Had anyone ever cared for her this much?

"No more waiting."

And then she pressed her lips to his in a soft kiss so much like their very first under the mistletoe.

Fifteen

Mary held tight to Jack's hand as they came down the stairs. By now, there were only a few people left in the lobby to see them together, but when she and Jack didn't rush into a taxi, several strangers came up to ask for her autograph. Throughout, while Mary made it a point to remain close to Jack, she noted that he was still being careful not to touch her too much or be too publicly affectionate. It was as though he knew one wrong move so close to her decision to share their relationship with the world would make her skittish.

It never ceased to amaze her how well he knew her... and how deeply he'd gotten into her heart right from the first day she'd met him.

Could he know that she was working overtime to try

to ignore the voice in her head that said she was moving too fast? Could he hear the cautionary whisper inside her that was trying to warn her she was making decisions too wildly where he was concerned? Could he see her worrying that she was letting her heart run away with her again...and that she would pay for her foolish romantic ideas in the end?

A part of her wished that he'd push her tonight, that he'd force her to admit all of her remaining fears—of being scared to trust him with her heart, and wondering if love could truly last forever...even whether she would still be someone who mattered to him or anyone else when her face was no longer on magazines and TV screens and billboards.

But in the back of the taxi on the drive back to her house, Jack didn't force her to admit her hidden fears. He simply pulled her close and held her.

Mary had been with men who were flashy, the life of every party, the head of every line, the first in front of every camera. Whereas Jack reminded her of her own father. Steady. Warm. Strong.

Solid, from heart to soul.

When the taxi pulled up in front of her house, she

slid her fingers through his. "I'm not ready for the most romantic date of my life to end."

Of course, she wanted him to come inside and spend the night with her, sweet hours of sinful lovemaking that stole her breath and set her heart to racing. But even more than that, after those moments when they'd temporarily sated their passions and he was holding her in his arms, she wanted to experience the feeling of deep, sweet closeness and joy.

Jack's dark eyes never left hers as he paid for the taxi, and then they were standing in front of her house once again, two lovers who she now understood had never had a chance of resisting the beautiful pull between them.

What sweet relief it was to allow herself to give in to the heady urge to kiss him out on the sidewalk beneath the moon and the stars for anyone to see. And when his mouth was against hers and his arms were around her, it was easy to ignore her lingering fears, the worries that she wished would stop trying to push their way to the surface.

"Thank you for the flowers, the movie, the popcorn and the company.... They were all wonderful." With each word, she drew him step by step up the stairs. "I'd offer to make you a cup of coffee, but I have a feeling I wouldn't give you a chance to let you drink it before it got really, really cold."

She was just opening her front door when he said, "We'll have it in bed," in that low voice that sizzled up her spine. *"After."*

Oh, yes. *After.*

As soon as they were inside, Mary started stripping away Jack's jacket and shirt, her lips immediately covering each patch of skin she bared. He was doing the same with her when her phone rang.

She'd never once let the phone go unheeded, even when the timing was as bad as it was now. What if it was her parents calling? What if they were hurt or sick? Or what if her mother was finally ready to talk to her again?

The men Mary had been with before Jack had never understood why she would drop everything to pick up the phone, but when she looked into Jack's eyes with an apology in hers and said, "I'm sorry. I have to get the phone," he didn't look upset.

Instead, she could see that he automatically understood. "I'm not going anywhere. Go see who that is."

She pressed a quick—and grateful—kiss to his lips before rushing off to grab the phone from its cradle. "Hello, this is Mary."

Yvette's cheerful voice came through the line and Mary had to smile at the girl's rush of excited words. "Slow down, Yvette," she said with a laugh. She grinned at Jack, who was in the kitchen filling her moka pot with water. "Start over at the beginning so that I make sure I get all the fantastic, exciting details straight. You were playing cards with your aunt and uncle in your Iowa farmhouse when you got a call about a last-minute shoot in Switzerland?"

Mary had just kicked off her shoes and was tucking her legs beneath her to relax on the couch when Yvette said the one name she never wanted to hear again, much less a name connected with one of her young model friends. "Romain?" His name followed a sharp intake of breath as Mary confirmed again, "You're working with *Romain Bollinger* in Switzerland?"

Yvette continue to chatter in her ear, while Mary's hand went numb on the phone as she was hit with a crystal clear flashback to that horrible day she'd walked into his penthouse and found him in bed with a much-younger model.

A young model who had looked an awful lot like Yvette...and one who hadn't lasted any longer in his bed, or life, than Mary had. Models, they'd all learned the hard way, were totally dispensable objects to Romain. He was, in fact, a thousand times more faithful to his French chef than he was to any of the women he brought in through his revolving door.

On a night when Mary should have been basking in the glow of finding a man like Jack Sullivan, she was forcibly reminded of what a fool she'd been when it came to matters of the heart. She'd believed every one of Romain's false promises and had been so desperate for someone to love her that she'd turned every one of his pretty lies and every single kiss into so much more than he had ever meant them to be.

Sitting on the couch speaking with Yvette on the phone while Jack was just feet away in the kitchen, Mary couldn't stop her past and present from getting all tangled up again.

Jack and Romain, Mary and Yvette, love and loss, heartbreak and recovery... She simply couldn't figure out how to separate them tonight.

Belatedly, Mary realized that Jack had left the kitchen and was kneeling in front of her, her free hand in his. His eyes were full of concern and silent support.

A week ago she probably would have run, would have done anything she could to push him away and escape from feelings that were too strong and too frightening. But, amazingly, as she stared into his eyes and felt his thumb stroke over the pad of her palm, she actually felt her insides begin to untwist. Enough that she finally realized Yvette was saying her name over and over, asking if their connection was still all right or if they'd been cut off.

Working to refocus her thoughts on the bright, vibrant young woman on the phone, Mary knew she needed to warn Yvette to be careful with Romain. She wouldn't be able to stand it if the fun, lively girl was drawn in by his false promises and ended up hurt and disillusioned. At the same time, however, Mary remembered all too well what it was like to be a headstrong young woman. Whenever anyone had told her to be cautious, there had been nothing more she'd wanted than to prove she could deal brilliantly with whatever risky situation had been thrown at her.

Very carefully, in as easy a voice as she could manage, Mary told Yvette, "I worked with Romain and his company a few years ago. The photo shoot was excellent, but—"

Oh, how she wished she could find exactly the right words to keep Yvette safe. Barring getting on a plane to

Switzerland and watching over the photo shoot to make sure he didn't try anything, it was simply impossible to play bodyguard to the young models who had come to mean so much to her. And wasn't it true that they would soon come to hate her for hovering?

Mary took a deep breath. All she could do was tell Yvette the truth of her feelings and then trust her to do the best she could with the information. "Romain is quite a ladies' man. I know that because I didn't just work with him," she admitted in a voice she worked hard to keep steady. "I dated him for a while, too." Jack's hand on hers kept her warm and grounded as she told Yvette, "It didn't end well, and the reason it didn't is because he cheated on me. To him, I was nothing more than an expendable pretty face. I could never forgive myself if something like that happened to you—I just wanted you to know."

"He sounds like scum," Yvette said in a passionate voice. "And stupid, too, for cheating on you. What guy could be that dumb when you're so amazing?"

Mary was more than a little surprised to find herself starting to smile at Yvette's reaction. And then when the girl said, "Besides, I'm not interested in old guys like him," she could all but see Yvette's nose scrunch up as she added, "Eww."

Mary couldn't keep her laughter from bubbling up and over as she agreed with a simple and heartfelt "Yuck."

All those years ago, when Mary had been telling her mother about her grand opportunities to model in New York City, all she'd wanted was for her mother to have faith that her daughter would make good decisions. Now, she realized, it was her turn to do that for Yvette.

Of course, Mary had known all along that Yvette had a good head on her beautiful shoulders. Which was why she meant every word when she told her, "You're going to knock them off their feet in Switzerland, honey. I can't wait to hear all about it when you get back. And thank you for sharing this great news with me."

When Yvette told her that of course she had to call, because Mary was family, her eyes finally teared up, but not with fear or worry.

With joy.

Women had often told Jack over the years that he didn't pay enough attention to their needs, their feelings, that he was too focused on his computers and circuits to understand them. And they'd been right, but only because none of them had captured enough of his heart to get all his attention.

But Mary had had his full attention from the first moment he'd set eyes on her. He'd watched her shift from an animated phone conversation with Yvette to turning pale as a ghost, and when he heard the name *Romain* fall from her lips, he immediately sensed her concern for the young woman she'd been watching over.

At the same time, he'd instinctively known that Mary's doubts and fears about their relationship had to be rising up again. What could have been a better reminder of the need to be careful with Jack than hearing about that bastard again?

Back at the movie theater, it had meant so much to Jack when she'd said she didn't want their relationship to be a secret anymore. And yet, even as she'd said it, he'd known that she was still holding something back from him, that final piece of herself...just in case.

Jack knew how badly she'd been hurt. Not only by the Swiss-watch mogul, but also by the way her own family had pushed her out of their lives. And he'd meant it when he said he'd wait as long as he needed to for her.

She'd told him that day in his garage that it would take her some time to heal all the way. Well, he was a very patient man when he needed to be…and he would just keep loving her through her doubts and fears until they were completely gone.

As she hung up the phone, Jack moved beside her on the couch and asked, "Are you okay?"

She put one hand on his cheek and held it there. "You know what? I am." She stroked her fingertips lightly over the stubble on his cheek. "I've never had a man to lean on," she said softly. "Not until you."

In that instant, all of the vows he'd just made to himself to be patient snapped in two.

He had to tell her how he felt.

She had to know.

"I love you, Mary."

She'd blinked at him in pain and confusion minutes earlier when Romain's name had left her lips. And then, when she'd put her hand on his cheek after she'd hung up the phone, she'd gazed at him with warmth. Now she was clearly shocked by his sudden declaration.

As an engineer, Jack understood precision and timing better than most. And yet, even if he was screwing up everything in this moment, he simply couldn't hold back the depths of what he felt for Mary one more second.

"I never want to keep anything from you, Angel."

Now he was the one cupping her face in his hands as he told her, "Even when my professional dreams stretched from a few years to a decade, I always felt like I was holding the reins of control. I could see steady progress, and I was certain that nothing would knock me off course before I achieved my goal. But then I met you, and from that moment I've been hit with countless feelings—and desires—that I never saw coming. Not just the desire to kiss you, to touch you, to make love with you, but the need to make a life with you. I want to know that you're mine and I'm yours and that everything we do from here on out, we'll do together. I want you to become a part of my family. I want to find a way to reconcile you with your family. And I want the two of us to create a family of our own together, too."

Jack hoped like hell that he was making some sense, but he'd never been caught up in a storm of emotions like this before. Only Mary could have unleashed such passion from a man who had always been so rational.

"I don't want to push you any faster than you're ready to go, and you've already given me so much more than I ever dreamed I'd have, but—"

Mary lifted her hands to touch his as they rested on her cheeks and, at that exact moment, her mouth covered his, and her kiss stole the rest of his words. His heart hammered in his chest as she stroked her tongue over his. Of course, he loved kissing her, but right now he needed to understand what her kiss meant. Was she trying to tell him she felt the same way…or was she trying to stop him before he said anything more?

Gently, he drew her back, but before he could ask her anything, she was looking at him with such open trust and so much emotion that his hands would have trembled if she hadn't been holding them.

"I love you, too, Jack."

For the first few seconds after she spoke, all he could do was stare at the most beautiful woman he'd ever known, and marvel not only that she was here with him but also that she'd actually said the three sweetest words he'd ever heard.

Finally, when he thought he'd found his voice again, he said, "You—"

He stopped, more than a little afraid to repeat the words out of fear that she'd take them back when she finally realized she'd said them aloud to him.

"I meant what I said earlier tonight," she said in a soft but steady voice. "I don't want to let what happened with Romain ruin the best thing I've ever known." Her eyes were the clearest blue he'd ever seen as she said, "I know you told me you'd wait for me, but I don't want either of us to wait anymore. Especially when I knew from the first moment I saw you that you were special. I feel like I've been running my whole life, speeding from a small town into a big city, jumping from one place to the next for years until they all blurred together. And right when I decided it was time to finally stop running and set down some roots, there you were. My new beginning." Her eyes filled with tears as she smiled up at him and slid her arms around his neck to pull him closer. "My love."

Jack sank down onto the couch with Mary, her curves soft beneath his muscles. "I'll always be yours, Angel. Forever."

Jack would never forget their first kiss under the mistletoe, and he would never forget this one, either.

Their first kiss after *I love you…*

Sixteen

The next day Jack was surprisingly full of energy as he went from meeting to meeting, despite the fact that neither he nor Mary had gotten much sleep, having spent most of the night discovering ever new joys of being with each other. Not even the string of corporate meetings he'd been in today could tax his strength when he knew Mary would be waiting for him at her house that evening with open arms.

Jack could still hardly believe he'd been lucky enough to stumble onto her photo shoot in Union Square that fateful afternoon, when all hope for his career had almost been lost. Just as she'd said, it had been a new beginning to something so much bigger, so much sweeter, than anything he could ever have imagined.

He'd been looking for a miracle to save his company... but in Mary he'd found far more than that.

This morning, when the first rays of light had come in through her bedroom window, he'd awakened with Mary spooned into his chest and hips, with his hand over her heart, and hers curled into his palm. Jack had been hit with a fierce need to keep her love all to himself, just for a little while longer. Soon he'd shout from the rooftops that Mary was his, but for just a few extra hours, he didn't want to have to answer the questions that would surely come from all quarters—from people who knew them and journalists who didn't—when their relationship was revealed.

"I know we're not hiding anymore," he'd said softly as she'd turned into his arms so that her head was in the crook of his shoulder and her hand was resting over his heart, "but I don't think I'm ready to share you just yet."

She'd smiled up at him, her olive skin and long, dark hair a beautiful contrast to the ivory sheets. "You know what they say about secret kisses, don't you?"

He should have been completely tapped out from their lovemaking during the night, but when she let the sheets slip from her shoulders and moved her gorgeous naked curves over him, then *showed* him exactly how good secret kisses could be, Jack knew he'd never get enough of Mary. Their lovemaking had also helped him to ignore the relief that had flashed across her face when he'd said he wanted to keep things private between them a little while longer.

Still, he knew they couldn't keep their love a secret forever. At some point in the very near future they'd have to weather the fascination that was bound to come from an international celebrity choosing to settle down with an ordinary man who fiddled with electronics for a living. Jack desperately hoped Mary would be ready for that when it happened....

With bumper-to-bumper traffic in the city that afternoon, Jack decided it would be faster to forgo a taxi to Walter Industries and head there on foot instead. Allen had asked to see Jack, Larry and Howie this afternoon so that they could touch base on the progress they'd made these past two weeks and to make sure they were all on the same page heading into the big pre-Christmas launch in a couple of days.

As he walked past a strip of high-end stores, the glint of light off a ring in a jewelry-store window stopped Jack in his tracks.

He'd often heard it said that the key to success was

never to make the mistake of letting something shiny along the path pull one's attention away from the end goal. But, as an inventor, Jack had learned the enormous value of paying attention to those little glimmers that arrived and surprised him. Because sometimes you were so busy looking for answers that you missed seeing them when they were right in front of you.

He was inside the jewelry store a moment later asking to see the ring in the window. The diamond at the center of the slender band had been cut into a perfect circle and was set with smaller diamonds in a delicate ring all around it.

"This is a traditional Italian engagement ring from our estate collection," the slim woman behind the counter told him. "It's approximately eighty years old and the woman who sold it to us said her grandmother wore it with great love her whole life. The smaller diamonds surrounding the center diamond symbolize the eternity of love."

No wonder he'd been so drawn to the ring. It was not only from Italy, but it had a history of great love.

The woman discreetly showed him the price and he had to blink a couple of times to process the large number before saying, "I'd appreciate it a great deal if you'd hold this ring for me. I don't have the money right now, but I'll get it."

"I can hold it until closing, sir."

"I'll be back for it before then," he promised.

It had been less than twenty-four hours since they'd declared their love for each other, but Jack had waited his whole life to meet Mary. Most people took a while to go from "I love you" to "Will you marry me?" But just as he couldn't have held back that love from her last night, he knew he wouldn't be able to wait for their new beginning to be official, either.

This was the ring he would give to Mary when he asked her to be his forever.

Fifteen minutes later, Jack walked into Allen's office, barely noticing the spectacular view of the Bay and the bridge from the chairman's windows.

"Great news, Jack," Allen greeted him as he came around his desk and shook Jack's hand. "We've got nearly all of the major retailers on board already, and we haven't even had our official campaign launch yet." Allen was as animated—and pleased—as Jack had ever seen him. "Mary's face and personal endorsement of the Pocket Planner has been pure advertising gold. You were right not to give up hope on your invention. I've got a very good feeling about what the Christmas season is going to bring for all of us."

Jack had a good feeling about things, too, but for different reasons. Because, while he was happy that their business was going well, solidifying his future with Mary now took precedence over everything else.

"I'm glad to hear things are going well," Jack said, and then in his characteristically direct way, he said, "I need an advance on my earnings, Allen. This afternoon, actually."

"You need money this afternoon?" The other man raised an eyebrow. "How much?"

Jack told him the number and Allen stared at him for a long moment before finally nodding. "Excuse me while I call my personal banker to let him know to have a cashier's check for that amount waiting for you immediately."

"Thank you." Jack had never asked anyone for a loan before, and he'd very rarely asked for a favor, either. But his pride could take a backseat for a few hours. Mary was more important.

After concluding the call, Allen sat back in his chair. "You don't strike me as the kind of man who would get himself into trouble gambling, Jack." Clearly, he was dying for more details, but in the end he simply said, "Whatever you're planning to use that money for, I hope it's worth it."

"I don't have a single doubt about that." Jack decided that Allen's vote of confidence in him deserved one in return. "I'm going to ask Mary to marry me. Your generous advance on profits has just made it possible for me to buy her the ring she deserves."

Allen's eyes grew big. "You're with Mary? Our Mary?" When Jack nodded, Allen had to clarify one more time, "Mary Ferrer?"

"I'm in love with her."

"Of course you're in love with her. Who isn't?" Allen replied, but his shock was already shifting to admiration. "I couldn't have written the headlines better myself: An Unexpected Christmas Romance between Our Brilliant Inventor and the Gorgeous Model. She was already the golden touch we needed for this campaign, but if she says yes to your proposal, the two of you together will be the best story we could ever have—"

Jack cut Allen off. "I appreciate your cashier's check, and that you're so excited about things working out between Mary and myself. But we'd like to keep things private between us for as long as we possibly can." The chairman had just done him a great favor by issuing the check, but Jack's gratitude didn't extend to selling their "love story" to the press, especially not given Mary's past with Romain. "I would *never* exploit our relationship for increased profits."

After a long silence, Allen spoke. "Very few people stand up to me anymore. I'm richer, smarter and more powerful than all of them. But you've surprised me from the start, Jack." Allen suddenly grinned, looking ten years younger as he waved Jack out of the room. "Go get your ring and the girl. I'd wish you luck, but I have a feeling you're not going to need it."

Jack thanked Allen again and was just getting into the elevator when Howie and Larry stepped out of it.

"Where are you going?" Howie asked. "Isn't Allen waiting for all of us in his office?"

"You two can take this meeting without me. I'll see you all tomorrow at the final shoot."

Where, hopefully, he'd arrive as a newly engaged man.

Mary had really enjoyed the mix of photo shoots and interviews while working on Jack's campaign, but tonight was her favorite moment so far. The ad agency had booked her to be a part of the Christmas-tree-lighting ceremony at Union Square, and she would be giving away twenty-five free Pocket Planners as early Christmas gifts to people in the crowd.

Already, Mary had spotted several people who she guessed would really benefit from one. A young mother trying to simultaneously hold the hands of three rambunctious children. A businessman who had arrived tense and harried but who, when he saw his kids in the crowd, immediately dropped his briefcase to the ground to catch their hugs. Even the teenage girl with the heavy backpack who was clearly dreaming of finishing her classes for the semester so that she could enjoy winter break with her friends.

The night air was crisp and the sky was clear and sparkling with stars. The only thing that could make Mary's night better was if Jack were here to share it with her.

For the dozenth time that day, she worked to push back her impatient longing for him...especially when there was only an hour left to go before she could meet him at her house.

Though the night was cool, remembering their lovemaking from the night before made Mary warm all over. How sweet Jack had been as he whispered "I love you" over every bare inch of her skin, then followed up his words with heated kisses that stole every last rational thought from her brain. Again and again they'd loved each other, until they'd finally fallen asleep in each other's arms. They'd awakened to tangled sheets and a sensual hunger that hadn't even come close to being sated. Mary had never known pleasure so sweet, so decadent or so overwhelming.

Deep inside, the still-wary part of her heart kept trying to warn her not to let bliss blind her to the possibility of future pain. But she refused to listen.

Jack was different. Yes, they were working together on his campaign, but every step of the way, he'd reassured her that his feelings for her had nothing to do with business.

And that he loved her.

Still, nothing soothed her lingering fears better than being in Jack's arms. Yet again she wished he were—

"Angel."

Mary looked up into the most beautiful face she'd ever set eyes on.

"Jack, you're here! I thought you had a meeting with Allen."

His smile as he drew her close was both warm and

filled with desire. "I couldn't stay away a moment longer."

He'd been the one to ask for a little more private time together that morning, but despite the dozens of eager and interested onlookers, how could she possibly keep from kissing him?

Mary was just moving to wrap her arms around his neck when a little girl pushed between them.

"Here are your candles for the ceremony."

Soon, Mary reminded herself as they moved apart to each take a candle from the girl, she and Jack would be alone again and then she could kiss him to her heart's content with no interruptions.

As their candles were being lit, a young boy walked onto the small stage beside the tree and began to carefully recite a Christmas poem he'd written about Rudolph the reindeer and Santa Claus. In the dark, Jack slid his hand into Mary's and she leaned into his warmth, loving how strong and steady he always was. Just as the boy finished his poem, the Christmas tree came to colorful, glittering life.

"Isn't it beautiful?" Mary said as she squeezed Jack's hand tighter.

"The most beautiful thing I've ever seen," he agreed. But he wasn't looking at the tree.

He only had eyes for her.

A children's chorus began to sing "Hark! The Herald Angels Sing," and when Jack joined in, his voice ringing out deep and true, Mary's heart swelled with love.

Seventeen

"I haven't enjoyed a Christmas celebration that much since I was a child," Mary said when they had finished distributing the Pocket Planners to the crowd. Mary had explained how the device worked to the mother, the businessman and the student, and they'd all been thrilled to go home and play with their unexpected gifts.

A short while ago she'd met Jack in this same spot in Union Square and he'd asked her to join him for pie and ice cream. Now she was the one saying, "I happen to know a great diner just around the corner from here. Want to join me for some of the best pie you'll ever have?"

Strangely, he gave her a slightly nervous look that confused her. She'd never seen Jack anxious before. Was he tired from the string of long days getting ready for the big holiday launch? Or was there something else going on?

Before she could ask him if everything was all right, he finally gave her one of his beautiful grins. "Great idea. In fact," he added as he took her hand and they began walking toward the diner, "I think pie and ice cream at the diner should always be part of our new post-Christmas-tree-lighting tradition."

Tradition.

Mary had thought she'd left tradition behind when she left Italy. The idea of starting a new tradition with Jack was at once terrifying…and wonderful. Because it meant that he really did intend to keep loving her past this first Christmas, when everything between them was so fresh and exciting.

She forgot all about his slightly strange initial reaction as they chatted easily about their busy days while they walked. They weren't just lovers; they were friends, too. Best friends who would do absolutely anything to make the other person happy.

Despite being fairly empty, the diner was cozy and warm. This time, they both sat on the same side of the booth and shared a supersize slice of pie. Her night couldn't get any more perfect than this, sitting with the man she loved while he fed her warm cherries coated in melting vanilla ice cream. They simply enjoyed being with each other.

She knew her life wasn't perfect, and there were things she would always wish she could have done differently, but for the first time in a very long time, she felt at peace.

"Mary—"

Something in Jack's voice as he said her name pulled her from her relaxed reverie. The note of anxiety she'd sensed earlier was back.

"Jack? What is it?" She'd seen him look intense before, but never *this* intense.

"I think we should go back to your place now."

He put a twenty-dollar bill down on the table and pulled her to her feet, quickly bundling her up in her coat and scarf. Moments later, they were out on the sidewalk, and he was all but dragging her along the street in the direction of her house.

Panic skittered down her spine. Just when she'd finally let herself relax, had something gone wrong?

"Jack." He was much bigger than she, but she was strong enough to tug him to a stop. "Tell me what's wrong. Please just tell me."

"I'm doing this all wrong." He cursed once in a low voice as he ran his free hand through his hair.

She shook her head in confusion. "What are you doing wrong?"

Before she knew it, he'd dropped to one knee in front of her.

Her mouth fell open. All the way open, in fact, as she stared in shock at Jack kneeling before her.

"I was planning to surprise you with rose petals and champagne and every other romantic thing I could think of. But I just can't wait another second to ask you to be my wife."

Mary's head and heart were spinning round and round so fast that she needed to make sure she'd heard him right. "You want me to be your wife?"

"I know I don't have much to give you, and that you deserve absolutely everything. Riches. Beautiful gifts. I can't give you any of those things. Not yet, anyway. All I can give you is my heart. And every last piece of my soul."

He reached with a shaky hand into the inner pocket of his blue blazer and pulled out a small black box wrapped in velvet. When he flipped the lid open, she gasped at the sparkle of diamonds in the light of the street lamp above them.

"And this ring."

Mary instantly recognized it as a classic Italian engagement ring. One that symbolized love for all eternity.

"Marry me, Angel, and make me the happiest man in the world."

"Yes." The word flew out of her mouth before she could think, before she could process anything more than how much she loved him. She tugged him back to his feet so that she could wrap her arms around him, the ring and box crushed between them. "Yes, I'll marry you."

Their mouths met in a kiss so loving, so sweet, so passionate that she could hardly believe all of this was real. It had happened so fast, from meeting Jack to falling in love with him, to being offered his heart and soul.

When they finally drew back from each other, he took her left hand in his and slipped the gorgeous engagement ring onto her fourth finger. Mary stared in wonder at it, thinking just how much her mother would have loved this moment. If only she could call her with the wonderful news…

But, suddenly, thinking of her mother brought more

than just a pang of longing for her estranged family. It also brought Mary's fears back to the forefront.

"I don't—" She swallowed hard as she made herself face Jack. "What if I don't know how to be a wife? What if I'm no good at being one half of a whole? I've only ever been on my own as an adult."

"So have I," he said in a soft voice, "but that's just because I was waiting to kiss the prettiest girl in the world under the mistletoe. Whatever we have to learn, we'll learn together."

Easy. He made it sound so easy. And because she badly wanted to believe that it would be, she echoed him. "I was waiting for you, too."

Mary and Jack stopped to kiss at every corner, so the walk back to her house took twice as long as it otherwise would have. By the time they made it to her front door, she was more than ready for a repeat of the wild against-the-door lovemaking from the night he'd taken her to see *Singin' in the Rain*.

But instead of tearing her clothes off the moment they were inside, Jack put his hands on either side of her face and held her gently.

"Mine."

He said the word softly, but she heard the possession—and the wonder—in the simple word as it fell from his lips.

"Yours." Emotion made her voice unsteady. *"Always."*

Slowly, reverently, he ran the tips of his fingers over her eyebrows, cheekbones, lips and earlobes. By the time he reached her neck and then the hollows of her collarbones, she was beyond desperate for more of him.

"Jack, *please.*"

He leaned forward and slid his bristly cheek against her smooth one. "I know I didn't do the proposal right," he murmured against her earlobe, "but I'll get this part right. I promise."

"Everything you do is exactly right," she insisted, just as she had the first night they were together, even though she knew that when Jack Sullivan made up his mind—especially when it came to giving her pleasure—nothing could deter him.

After slipping off her scarf and coat and then his own, he slid his fingers through hers and led her into the bedroom. For so long her bed had seemed too big, but it was just the right size for the two of them.

"Undressing you is one of life's greatest pleasures."

He moved behind her to gather her hair up over one

shoulder and began to pull down the zipper that ran from her neck to the center of her back. She could feel the heat of his fingertips through the silk chemise she was wearing.

Slowly, so slowly it made her breath catch in her lungs, he slid the wool off her shoulders and arms so that it bunched at her waist before he finally gave it an impatient shove down over her hips. A moment later, she felt the warm press of his lips against her neck, and then she was arching into his touch as his large hands slid from her waist up to her ribs to cup her breasts. She gasped when his thumbs brushed over the taut peaks.

Turning her head so her mouth could find his, she might have kept kissing him forever had his roaming hands not made her so breathless that she had to pull back to drag much-needed air into her lungs.

Holding her still with one large hand over her stomach, he slid the other between her thighs, brushing his fingers over the bare skin at the top of her stockings. In her girlish dreams of love, and then later, in her adult experience of real-life passion, she'd never expected to feel this much…or to *want* this much. But every time Jack touched her, she sparked, lit into flames and then melted for him.

Slowly, seductively, Jack moved his hand higher to cover the damp material between her legs, then slid his fingers beneath it as he breathed the sweet endearment. *"Angel."*

She shook, then shattered against him as he took her even higher with a kiss that rocked through her as deeply as the caress of his hand just had.

The next thing she knew, she was in his arms and he was laying her down on the bed. After he quickly unzipped her boots, he unhooked her garters to roll one stocking down her leg. Her breath was coming fast by the time he'd bared her other leg.

He was still wearing his sports coat and slacks and she felt deliciously naughty in only her bra and panties as she rose to her knees to take off his jacket.

"One of life's great pleasures," she agreed as she unbuttoned his shirt. Even the sound of his belt buckle coming undone excited her, as did the caress of his hands over her skin as he stripped the final bits of lace from her body.

Need fed need, desire stoked desire and love fueled love as they fell back onto the bed into each other's arms.

A long while later, Mary lay on Jack's chest, working to catch her breath, while he stroked his hand over her hair, soothing her even as he inflamed her again.

"I love you."

She nestled in closer to him, loving the way his voice rumbled through his chest to hers when they were this close. "I love you, too."

The ring glinted in her peripheral vision and happiness swelled inside her. Everything was so great, almost perfect, as long as she didn't think about…

As if he could read her mind, Jack suddenly said, "I think you should call your mother and father to tell them about us. They've got to want to know how happy you are."

Mary was tempted, so tempted to pick up the phone and share her joy with the two people who had been the center of her world for nineteen years. Her heart raced just thinking of it.

"No," she finally said, shaking her head against his chest. "I can't."

"Why not?"

Her parents had always expected her to be the perfect little girl and to only dream the dreams they allowed her. Clients and photographers had always expected her to be flawless and poised.

Only Jack, Mary believed, loved her for who she really was.

"Because if I call and they aren't happy for me, it will ruin our perfect night. And I don't want anything to touch us tonight." Mary lifted her head and shifted her weight over his so that her thighs were on either side of his, her breasts pressed to the dark hair on his chest. She lowered her mouth to his and whispered, "Tonight is only for us. Only for love." And then she let passion—and the joy of knowing she was with the one person on earth who loved her for herself—sweep her up all over again.

Eighteen

Mary felt as though she were floating the next morning as she and Jack got out of the taxi, hand in hand, in front of the studio where they were going to shoot the final photos for the campaign. She thought she'd been in love before, but now she knew she'd never been anywhere close to it. Just being near Jack sent her heart racing and every inch of her skin heating up. And though it had been an hour since they'd made love that morning, when he took her hand in his and gently rubbed his thumb across her palm, she felt as if he was still holding her in the warm, strong, safe circle of arms, naked and sated.

And loved.

Mary was known for her prompt appearance at every booking, unlike many of the models who rolled into the studio when it suited them. Today, however, she and Jack had arrived a good fifteen minutes after everyone else, and she didn't care that they were late. Not when every extra moment in Jack's arms had been utterly precious.

Jack gently brushed a lock of hair away from her forehead. "I love you." His voice was soft but oh so steady as he brought his lips nearly to hers. "I can't wait to let everyone know that you've agreed to be my wife. Are you ready?"

She absolutely refused to acknowledge the nerves jumping inside of her as she said, "Yes."

It was so easy to get lost in him, she thought as he kissed her. But before she could get more than one too-short taste, the door opened...and Howie discovered their big secret before they made their big announcement.

Mary was glad to see more delight than shock on Jack's partner's face as he happily ushered them inside the building. The beautiful diamond ring on her left hand was hard to miss, and before Mary knew it, Howie was giving her a congratulatory kiss on the cheek and clapping Jack on the back.

"Everyone," he called out, "I believe Jack and Mary have a very exciting announcement to make!"

It had all happened so fast, a whirlwind from having

pie and ice cream with Jack to swearing she wouldn't mix business with pleasure, and then not being able to stop herself from doing just that as she fell head over heels in love. More than once she'd worried that she was in too deep, and that it had happened too fast, but each time Jack's constancy had reassured her. Every step of the way, he'd been so sweet, so patient with her, even when they'd both been driven to the edge of madness with desire.

How, she wondered as they stood on the precipice of announcing not only their relationship but also their engagement, could those long-held fears rear up again?

Love, in her experience, had always been conditional. But Jack wasn't like that. He could never treat her that way…could he?

"Mary?"

Though everyone was waiting for their big announcement, Jack was looking at her as if they were the only two people in the room.

She remembered the way she'd felt in Union Square that first time she'd seen him in the crowd of strangers. From that first moment she'd felt as if she knew him… and she had known that he was special.

Just because other people in her past had disappointed her didn't mean that he would, too. Plus, she'd seen him with his family, the way he and his brothers had always been there for one another, no matter what.

Telling herself that trusting Jack couldn't possibly be the wrong decision, Mary squeezed his hand and let his steady warmth settle her nerves. "Let's tell them, Jack."

In all her dreams of love, she'd never envisioned a man like him could exist, one who was completely open every single moment about his feelings for her. She'd never been one for public displays of affection—in the entertainment business they were almost always false—but now she couldn't resist leaning in to kiss him.

When she drew back, Jack pulled her close against him, then he finally told the group, "I'm extremely pleased to let all of you know that Mary has agreed to become my wife."

The next thing she knew, Allen had popped a bottle of champagne and was pouring a glass for everyone. How, she wondered, could Allen have known to have champagne ready?

Realizing it was just the cynical part of her that kept trying to rise up to ruin everything, she figured it wasn't at all impossible that Allen had the champagne on ice to celebrate the end of their successful campaign and their upcoming launch.

"I'm so happy that you found true love," Gerry said as he drew her into his arms and hugged her tight.

While it occurred to her that Gerry was the only one in the room who had truly looked surprised at Jack's announcement, she assumed that was because he was the only one of them who knew her history and how badly she'd been hurt before.

When he moved away to finish setting up his cameras, though she was only a few sips in, Mary could already feel the champagne going to her head, so she put her glass down.

She was just about to head into her dressing room to do her hair and makeup for the photos when Larry said, "Hey, now that you and Jack are engaged, what do you guys think about taking some shots of the two of you together with the Pocket Planner?"

Mary's gut twisted reflexively at the suggestion that they use images of the two of them as a couple to sell Jack's invention, but even as she was working to push away the twinge, Jack was shaking his head.

"Mary's the face of our product. She's the one people want to see using the Pocket Planner, not an engineer who's worked out of a garage for the past ten years."

"Actually," Howie said as he rubbed his chin thoughtfully, "you two do look good together. Really good. Layla even pointed it out to me after that night at the bar. I wouldn't be at all surprised if people responded just as well to the two of you as they do to Mary. And maybe Jack's ugly mug could help pull in even more female buyers."

Mary felt torn right down the middle. Old fears were screaming at her, warning her not to be so stupid a second time by shooting pictures for a campaign in which falling in love with the founder of the company played any part. But she loved Jack and wanted the very best for him. And her experience with advertising over the past thirteen years told her that the two of them posing together would be good. Really good.

She looked at Jack and smiled. "It's a good idea. Let's do it."

Jack took her in his arms, clearly concerned about the decision she'd just made. "We should stick to the original plan, Mary. I don't want you to have any regrets. Not now. Not ever."

For his ears only, she said, "Your dream is just as important to me as it is to you. I think we owe it to all those years of working in your garage to convince people to give your invention a chance any way we can." She lifted her hand to his face and smiled. "Plus, just like Howie said, women are going to go wild for this face of yours."

Gerry had picked up his camera and moved over to them in the hopes of capturing the poignant moment. "Mary? Jack?"

Finally, Jack gave a small nod. Larry handed them the Pocket Planner and she held on to both Jack and his dream as the camera bulbs started flashing.

Several hours later, Gerry declared that they had more than enough fantastic pictures and headed out to develop them immediately in his darkroom so that they could create the final ad in time for the launch.

Mary realized she'd never had that much fun in front of the camera before. She'd always been able to perform with people watching her, but when she was in Jack's arms, everyone and everything else truly disappeared. It had been totally different from the way things had been when she'd shot the ads with Romain. Fun, rather than serious. Impromptu, rather than planned.

Jack was, as she'd suspected, a natural in front of the camera. Gerry was practically drooling over every frame that Jack had been in, and she had a feeling the photographer wouldn't be the only one. Rugged, mature men like Jack were always in high demand in the print-ad industry. Clearly, if he ever wanted to give up engineering, he could walk right into a very lucrative career in front of the camera. Of course, she knew he'd never give up his work, not when his brilliant mind would always be racing ahead to the next invention.

Mary went into the dressing room to change back into her street clothes and was just coming back out when she overheard Larry and Howie talking excitedly, their voices traveling down the hall to her.

"Can you believe how well this is all going?" Larry said to Howie. "Thank God we walked past Mary's photo shoot that day in Union Square."

She smiled, agreeing with them. Meeting Jack that day had changed her life, in the *most* wonderful ways.

"And thank God she agreed to Jack's marriage proposal," Howie added. "Allen was completely right when he told us yesterday afternoon that the press is going to eat up the way the two of them met and fell in love while working on this campaign. He's already put out some feelers and it sounded like there is going to be lots of interest already. That's probably why he left so fast after the celebration this morning—to go make all those calls to confirm the news that she's wearing his ring."

Allen had known about her and Jack yesterday afternoon? He'd talked to Howie and Larry about it and how the press was going to love seeing Jack's ring on her finger?

But he hadn't asked her to marry him until that evening. And on top of that, they'd agreed to keep their relationship private, just between the two of them. In fact, Jack had been the one who'd said he wanted to keep things private a little while longer once they'd declared themselves to each other.

So how could all of them have already known?

"It's been the perfect plan from start to finish," Larry agreed happily.

Plan. Mary felt as if her heart was tearing in two right where she stood. *It had been the perfect plan.*

She braced herself against the wall and forced herself to take a deep breath. Now that she knew what a fool she'd been, it would be easiest to run, to leave, to get on a plane to somewhere, anywhere, and never see Jack again.

But even bigger than her shame at how easily she'd been duped was her anger. And right now, fury was all that stood between her and the bitter pain of a broken heart.

She moved quickly from the hallway to where Jack

was standing with several Walter Industries board members. "We need to talk."

She didn't wait for him to respond as she headed back into her dressing room. When she heard the door close behind her, she whirled.

"When did you tell everyone we were together? Did you brag about it the first time we kissed? Did you give them a play-by-play of the first time we made love? Did all of you toast the way you'd gotten me to be both the face of your product and your pretty little plaything—two for the price of one?"

"Mary?" He started to reach for her, but when she flinched away from him, he dropped his hands. "What's going on? What happened?"

"How dare you act like you don't know what's going on!" The words erupted like a snarl from her lips. "I thought you were such a gentleman, that you were one of the rare men who actually cared about what I wanted. What I needed. I thought I was more than a pretty face to you, more than just another couple of digits added to your bottom line." Her chest was so tight she felt as if she could hardly breathe. She took several steps away from him, as if that might help her find some oxygen. "When were you going to ask for the ring back? Were you going to wait until sales were steady enough that it wouldn't matter to anyone that we weren't together anymore?"

"Damn it, Mary, what are you talking about?" A muscle was jumping in his jaw. "Why would I want the ring back?"

He started toward her again, but she knew the moment he put his arms around her she'd forget to protect herself again…and that she'd give in to her foolish heart and keep loving him anyway.

Panicking, with her Italian temper rising up and clouding her better sense, Mary took off the beautiful engagement ring and threw it at him.

Nineteen

What the hell just happened?

Jack stood in the middle of Mary's dressing room, stunned that she had yelled at him about using her and then nailed him in the head with the engagement ring he'd given her.

He had never been an angry man, had never fought at school or raised his fists for anything but the boxing training at the gym. Most disagreements, he figured, could be worked out with a rational conversation or two. But Mary hadn't even come close to trying to talk to him about what was bothering her. She'd flat-out erupted.

Though he'd often seen and felt the flashes of fire while they were making love, he'd never seen her like this. So furious—and so hurt—that she seemed to have shut herself down to him completely.

His eyebrow was throbbing from where she'd nicked him with the ring, but it was nothing compared to the heavy twisting in his gut at the thought that she might leave him.

Her hand was already on the doorknob when he caught up with her. Fear that he was losing her made it hard to think, to do anything but grab her around the waist and pull her against him.

Her breath rushed out in surprise at the hard press of his arms around her. "Tell me what happened to make you so upset with me." Her fury had stirred up his, but he worked to keep his voice even. She tried to push out of his arms, but he wouldn't let her go. "Tell me what's wrong."

"You *used* me."

Her sentence ended on a sob, and even though he knew she was furious with him, he had to kiss the top of her head. When she was hurting, all he wanted was to help her. To ease her pain. Even if he was suddenly the last person on earth she wanted doing that.

"I've spent so long staring at circuit boards and computer screens that I know I often miss what's happening in real life." Gently, he turned her in his arms so that he could look into her eyes. He put his hand beneath her chin and tilted her face up to his. "If I've made a mistake with you, I want more than anything to make it right. Please just tell me what I did and how I can make it right."

But as she looked up at him, her eyes went wide. "You're bleeding." She covered her mouth with a trembling hand and her eyes filled with new tears.

A knock came, the door opening before Jack could warn whoever was outside to stay there.

"There you two are." Larry was too high on the thrill of success to notice that anything was wrong as he said, "A journalist and photographer from the *San Francisco Chronicle* were hoping to get some shots and an interview with you both. I figured you two lovebirds were stealing some time alone."

Jack didn't take his eyes from Mary's as he said, "We'll be out in a few minutes."

"Oh." Larry looked between the two of them with a sudden frown. Looking terribly uncomfortable, he backed away from them. "Sure. Okay. Great." He closed the door with a click behind him.

Mary's mouth trembled as she stared at the cut on

Jack's eyebrow. "Oh, God, I'm so sorry. I didn't mean to hurt you."

"I am hurting," he told her as he took both of her hands in his, "but not because you threw the ring at me. What hurts more than anything is that you've doubted for even one second that the love I feel for you is real."

She took a shaky breath. "I need to know why you didn't wait until the product was launched to ask me to marry you."

"I had to ask you because I couldn't wait one more second to know that you'd be mine. Forever. I know the timing was bad, that there's so much going on already—"

"Wait," she said, interrupting him, "don't you mean the timing was perfect?" She gestured toward the other room. "That way we could do this photo shoot and interviews today to sell your invention as a couple."

Awareness dawned with the suddenness of a hammer knocking him on the head. Even though Jack loved her more than he had ever loved anyone else—or ever would—he wanted to shake her. "You think I was using you like Romain did."

Her beautiful eyes flashed with an array of emotions. Fear. Hope. And something that looked a little like shame. "Everyone was so happy for us today, and that was lovely, but then I started putting the pieces together. Allen already had the champagne. How easily you stepped in front of the camera. And then I heard Howie and Larry talking about how perfect the timing was, and how the news of the fairy-tale engagement between the model and the engineer was going to get even more press and sell even more units than I would have representing it alone. What else was I supposed to think?"

"That I loved you. And that I would never hurt you like that spineless scumbag did."

Mary had made her living with her expressive, beautiful face for over a decade. She knew how to change her look from happy to sad to pensive between one frame and the next. But she'd never hidden her emotions from Jack, which was why he could easily read the hope on her face along with the continued fear.

"But the first time you saw me, the first time you spoke to me, you wanted me for your business."

"That day I saw you in Union Square, I felt as if a lightning bolt had stopped me dead in my tracks. I knew you'd be perfect to represent the Pocket Planner, but more important, I knew you'd be perfect for me." He held her gaze, forcing her to recognize the truth in his. "I know I fumbled in the diner and said everything wrong, but business never came first. *Never.* And I *always* wanted you for you."

"But you didn't even know me that first day."

"Yes, I did. I've always known you, Mary."

"How?" she asked in a whisper, as if she still couldn't possibly believe that he loved her.

Last night after he'd proposed and she'd accepted, she'd said, "I can't believe you love me. I can't believe this is real." Caught up in her kisses, in the heat between them, he hadn't wanted to read too much into it, hadn't wanted to admit that there was anything wrong.

But now he knew. She'd still doubted his love.

"I know you, Angel, because every time you smile I see the honest warmth in your eyes. And that first day in Union Square, when you picked up that little girl who ran onto the set and laughed with her, I saw that your beauty ran much, much deeper than the surface. Every moment I've spent with you since then has made me love you more."

"But I just accused you of hurting me and then I threw your ring at you and *I* hurt *you*." She looked up again at the nick on his eyebrow with deep regret. "How can you forgive me?"

"Because I love you."

"I thought my mother loved me, too, but she never forgave me for the way I behaved. For the things I said."

Everything became clear in an instant. Mary had been told she was loved and had loved back with an open and honest heart, first with her mother, and then with Romain...only to have her love thrown away as if it were worthless.

"I don't care how much you yell," he told her. "I don't care how many things you throw at me. I'm not going anywhere, Mary. Not now. Not ever. I loved you from the first moment and I will love you until the last."

She reached for his face, held it in her hands. "That's why it hurt so badly to think that what you felt for me might not be real...because I knew it would never change what was in my heart. Because I knew I would still keep on loving you. And while I can't promise not to yell sometimes, or lose my temper, or to make assumptions that are completely wrong because I'm frightened, I can promise to never take your ring off again. Please," she said softly, "will you put it back on my finger?"

Not wanting to let each other go, she moved with him so that he could still hold her hand while reaching for the ring on the floor.

He looked deep into her eyes as he slid the ring back into place. *"Forever."*

She echoed the word against his lips. It would have been easier to just keep kissing her, to lose himself in her warmth, her softness, and save everything else for later. But he had always been honest with her, and he always would be.

"You need to know why Allen knew I was going to ask you to marry me." Jack had never worried much about pride, but for the second time in twenty-four hours, he found himself swallowing it. "The moment I saw the ring, I knew I wanted you to have it, and I wanted you to wear it as a symbol of our love for each other."

He shook his head, hating having to admit that he hadn't had enough money for the ring. Money had never seemed important before, not when all he'd ever needed was enough to keep a roof over his head and to be able to buy the hardware he needed for his research and development.

"I went to Allen and asked him for a loan, one that would, hopefully, be an advance on profits. When he asked why I needed the money, I told him I had fallen in love with you...and that I wanted to ask you to marry me."

"Oh, Jack, I love the ring, but you could have put a dime-store ring on my finger and I would have loved you just as much."

"I know you don't need fancy jewels, that you must have a hundred already, but that's not why I wanted you to have it. A diamond," he said softly as she splayed her hand across his chest, right over the heart that would always beat harder when she was near, "is nearly impossible to break, no matter how hard you try."

She lifted her gaze to his. "Just like us."

Twenty

For the next several hours, Mary and Jack went from one interview to the next, answering questions not only about why the Pocket Planner was the must-have Christmas gift of the year but also about their whirlwind romance. Allen had been right that the press couldn't get enough of their human-interest story.

No matter how different people were, they all had one thing in common: a dream of finding *the one.*

Mary told the journalists how she'd set eyes on Jack in Union Square at what was supposed to be her final photo shoot and had instantly known she'd fall in love with him. But what she didn't say to anyone was how sure she'd become over the years that she would never find a man like Jack.

Throughout the hours, Jack continued to hold on to her hand. She wondered, did he realize how much he touched her as he spoke? Her face, her hair, his forehead pressed against hers as they laughed together. He was so free with his affection, so unafraid of giving too much.

She'd learned so much from him already—not only how to love, but what forgiveness looked like.

A familiar pang resounded within her chest as she thought about her mother...and how happy she would be to see an engagement ring on her daughter's finger, at last. Of course, Mary knew that her mother would be even happier about the man her daughter was marrying. Jack was such a good man. Such a solid man.

Such a beautiful man, inside and out.

Tonight. She'd call home tonight with the good news. And even if her mother still wasn't ready to forgive, Mary told herself it would be enough just to know their engagement was the news her mother had longed to hear.

When the last journalist finally left the boardroom, Jack's eyes were warm as he smiled at her. "We should probably make a run for it before Allen scrounges up another twenty journalists."

They gathered their coats and she felt like a little girl

again, trying to sneak out of her room to play when she was supposed to be taking a nap.

Mary was used to this kind of intense photo-and-interview schedule, but considering it was all new for Jack, she thought he'd held up remarkably well. Especially considering the big launch was the following day and Mary knew it would be even busier. But Mary had no problem with hard work, especially when the man she loved would be reaping the rewards.

Allen caught them both before they could escape out the side door. "You two were marvelous today. I'm very happy for both of you. And I'll admit to being rather pleased that your engagement is a PR dream come true," he added with a grin.

Earlier that morning, Allen's words would have driven fear through every part of her. But not anymore. Not now that she finally believed that the love she and Jack shared was real.

"I'd love to take both of you out to dinner, if you're not too tired from the interviews," Allen offered.

Mary appreciated the offer, but after giving a long day to the campaign, what she wanted was to be alone with Jack tonight before they started all over again tomorrow morning with the launch-day festivities. Because while they'd made up after she'd thrown the ring at him, she very much wanted to show him with more than words how sorry she was for ever doubting his love…and that she never would again.

"Thanks for the invitation, Allen," Jack said, "but I'm going to take Mary home so she can rest up a bit before tomorrow. And thanks again for getting behind the Pocket Planner in such a major way. We'll see you bright and early at the launch."

Even though Mary was easily strong enough to keep from being swept away by a powerful man, she was thrilled to let Jack lead her out of the building, his large hand on the small of her back.

He hailed a cab outside the corporate offices, and when he slid in beside her, she couldn't wait another second to do what she'd been longing to do since the moment Jack had slid the ring back on her finger. Putting her hands on his gorgeously scruffy jaw, she brought his face down to hers and kissed him. Despite the cold, his lips were warm and more delicious every time she tasted them.

"I love you." She whispered the words against his lips between kisses and he whispered them right back.

They couldn't get to her house fast enough. She

wanted to be as close as she could to Jack. She wanted to strip off his clothes and then her own and wrap herself all around him…and never, ever let go.

They paid the taxi and then kissed their way up her front steps, navigating by feel alone. Somehow she was able to find her key in her purse, without breaking apart from him, and open the door.

The second they were inside and alone, Jack pushed her back against the door and slid both his hands into her hair. Their earlier kisses had set her heart racing and her blood pumping in the taxi and on the sidewalk and steps.

But this kiss lit a fuse in her very soul.

During each photo they'd taken and during every interview they'd given today, she'd been dreaming of falling into bed with Jack. But there was no way they were going to make it that far.

She raked her hands over his broad chest to tear open the buttons on his shirt, and his hand slipped up her thigh to undo the clasp on her garters. Every touch, every gasp of pleasure as bare skin met bare skin, was absolutely perfect. Especially when Jack began kissing his way from her mouth, across her jaw to her neck and into the hollow behind her collarbone. She was tilting her head back to give him better access when her phone rang.

"Damn it," he growled against her skin, letting go of her to snatch the phone out of its cradle. "I told you, Mary is done working for the night." But listening to the person on the other end of the line had his expression changing in an instant. "Hold on a moment." He covered the mouthpiece and held out his free hand to her. "I think it's your father." Concern furrowed his brow. "He sounds upset."

Mary's heart dropped into her stomach and her skin, which had been so warm just seconds before, was suddenly ice-cold.

"Papa?"

Her father's words came out in a rush of anguish. She worked to stay calm to listen to the details, then told her father in Italian, "I'm coming right away on the night flight from San Francisco. I will be home tomorrow."

The phone would have fallen from her numb hands had Jack not taken it from her.

"My mother is sick. Papa was calling from the hospital." Mary pressed her hands to her churning stomach. "She's never sick. Never." Her father hadn't stayed on the line long enough to tell her much other than that her mother had been coughing so badly that he'd decided to take her to the hospital. "I need to go to her. To them. Tonight."

She started to move toward her bedroom to pack, but her legs were trembling so hard that when Jack brought her over to the couch and made her sit, she didn't try to fight him.

He knelt in front of her. "First, I'm going to get you a drink to steady your nerves, and then I'm going to book our flight and pack your bag."

Again, she was too shell-shocked to argue, to do anything but accept the glass of whiskey he handed her a few seconds later. But just as she was lifting it to her mouth with a shaky hand, she realized what he'd said: *our flight.*

He had already picked up the phone and was dialing the airline when she put down her drink and went to him. "Jack, are you planning to come with me?"

"Of course I am."

He said it as if there had never been any doubt that he would, but she'd been alone for so long that she'd immediately assumed she'd be alone in this, too.

Only, she wasn't alone anymore, was she? Not now that Jack loved her.

But though the trip back to her childhood home would be a thousand times harder without Jack by her side, it was her love for him that had her trying to take the phone from his hand.

"Your launch is tomorrow. I'm so sorry I'm going to miss it, that I won't be there for you to celebrate your dream coming true, but I can't let *you* miss it. Not when you've worked so long and hard for this day."

"My dream came true the moment I found you, Mary. And we both know that family is what matters most. We're going to Italy together to see your parents."

He kissed her then, a soft press against her lips that was at once empathetic and passionate, before he put the phone back up to his ear and booked two tickets to Rome.

Mary hadn't thought she'd be able to sleep a wink on the airplane, but with Jack sitting warm and steady beside her, his arms holding her tight, she was asleep almost as soon as she closed her eyes. By the time she woke, they were flying over Rome. Hand in hand, Mary and Jack got off the plane with their carry-on luggage.

Fear that they were already too late sent her to the first pay phone she found in the airport. But when she called the hospital, an old childhood friend who was now a nurse gave her a very welcome piece of good news: her mother had been diagnosed with pneumonia and had spent the night at the hospital, but had been discharged this morning.

Mary told Jack, "My parents left the hospital an hour ago."

Jack dropped a kiss onto her mouth. "Whatever you just said, I'm glad it's good news."

She'd been so relieved by the news her old friend had given her that she'd forgotten to switch back to English after getting off the phone.

She repeated what she'd just told him in English. "They've diagnosed her with pneumonia, which I know is still dangerous, but would they have sent her home if she wasn't well enough to recover there on her own?"

"From everything you've told me, your mother sounds like a very strong woman."

He was right. Lucia Ferrer was too strong willed to let illness get the best of her. Then again, Mary thought as panic rose again, she was also so stubborn that she might have left the infection too long.

Jack pulled her to him and kissed the top of her head. He didn't give her a bunch of empty words that she would have been too anxious to take in anyway. He simply told her with his steady warmth, just as he had a hundred different times since she'd met him, that he was there for her.

Now, and always.

When she felt stronger and calmer, they found a taxi to take them to her hometown. She'd been back to Italy many times during the past thirteen years, but she'd never been brave enough to cross into the border of Rosciano. Once, twice, she'd come close. But each time fear—and pride—had her turning back.

She wouldn't turn back today.

Mary was holding Jack's hand so tightly in the back of the airport taxi that he should have been complaining, or at least trying to pull free. He did neither; he simply held her right back, letting her know that he truly was there for her when she most needed him.

Trying to keep panic at bay, she looked at her watch and calculated the time difference. "The launch has just begun in San Francisco. Maybe we should stop at another pay phone and call Allen's offices to check in with everyone."

She could tell by the look in Jack's eyes that he knew exactly what she was doing. "We don't need to stop. We don't need to call. I'm sure everything in San Francisco is going just fine without us." He gently squeezed her hand. "Your hometown is beautiful, just like you described it. One day soon, I'd like my own mother to come and see this winter wonderland."

Mary forced herself to look out the windows of the taxi. To stop and really see where she'd come from.

Christmas in Rosciano had always been the event of the year. From the strings of lights crisscrossing overhead to the beautifully built nativity scene in the center of town, every inch was transformed with light and color. As a child, she'd spent eleven months of every year looking forward to the twelfth, and though she wasn't a child anymore, she wasn't at all immune to the wonder of the holiday season.

Everything, it seemed, was exactly as it had always been. The boys and girls out picking up a big tray of pastries at the *pasticceria* for the family lunches that would stretch on for hours. The young women, some of them barely out of their teens, cradling small babies in their arms as they met with friends by the fountain for a few precious moments before finishing the marketing and returning to their familial duties at their mother-in-law's house. The men meeting in the bar first for an espresso and then a glass of grappa to talk of old sports dreams while making bets on teams they'd laid their new dreams of glory on. The stone buildings stood just as they had for hundreds of years. The grapevines just beyond the buildings were groomed back for winter and the sky was a clear and crisp blue.

Mary felt as if she'd blinked at nineteen and woken up thirteen years later in the same exact place. How, she wondered, could it feel as if nothing had changed when she had changed so much, in so many ways?

She'd left Italy as a naive girl full of a hunger to experience life. The beauty she'd seen, the thrills she'd experienced as she'd flitted from one spot on the globe to the next, had far exceeded her dreams. And yet, all that time, she'd still been searching, longing, for something she had never been able to find by getting on another airplane or seeing another amazing vista.

As if he could read her mind, Jack stroked his hand down over her hair and shoulders.

Love.

It was all she'd ever truly wanted, the only thing that could have made her feel whole again when she'd been broken for so long.

Jack's love had filled so many empty places inside of her...but that hollowness right in the center that had begun to burrow into her soul as a little girl when she'd realized that she could never be what her mother wanted her to be was still there.

Finally, the taxi pulled up in front of her childhood home. And as Jack helped her out of the backseat and the driver took their bags out of the trunk, all she could think was *Oh, God, this is such a bad idea. Why have I come back? Why don't I know better?*

She wanted to dive into the taxi and have it take her down the narrow cobblestone street and away from everything she was afraid of facing.

"I'm scared." She reached for Jack's hands and pulled them into her chest as if he could somehow get her heart to stop racing so fast. "What if my mother sees me and tells me to leave again? What if my coming here, being back in her house, makes everything worse instead of better?" They'd been in the country barely over an hour, and yet she couldn't stop the Italian accent from quickly seeping into her words. "What if—" The fears crowding her mind piled on one another too fast for her to clearly put a voice to them. "I made so many mistakes, Jack. I can see that now. What if it's too late to undo them?"

"Everybody makes mistakes. But that's the magic of family—knowing that underneath whatever you've said and done, you are still loved. And that you always will be, no matter what."

Jack had been right about everything else so far. She wanted desperately to believe that he was right about this, too.

Knowing she needed to be brave enough to find out, she lifted a hand she couldn't stop from trembling to knock. Before she could make contact with the old wooden door, a gray-haired man opened it.

Her father's face was just as she'd remembered it, with perhaps a few more lines, but his expression was one of a man who had just witnessed a miracle.

Oh, how she'd missed him, every single day since she'd left.

"*Carissima,* you're finally home!"

On a joyful sob, Mary threw herself into her father's open arms, still—*always*—his little girl.

Twenty-One

"Papa, this is Jack. Jack Sullivan. He's the man I love. We're going to be married."

Despite the fact that she'd spoken in Italian, Jack didn't seem at all surprised when her father grabbed him by the shoulders and kissed him on both cheeks.

"Your mother will be very happy." He took both of her hands in his. "Come see her."

Mary's feet felt as if they were filled with lead. "Papa? When she asked for me to come see her, was she—" She stopped speaking when she saw the guilty look on her father's face. "She doesn't know you called me, does she?"

"Your mother has too much pride. So do you. Your

silence has gone on long enough. Come, it's time to see and to talk to each other again."

Perhaps her father had been wrong not to tell either Mary or her mother about what he was doing, but he'd been stuck in the middle of things for too many years. So when he pulled her through the living room and down the hall to the bedroom he shared with her mother, Mary let him. But since she knew she couldn't do this without Jack, she reached for his hand with her free one so that the three of them were a connected chain.

Her father gave a soft knock on the door before looking inside the bedroom. "*Tesoro,* I have someone here to see you."

A half-dozen questions flew through Mary's head as her father slowly opened the door. How much would the years—and illness—have changed her mother? Would she see that her daughter was no longer a girl but a woman now? Would there be softness in her mother's eyes? Or would her gaze be just as cold as it had been that horrible day so many years ago?

As Jack squeezed her freezing-cold hand with his warm one in a show of support, Mary knew there was only one way to find out. She sucked in a deep breath and threw her shoulders back, calling on years of poise in front of the camera to get through the hardest moment of her life.

Lucia Ferrer had always been a beautiful woman. Thirteen years had turned her dark hair fully gray, but her skin was still relatively unlined, her mouth still full, her limbs long and firm. Mary had been a girl when she'd left, but now that she was an adult, she saw in her mother's face the same eyes, nose and chin that she saw every time she looked in the mirror. How could she have forgotten how similar they were, not just in temperament, but in looks, too?

Mary couldn't remember her mother ever being sick when she was a child. She'd inherited that from her, too—good, healthy genes that meant she'd never once called in sick. For Lucia to spend any part of the day in bed meant that she was really and truly not well.

"Mama."

The short, simple word sounded raw and uncertain from lack of use. Her mother looked shocked, so stunned by her daughter's sudden reappearance in her life that she couldn't yet speak.

How Mary longed to run into the room and reach out to her. But Lucia had yet to give any sign that she was happy to see her daughter, and the pride that was never far from the surface began to bubble up again inside Mary as it had so many years before.

Only, she was no longer a headstrong, foolish girl with only dreams and adventures ahead of her. This time, Mary was a woman who had experienced some dreams coming true and others crumbling. She'd known terrible heartbreak and then had been lucky enough to find a love that would last forever.

And, most of all, for thirteen years, she'd longed for the family she'd left behind.

Her father was right: pride had kept her away for too long. If her mother wasn't ready to see her again, well, that was too bad. Because it was long past time for this nonsense between them to come to an end.

Decision made, Mary quickly moved into the room, holding her mother's gaze all the while. But before she could take more than a couple of steps, pure joy moved across her mother's face and her arms lifted from the covers, wide-open for her daughter.

Her emotions bubbled to the surface, and Mary felt incredible release as she ran into the room and put her arms around her mother. Despite her not being well, her mother's arms pulled her even closer. Sitting on the bed together, Mary breathed in the familiar smell of her perfume and felt how strong and warm her arms still were.

Her tears fell then, not just for all the years they'd lost, but because between her and her mother, Jack and her father, the small room was overflowing with love.

Mary and her mother held each other close for a long time, and when they finally drew back, Lucia framed Mary's face in her hands. "Let me look at you, my beautiful girl."

There was so much Mary wanted to say to her mother, and she was sure there was at least as much that her mother wanted to say to her, but for now, just being with each other again was enough.

"You're not a girl anymore." Mary could read her mother's regret at losing those years just as clearly as she could see the pride in what she'd grown to become. "You are a woman now."

Another tear slid down Mary's cheek. Of all the things she needed to say, two stood out above all the others. "I love you."

"I love you, too. More than you'll ever know."

Her heart so full she thought it might burst, Mary said, "Jack came home with me, to meet you and Papa. I love him, too."

Hearing his name, Jack came closer. Mary took his left hand in hers even as he held out his right hand for her mother. "It's very nice to meet you, Signora Ferrer."

Mary was amazed to hear him speak Italian, however halting. Was there nothing he wouldn't do for her?

As her mother studied Jack carefully, Mary could almost read her mind. He wasn't Italian or one of the men from the village, but he was clearly solid…and handsome enough to make even a happily married woman's heart beat a little faster.

But instead of taking Jack's hand, Lucia said, "You need to promise me you will always be a good husband to my little one. That you will never hurt her. And that you will love her even when she makes mistakes."

Mary flushed as she translated her mother's demands. All the while Jack never took his eyes from Lucia, and his gaze remained as serious as hers.

"I love your daughter." He spoke in English this time and paused so that Mary could translate. "I will always put her and our family first." Again he paused while she translated his sweet vow in a voice that grew thicker and thicker with emotion. "And I promise you, I will never, ever hurt her."

Finally, Lucia smiled. But instead of taking his hand,

she opened her arms and hugged him as if he were already her son-in-law.

That was when her mother began to cough, a deep rattling sound that jarred Mary's heart just as badly. "Mama, you need to rest."

"No, I need you here with me. I need you to stay."

It was what her mother had said thirteen years ago, but instead of feeling trapped by the words this time, Mary felt only the sweet warmth of knowing she was loved.

"I'm not going anywhere, I promise." Brushing the hair back from her mother's forehead, just as her mother used to do when she was sick, Mary said, "Rest now, and when you wake up I'll have made you *pastina in brodo*. We'll eat together."

"I don't want soup. I want to talk to you. I *need* to talk to you." Her mother coughed again, this attack longer as she was obviously too exhausted to be able to fight it. "I need to tell you everything I was too proud to say before."

Both men had left the bedroom by then. "I love you, Mama," Mary said again. "I never stopped loving you, not for one single second. How could I?"

Mary pressed a kiss to her mother's soft cheek. She could see the pill bottles by the side of the bed for antibiotics and cough suppressants, but while she prayed they would do the job of healing the infection inside her mother's lungs, there was one thing she knew would likely be more powerful than any drug in inspiring her mother's recovery.

"I need you to be healthy and happy at my wedding."

"Your wedding!" Her mother smiled then and finally sank back into the pillow to let Mary tuck her in. Lucia's voice was heavy with drowsiness as she said, "Yes, we'll give you and your Jack a perfect wedding, on the day before Christmas Eve." Mary could see the pride sparkle in her mother's eyes as she declared, "You will be the most beautiful bride in the world."

When Jack saw that Mary and her mother were going to be just fine, he followed Mary's father, Marco, out into the walled garden. Although it was barely noon, when her father handed him a glass of prosecco, Jack took it with a smile.

Her father lifted his glass. *"A amore!"*

Jack could easily translate—"To love"—and repeated the sentiment as he raised his glass.

It was amazing how much could be said with so few words. Jack could see, could feel, how much Mary's father loved his daughter, and he could clearly see the same thing in Jack.

Mary found them sitting in a patch of winter sun, sharing a companionable drink. "Of course I should have known you'd fit right in," she said to Jack as she walked outside and pressed a kiss first to his forehead and then to her father's. "I'm going to walk into town to pick up a few things to make soup for Mama. I can see how much my father is enjoying having a man around the house. Stay with him. I'll be back soon."

Jack knew that she needed a little time alone to process everything. Not just making up with her mother and seeing her father again, but coming back to her childhood home. She'd made it over the first hurdle, but Jack knew she wasn't done yet. Forgiveness had been freely given, thank God, but both Mary and her mother still needed to explain and understand each other's behavior over the past thirteen years so that old wounds wouldn't ever accidentally open up.

Taking a moment to think of everyone back in California, Jack realized that the Pocket Planner was now officially on sale. Finally, people would be using the invention that he and his partners had created. And he hoped it would be a gift found under many Christmas trees this year.

From a sunny walled winter garden in Italy, Jack Sullivan silently toasted the hope that sales were going well and that customers were pleased with the value of their new purchase. Then he turned back to Mary's father to continue their extremely enjoyable conversation—one comprised of simple gestures and laughter.

Twenty-Two

Mary wrapped her winter coat tightly around her as she set out on foot through town. Tomorrow, she'd show Jack all of her favorite childhood haunts, but right now she appreciated the fact that he understood she needed to see them again for herself first.

Young children playing by the fountain stopped their game to point at her. The girls chattered excitedly about her boots, her outfit and hairstyle. The boys wondered what the big deal was. When she smiled at the girls and waved at the boys, their cheeks colored and they quickly turned back to their game.

Already she longed for little boys with Jack's smile and focus and little girls with her passion and determination.

Love had come quickly for her and Jack. She hoped a family would, too.

Mary put a hand over her flat stomach. She and Jack hadn't yet said their "I do's," but Mary had never been one to wait when there was something she wanted.

Her father, she thought with a smile, was likely getting their separate bedrooms ready right now. Well, she'd mastered the art of sneaking out of her bedroom as a girl. Tonight, she decided with a flutter of anticipation, she was going to sneak into the bedroom on the other side of her parents' house to seduce her fiancé.

The butcher was her first stop and she was barely in the door when Antonio exclaimed with delight. Mary had been afraid that people would be wary of her—after all, she'd left without a backward glance thirteen years ago and it had taken her mother's illness for her to finally return. But with each stop she made during the next hours, she felt as if the years she'd been gone were slipping away one by one.

From the butcher to the vegetable stand to the florist and then the cheese shop, none of the proprietors would let her pay for what she needed. A half-dozen invitations came for coffee and dinner and she was thrilled to get to hold her friends' new babies and admire their beautiful older children, as well. By the time she turned to head back to the house, her heart was as full as the bags of food and flowers she carried.

Jack was playing scopa, a game similar to gin rummy, with her father in the living room when she returned and her heart hitched in her chest at what a beautiful picture they made, the two men she loved most in the world.

Jack quickly put his cards down to take the bags from her and bring them into the kitchen. Once she'd taken off her coat, he took her hands in his and pulled her close.

"You look happy."

"I am. And tomorrow, I'll introduce you to everyone in town. I told them all about my gorgeous, brilliant American fiancé. They can't wait to meet you."

His mouth was warm over hers, and when he let her hands go to slip his around her waist, she slid her fingers into his soft, dark hair and pulled him even closer. She'd never kissed a boy in her parents' kitchen before, and when she heard her father's footsteps—made purposely louder, she was sure, because he could guess what she and her fiancé were up to—she drew back with a laugh.

"I hope your jet lag isn't too bad," she said to Jack in a

low voice, "because I don't know how much sleep you're going to get tonight."

His eyes darkened with so much desire—and the love she felt from him in every moment—that she lost her breath as he whispered, "Your room or mine?"

Ah, so she'd been right about her father setting up separate bedrooms for the unmarried couple. "Yours."

Her father came into the room then, and for the next hour Mary cooked and translated the conversation back and forth from Italian to English. Her mother had made this sickbed meal for her several times when she was a child. This was the very first time Mary had ever made it for her mother.

A short while later, when she'd set heaping plates in front of Jack and her father, Mary made up a tray with a full bowl of soup and a warm cup of tea. Her mother stirred as she walked in, as if she'd simply been lying in bed waiting for Mary to come back.

Helping Lucia sit up comfortably with a few thick pillows behind her, at her mother's protests that she wasn't hungry, Mary said, "You need to eat a few bites to build your strength up."

Her mother took a small sip of the soup. "It tastes just

like mine. Maybe," Lucia said as she took another sip from her spoon, "it's even better."

It was amazing how such a small compliment could mean so much. "I learned from the best."

Her mother put down her spoon. "*Cara,* I have much to apologize for."

Mary was nearly bursting with the things she wanted to say to her mother and that she wanted to know—but not only had she learned unconditional love from Jack, she'd learned patience, as well.

"I do, too," Mary said in a soft voice, "but tonight all you should be doing is eating and resting. In the morning, when you're stronger—"

"I'm strong enough now to tell you how much I've missed you. How much your father has missed you. I'm strong enough now to tell you how much we both love you and that if I could rewind the clock back to that day when you were nineteen, I would do it better this time. I would do it right."

Her mother began to cough and Mary handed her the mug of tea. "Mama, I can't tell you how much it means to hear you say these things, but I promise you, I know how much you love me, because I love you just as much.

I don't want you to wear yourself out. We have time to talk about all of this later, once you're well."

"We've wasted enough time," Lucia insisted, and Mary had to smile at the stubborn expression so similar to her own. "I will talk and you will listen."

"Okay, Mama."

"Before I met your father, I had dreams like yours—to travel, and to have people applauding for me as I sang and danced on the stage."

Of all the things Mary had thought her mother would tell her tonight, learning that they'd shared similar dreams had not been anywhere on the list of possibilities. Lucia had always hummed as she worked in the kitchen and the garden, and Mary had found her parents waltzing together in the moonlit garden more than once as a child, but she'd never realized that performing had been her mother's dream. Yet again, they were more alike than she'd ever realized.

"What happened? Why didn't you follow your dreams?"

Her mother lifted her hand to Mary's cheek. "I found a new dream. Your father was so handsome, so much more exciting than any stage had ever been, that he swept me off my feet. And then you came, exactly nine months to the day after we were married. My greatest achievement. My biggest joy. I saw those same dreams in you, watched them grow bigger with every year. Your beauty was so stunning that the other mothers would make jealous comments sometimes. Did you know, strangers passing through town would often stop on the street to take your picture?"

Mary shook her head. "No. I didn't know."

"You were too beautiful for the nice boys in town to have the nerve to approach you, but I saw the way the dangerous ones watched you. I was terrified that you would be swept off your feet, but not by a good man like your father. He often told me you had a good head on your shoulders, but he didn't know what it was like to be a young girl, especially one who wanted so much, who longed for everything life could give her. All I wanted was for you to find true love and have a family that would give you as much joy as you and your father gave me. But when you came home that day to tell us you had been discovered by an agent and that he wanted you to come to New York City with him—"

"All of your fears came true."

"With every awful word I hurled at you, it was as if I was watching myself from a distance, knowing the tighter I tried to hold on to you, the further you were going to slip away."

"I'm sorry," Mary said, "so sorry we both hurt each other so badly."

Lucia gently wiped away the tears falling down Mary's cheeks. "Go to the closet and bring me the red box on the top shelf." The box was the size of a large hat and was quite heavy. "Look inside."

Inside the box was a photo album her mother had put together of photos from Mary's childhood. She smiled as she looked at the photo on the cover—herself as a chubby-cheeked baby. Her first thought was that Jack would love to see it.

"You and your Jack will have beautiful children. Smart, lively, passionate girls and boys that will fill your arms and hearts with endless joy."

As they went through the pictures one by one, Mary watched herself grow from baby, to toddler, to school-age girl with skinned knees, to lanky teenager, to young woman. The last few pages of the photo album were empty and her heart twisted yet again as she closed the leather-bound book.

"I never stopped collecting pictures of my baby," her mother said as she lifted a thick divider from inside the box and revealed hundreds of glossy magazine covers and photo spreads.

Mary was beyond amazed to find a print from her very first photo shoot. "Where did you get these?"

"Your agent, Randy, mailed these to us. At first, I think it was to reassure us that you had come to no harm with him. But when your father wrote to tell him how much we appreciated it, he mailed us a new package every week."

"I can't believe he never told me." Then again, if he had, wasn't it possible that she might have insisted he stop, simply because she'd nursed her anger and hurts for so long that she couldn't see beyond them?

"I should have come back long before now, Mama." Just as Jack had told her, family was what was important. Both she and her mother had done what they felt they *had* to do, and both of them had made the mistake of being stubborn or holding a grudge about decisions they'd made while simply being true to themselves. "I never meant to stay away this long."

Again, her mother wiped away Mary's tears, even though she was crying, too. "You're home now." Lucia suddenly smiled through her tears, as happy as Mary could ever remember seeing her. "I've been thinking about your wedding," she began, and this time Mary knew better than to try to get her mother to save her breath and rest.

Lucia Ferrer had been waiting for more than a decade for this wedding, and Mary knew her excitement and joy over the celebration would heal her illness faster than any pills or hours of bed rest possibly could.

Twenty-Three

The moon had fully risen in the winter sky by the time everyone in the house settled down to sleep. Mary had waited impatiently for her father to finally tire and join her mother in the master bedroom.

It had been less than a month since she'd met Jack in downtown San Francisco, but there was no question in Mary's mind that she was utterly, completely addicted to him. She'd enjoyed her solo walk through town and the time she'd spent reconnecting with her mother, but though it had been only a matter of hours since Jack had been holding her close on the airplane and in the taxi, it felt like forever. And if she wasn't mistaken, from the way he'd been looking at her in the living room when her father had insisted on one more round of cards, he was just as addicted to being with her.

That evening, she'd told him and her father about her conversation with her mother, about seeing the pictures her parents had collected of her over the years. Her father had teared up with the same tears of joy she'd been crying herself all day. Jack's eyes, and his hand over hers, had been full of so much love for her that she could still hardly think what she could have done right in her life to find him.

Now Mary stepped out of the cooling bath, dried off, then wrapped herself in the soft silk robe she'd packed in her bag. Feeling like a naughty teenager, instead of heading for her own bedroom, she tiptoed down the hall, through the kitchen and living room until she reached the guest room on the far side of the house. Her heart pounded hard with delicious anticipation as she put her hand on the doorknob.

Making sure to open the door quietly so that the hinges didn't creak and give her away, she almost forgot to close the door as she stared in wonder at the beautiful man waiting for her on the bed, the sheets at his hips leaving his chest gloriously bare. Jack was smiling at her, but desire was simmering just beneath the surface.

"I thought my father was never going to let you go to bed. All this time I believed my mother was the one desperate for me to marry. Now I realize my father was quite possibly even more desperate for a son-in-law."

She'd spoken in a whisper, but she and Jack were so attuned to each other that she knew they could probably have read each other's lips—or minds—if they'd needed to.

"Your father is a good man. He's agreed to teach me some Italian. Want to hear what I've learned already?" She laughed softly at the list of sports terms he rattled off in perfectly accented Italian.

When she stood at the bed and slipped off her robe, he said, "But he forgot to teach me how to say 'you're beautiful.'"

"Sei bellissima."

After Jack repeated the words she'd just taught him, he reached for her. "Come to bed, Angel."

Sliding beneath the covers into his open arms made an already amazing day even better. "You and my father are so much fun to watch together, especially when you're communicating with increasingly wild hand gestures."

"Funny you should mention my hands, because I've got a great idea for what I could do with them tonight."

Jack slowly skimmed his large, warm hands down over her curves, from breasts to hips.

Mary was a heartbeat away from being lost to everything but sensation, to everything but how much she loved him. Forcing herself to keep her eyes from fluttering closed with pleasure for just a little while longer, she said, "My mother is just as excited about you as my father is. In fact, she's hoping that we'll—"

"Get married."

"Well, yes, of course she's expecting that," Mary said with a tap of one finger to the top of her engagement ring. "But more than anything, she'd like for us to—"

"Have the wedding here in Italy."

Would he ever stop surprising her...and pleasing her in equal measure?

"That's exactly what she's hoping. And it would truly be a dream come true for her if we decided to have the ceremony—"

"Just before Christmas."

Awareness finally dawned. "My father must have said something to you, didn't he? Did he draw you a picture of a bride and groom standing in front of a Christmas tree?"

Jack grinned. "Actually, I'm the one who drew him

the picture. It seems your mother and I had the exact same idea for how to make this a perfect Christmas."

Mary's heart skipped a beat as she shifted against him so that she could look into his eyes. "You did?"

Jack's expression grew serious. "I know I only just convinced you to wear my ring, and that most people wait a year between getting engaged and getting married, but I've been waiting my whole life for you." He stroked the back of his hand over her cheek. "I don't want to wait anymore."

"I don't want to wait, either."

"So you'll be my Christmas bride?"

Tears threatened even as she teased, "Just as long as you promise not to dress up in a red suit and long white beard for the ceremony."

The next thing she knew, she was lying back on the bed and his big, strong body was levered over hers. "How did you know that's what I was planning to do at our wedding?" he teased back.

"You're not the only one who can read minds."

"How about we do a little scientific experiment, then?" he asked, her skin heating from the sensuality underlying his question. "Tell me, what am I thinking about right now?"

She made a show of mulling it over as she ran her hands down from his broad shoulders over his well-defined abdomen to his hips. "You're thinking about kissing me right here," she said as she lifted one hand to her face and lightly touched the tip of her index finger to the center of her lips. "Did I guess right?"

"You did."

Running his hands back up her naked curves, he slid them into her hair. As he lowered his mouth to hers, she met him in the middle, more desperate for his kiss than she'd ever been for anything in her life.

The first touch of his lips to hers was gentle. Sweet. But the long hours apart had taken their toll on both of them, and though pure love was at the heart of every moment they shared, and they knew they needed to make love as quietly as possible in her parents' house, desire's demands couldn't possibly be ignored.

Mary didn't know who nipped at whom first, just that she needed more than gentle or sweet. She needed to devour and be devoured, needed to fill her senses with as much of Jack as she could take in tonight. With tongues and teeth, they both took what they needed so badly. There were no boundaries, no rules left between them, their passion so pure and true that they each gave more than they took.

They were both breathless when they finally pulled apart. He was hot and hard against her and it would have been so easy, so good, just to open herself up to him and take him inside. But when he asked, "What else am I thinking?" she knew it would be even better to hold out just a little while longer, until anticipation hit its breaking point.

"You're wondering what it would feel like if you ran your tongue over the swell of my breasts—" she lightly swept her fingertip over her skin "—from here to here."

On a growl of assent, he lowered his head to her chest. The warm, wet slide of his tongue across her very sensitive flesh sent thrill bumps running over her skin, and she clutched at his shoulders, trying to bring him even closer. But instead of just licking across her breasts once, he followed the same path back and forth, one time after the next, until she was nearly delirious with need.

"Jack."

He lifted his head to gaze down at her, his pupils dilated with his own need. "If you can guess my next move right, I'll give you a special prize."

Her brain felt fuzzy now, her limbs heavy with desire. Somehow she managed to reply, "I like prizes." Her hands trembled as, feeling naughtier than ever, she slid them beneath her breasts and cupped them. "You're thinking of using more than your tongue now, but it's driving you crazy trying to decide where to taste first."

"You really must have ESP," he murmured as he covered her hands with his. And then his tongue was laving an incredibly sensual figure eight around her nipples, coming closer to them with each seductive trip. When he blew lightly over the tightly puckered, damp skin, she couldn't remember ever feeling this aroused before.

When his lips closed over her nipples, Mary barely remembered in time to tamp down on her moan of pleasure as he used the pads of his thumbs to caress the soft flesh in his hands at the same time.

Teetering on the edge of release already, she gasped, "Is that my prize?"

"No," he said as he moved down her body to lay one kiss after another onto her overheated skin. "This is."

His mouth was warm and hungry as he lowered himself between her legs. At the same time that the sensuality of what they were doing together rocked through her, he found her hands with his and slid their fingers together.

If she'd been close to coming apart before, it was the

love that he gave her even during the naughtiest sex that sent her hurtling over the edge. Her lungs burned as she tried to gasp in air; her skin was slick with sweat, and her heart was racing as if she'd just sprinted from one end of town to the other.

The intensity of the final San Francisco photo shoot with Jack, combined with the anguish of her father's phone call, the long red-eye flight to Italy, and then the emotional reunion with her mother and her trip into town, should have left her limp and exhausted. But instead of her climax using up the last of her energy, Mary suddenly felt stronger than she'd ever been.

Tugging on Jack's hands, she pulled him back up her body, then rolled them over so that he was the one beneath her. Mirroring the kisses he'd given her, she started at his mouth, then moved from his face to his chest, then down lower, still mirroring the way he'd been loving her minutes earlier.

"Angel."

She ran her tongue over him and his fingers clenched hers as she took, tasted, gave. She loved knowing how close she brought him to the edge, that she could make him lose control with every press of her lips against his hard heat.

But as he effortlessly dragged her back up to spin them again so that his heavy weight was over her once more, she knew the time for teasing, for ratcheting up anticipation to even higher heights, was long past.

She gasped as he slid into her, then lost her breath entirely as she arched to take him deeper. Her name was on his lips, a caressing whisper across her overheated skin in the moonlight that was streaming in through the window.

And as her climax spiraled into his, feeling safe and comforted and cherished with Jack's hands in hers and his loving eyes dark and intense as he gazed down at her, Mary drank in the perfect beauty of knowing she'd finally come home.

Not just to Rosciano and to her family...but to the most wonderful man in the world.

The first times they'd made love, he'd been her secret lover, then boyfriend. Now he was her fiancé. In just a few days, she thought in wonder as she put his hands over her heart, he'd be her husband.

She'd been Mary Ferrer for thirty-two years.

She couldn't wait to be Mary Sullivan for all the rest.

A long while later, just as the first rays of morning light were starting to sneak in the bedroom window, she slid from beneath Jack's strong arms, tied her robe on and tiptoed back down the hall to her bedroom. A naughty—and well-pleasured—smile remained on her face all morning as she dived headfirst into putting on the Christmas wedding her mother had always dreamed of.

Twenty-Four

Mary's first memories were of sitting on the floor at her mother's feet, surrounded by what seemed like acres of lace and silk as Lucia transformed them into dreams come true. Her friends had always fantasized about the day Mary's brilliant seamstress mother would make them their wedding dresses, and before Mary had left Italy, she'd had the pleasure of watching her closest girlfriends walk down the aisle in the beautiful gowns her mother had so lovingly made for them by hand.

At long last, it was her turn.

With her arm around her mother's waist to keep her steady, Mary walked slowly into the bride's dressing room in the back corner of the church. Her father had brought over the beautiful wedding dress earlier and had hung it from a strong hook in the middle of the stone wall.

"Sit, Mama." Mary helped settle her mother into the most comfortable chair, still concerned that she was too weak from her illness to be expending so much energy.

Lucia should have spent the days before the wedding resting, but despite how many times Mary tried to pry the needle and thread from her fingers, she'd never succeeded at getting her to stop. Mary didn't have her mother's incredible skill, but she was proficient enough to work on the gown's lining that no one would see. Together, the two of them had sat by a blazing fire in the living room and worked on her wedding dress, made from combined pieces of her mother's wedding dress and new fabric to create a style that would be Mary's alone.

They filled up the hours with stories from the past thirteen years of each other's lives. Her mother asked her about the various celebrities she'd met and Mary made sure not to leave out one single glittering detail. Likewise, her mother left no stone unturned in their town, and as old friends and neighbors she'd grown up with came by one after the other to visit, she was amazed by how easy it was to rekindle those relationships, as if she'd been gone only thirteen weeks instead of thirteen years.

And, of course, everyone adored Jack. As Mary and her mother had worked on her dress, Jack and her father had worked on Jack's Italian language skills. She'd known her fiancé was a brilliant man, but that didn't make her any less surprised two days later when she walked into the living room and realized he was actually having a conversation in Italian with the little four-year-old girl from across the street who had been sent over with her mama's panettone, a classic Italian Christmas cake. For a moment, Mary wondered if jet lag had finally gotten ahold of her brain.

Jack's use of her native language was still halting, of course, and he had to ask the girl to repeat herself a half-dozen times, but from moment to moment the man she loved continued to astound her. The little girl watched with big eyes as Mary moved to his side and kissed him right then and there in the middle of the living room with the cake in his hands and the midday sun streaming in through the window.

That night, when she sneaked into his bedroom, she taught him the romantic, sexy phrases her father had left out of his schooling. And as Mary and Jack loved each other, Italian and English endearments fell from their lips in a seamless blend of cultures and backgrounds.

She didn't realize she was standing and staring at her wedding dress until her mother gently said, "It's time to put your dress on now, *cara*."

Mary could no longer imagine her life without Jack in it, and yet up until this week, past hurts and fears had kept her from being absolutely certain that she could give her entire heart to him. She'd told him that night in his garage full of computers and circuits that she was still waiting for the cracks in her heart to heal, but he'd done so much more than just heal her broken heart.

He'd given her his heart, too.

Joy coursed through her as she undressed and folded the clothes she'd worn to the church in a neat pile. She reached for the beautiful dress she and her mother had made together and carefully slid it over her head and shoulders. Her mother rose then to help her with the dozens of tiny pearl buttons that ran down the length of her spine.

After helping her mother to sit back down, Mary moved in front of the full-length mirror. She'd modeled wedding gowns many times during her career, but they'd only been costumes she'd worn for the camera.

As she gazed at herself in the dress in which she'd promise forever to Jack, Mary finally understood why women spent so much time and money and energy on their wedding gowns.

One day in the future, will my own daughter wear this dress?

As if her mother had read her mind, Lucia said, "You're a beautiful bride, and you will be an amazing mother."

"I hope so." Both she and Jack had agreed they wanted a large family, one full of laughter and love. She could see their family already, little boys full of boundless energy and mischief, little girls that wrapped everyone around their fingers with big eyes and laughter.

Her hands trembling with emotion, Mary reached for her veil, but her mother said, "Not yet. Bring me that box first."

Mary had wondered if the medium-size box tied up in red-and-gold ribbon had been a wedding gift dropped off here instead of at the reception hall where they'd be later. Now she realized it was a gift from her parents.

Just as she had so many times as a little girl, it was natural for her to sink to her knees in front of her mother as she put the box in her lap.

"Your Jack told me about your first kiss."

Mary felt her face flush at the potent memory of Jack's lips against hers in the San Francisco bar, beneath the mistletoe. "From the first moment we met, even though I was frightened by what I felt for him, I think I already knew I would love him. But when he kissed me…"

Her mother's lips curved up into a soft smile. "When I met your father, he was eighteen and so sure of himself. I was a headstrong fifteen-year-old who couldn't wait to have a dozen men fall at my feet. It was Christmas Eve, and when we ran into each other in front of the fountain, the kiss he gave me was the best Christmas present I'd ever had." Lucia put her hand on Mary's cheek. "Your first kiss with your true love is something you will cherish forever. Your father and I were hoping you would want to wear this for your wedding."

As Mary carefully removed the top from the box, she truly had no idea what she'd find inside, only that it was meant to remind both her and Jack of their very special first kiss.

What she found atop a layer of red velvet was a beautifully made tiara of mistletoe, the plump white berries woven around bright green leaves in an intricate pattern.

With steady hands, her mother lifted the tiara from the velvet and placed it on Mary's head. "Today, when your true love kisses you under the mistletoe, it will be forever."

"I love you, Mama."

Her mother held her close. "I love you, *cara*."

Jack stood at the front of the beautifully decorated church, his heart pounding hard and fast with anticipation as he looked out at the large crowd. Mary's hometown had not only welcomed her back with open arms, but they'd thrown their arms around him, as well.

Through every conversation he'd had with one of her friends and neighbors during the past week, he had gained a little more insight into the woman he loved. She'd grown up surrounded by so much love that it was no wonder she was overflowing with it herself.

Lucia Ferrer was holding court at the front of the church, beaming with the joy of her dream for her daughter finally coming true. Jack had come to love his soon-to-be mother- and father-in-law a great deal during the days he'd spent in their house, so much that he was more than a little tempted to remain in Italy for a while. Larry and Howie had been extremely happy to hear that Mary's mother was doing well and that he and Mary had decided to tie the knot right before Christmas. As soon as they'd filled them in on the incredible sales and response to the Pocket Planner, Mary had taken the phone from him and promised she'd have Jack back in California and behind his computer by January second.

Jack's thoughts were brought back to the present as his gaze was caught by movement at the entrance to the church, where the little girl from across the street was waving at him from the doorway. As their flower girl, she stood proudly in a pretty white dress with a heaping basket of poinsettia flower petals in her sturdy little hands.

Again and again throughout the week, Jack had caught himself dreaming of the children he and Mary would have. Her mother had made him a photo album of Mary's childhood photos, from birth until she'd left to pursue modeling, and he could so clearly see himself lifting a little girl in his arms who looked just like her mother.

Everyone in the church was dressed in their best clothes, with holly decorating the ends of every pew. He knew the children must be counting down the hours until Christmas Eve and they could open the packages under their Christmas trees. But, considering all the excitement, they were an extremely well-behaved bunch.

Just then, Jack's brother Ethan walked in through the side door with a huge grin on his face. Jack had called his family to let them know about the wedding, and though he hadn't expected any of them to be able to make it to Italy on such short notice, as luck would have it, Ethan had already been in London and promised to make the trip to Italy to support Jack at his wedding. True to form, Jack thought with a matching grin, Ethan had squeaked in just under the wire.

Mendelssohn's "Wedding March" rang out loudly from the organ high above the pews and Jack instantly turned his focus back to the front doors of the church.

The flower girl skipped down the aisle tossing petals from her basket on the delighted crowd, and then everyone gasped with awe as Mary appeared on her father's arm.

Everyone and everything but Mary and the soul-deep love he felt for her fell away. Wonder wove through him as she slowly came up the petal-strewn aisle on her father's arm.

She was impossibly beautiful in her wedding dress, a dark-haired angel in lace and silk. Even through her veil, he could see all the love she felt in her eyes as she smiled at him, her joy a living thing. She was wearing a crown made of bright green leaves and berries, and as he worked to recover his senses, it took him a few beats longer than it should have to realize it was a crown of mistletoe.

I love you, Angel. I'll always love you.

He knew he didn't need to say the words aloud for her to hear them pass from his heart to hers.

At the final pew, Mary's father pressed a kiss to her cheek, but she never took her eyes from Jack's. Moving down the few steps that separated them, Jack held out a hand for his bride, and when she took it, instead of drawing her up to where the priest was waiting for them, he couldn't stop himself from lifting her hand to his lips.

A moment later her arms were around his neck and her mouth was soft against his in a promise of love that had nothing to do with priests or wedding gowns. They'd come so far, from their first kiss under the mistletoe when they were two strangers drawn to each other, to this beautiful day when they would make vows of forever.

Everyone was waiting to hear those vows, but Jack decided they could wait a little while longer as he pulled her flush against him and deepened the kiss. When they finally drew back from each other with bright eyes and flushed faces to take their places before the priest, the crowd was quite happily scandalized.

As Jack held both her hands in his, the priest led them through the traditional ceremony that they had learned during the past few days of *matrimonio* classes as the priest prepared them for their marriage and the vows they would be making to each other. Jack drank in every breath, every tremble, every flush of heat across Mary's soft skin.

Taking the simple gold wedding band from the intricately stitched pillow the priest held in his hands, Jack slid it onto Mary's ring finger. *"Tu sei tutto per me, la luce dei miei occhi, sei mia per sempre."* She was his entire world, the heart of his heart.

When two tears slid down her cheeks and he gently reached out to wipe them away, she pressed her face to his palm in a gesture of boundless trust.

"All my life I dreamed of adventure and I thought all of my dreams had already come true," Mary said softly as she slid the gold band she'd had made for him onto his ring finger. "But then I found you and realized you were the dream I had been waiting for all my life. *Ti amo dal profondo del cuore e non vedo l'ora di cominciare quest'avventura con te, amore mio.*" Everyone in the church sighed as they heard her tell him that she loved him with all of her heart and soul…and that she couldn't wait to take this adventure with him.

They were already kissing to seal their vows by the time the priest declared them husband and wife, and as applause rang through the centuries-old church, Jack knew that theirs was a love that would transcend time.

Twenty-Five

Mary and Jack's wedding reception was a glorious blur of music and laughter and hugs and dancing and bites of cake…and dozens upon dozens of stolen kisses from her new husband that made her lips tingle and her heart race with joy. Throughout the celebration, Jack almost never let go of Mary's hand, and as the sun fell lower in the sky, his gaze grew more heated and full of love every time she looked in wonder at the man who had just become her husband.

Jack was beyond gorgeous in his dark suit and tie, and Mary couldn't blame every woman at her wedding—even the married ones—from drinking him in with clear appreciation. He'd remembered to shave this morning, but his jaw was already covered with a dark shadow.

When she'd seen him waiting for her at the altar, her legs had nearly given out on her and she'd had to cling to her father's arm for support. A moment later, she'd wanted to pick up her skirts and run to him so that she could throw herself into his arms.

Now, as they stood surrounded by everyone in her hometown, and he moved his hand to the small of her back to lightly stroke across the curve of her hips through her wedding dress, she wanted badly to tangle her hands in his hair and yank his tie off and kiss him until they were both breathless.

Mary Sullivan. Love had given her not only a new name...but a new future, as well. Sullivans were determined and focused, loving and supportive. It was exactly right that she should embark on her new future as a Sullivan, and that the children they hoped to have in the near future would grow up knowing they were loved and supported, no matter what.

Mary had been very glad that Jack's brother Ethan had been able to come to support Jack as they'd made their vows, even if he was an irrepressible flirt who would leave more than one broken heart behind in Italy when he headed back for London the following day. After a lifetime as an only child, she couldn't believe how blessed she was now to have a sister and four brothers, and she couldn't wait to finally meet his parents as their newest daughter-in-law.

With Jack's hand in hers and the love of the friends she'd grown up with in every smile and hug and handshake, Mary worked to push away her impatience to be alone with him. This celebration was extremely important to her mother and father. Surely she could continue to smile and chat with everyone for another few hours without counting down every single second until she could be alone with Jack again?

Taking a deep breath, she made certain her smile remained firmly in place as one of her old friends from school began to walk toward them. But before her friend was even halfway across the reception hall, Jack lifted Mary into his arms.

Only by sheer force of will did she stop herself from laughing out loud. Her husband—*oh, wasn't that a beautiful word?*—didn't stop to speak with anyone, didn't say any more thank-you's or nice-to-meet-you's, just carried her through the reception hall, out the front door and down the steps to the cobblestone street below.

"I was hoping you'd run out of patience soon," she confessed as he practically ran down the street toward the small inn where they'd be spending their first night together as husband and wife. Holding on even tighter to him, she buried her face in the crook of his neck. He smelled like spice and heat and the man she couldn't live without.

During the ceremony, she'd loved how sweet and gentle he'd been. Tonight, she loved his demanding passion as he slid the old key into the lock and roughly opened the door, kicking it shut behind them.

Despite the need she could feel rumbling through every inch of her husband, he lowered her feet to the ground with infinite care. Every inch of her body that pressed against his ached for more.

"This is the most beautiful dress I've ever seen," he told her in a voice made raw with emotion. "The only reason I'm not going to rip it off you tonight is so that our daughter can wear it one day."

"I've gotten much better with a needle and thread this week. I can stitch it back together."

His eyes flared with heat, but instead of tearing the fabric from her in one swift move, he gently turned her in his arms so that her back was to him. The brush of his fingertips across her spine and shoulders as he lifted her dark hair away from the long row of small pearl buttons made her shiver.

He slid one of the buttons free. "Beautiful." Another two came loose and he leaned forward to press his lips to the small patch of skin he'd just bared. *"Sei bellissima."*

Mary's breath stuttered in her chest as he worked his way down the row of buttons with steady hands that also teased and caressed. How, she wondered, was she ever going to make it through his wedding-night seduction in one piece?

Finally—*finally!*—he slid the bodice of her dress off over her shoulders, and his large, strong hands stroked her muscles, cherishing every inch of her skin.

Needing more, needing *everything,* Mary shifted her torso and arms so that the dress slipped all the way down to her waist. Groaning against the curve of her neck, Jack immediately slid his hands around to cup her breasts. Arching her head against his shoulder, she turned her face so that their mouths could meet in a heated kiss. Her breasts felt heavy and sensitive against his fingertips until—*thank God*—he was turning her in his arms again with his hands on her hips and dropping his head to her chest to take first one peak, and then the other, into his mouth. Wild, sweet love poured from husband to wife and wife to husband as she arched closer.

Even as his lips worked magic over her breasts, his deft fingertips made short work of the rest of the pearl buttons at her hips, and moments later the beautiful silk-and-lace wedding gown was pooled at her feet.

"Were you—" He ran his hands over her bare hips and then the delicate white garters that held up her silk stockings. He was clearly stunned—and extremely aroused—at the realization that she hadn't been wearing any panties beneath her wedding dress. "You didn't—"

Though they wouldn't be opening their gifts for each other until the following day, Mary had wanted to give herself to Jack as an early present. "Merry Christmas."

He dragged her hard against him at the same moment that he crushed his mouth to hers. And then they were falling back onto the bed and his mouth and hands were seemingly everywhere at once.

Loving words spilled from their lips in a mixture of English and Italian.

"I adore you."

"Ti amo."

"You're mine."

They'd shared their first kiss under the mistletoe.

Wearing only the tiara of mistletoe leaves and berries, Mary reached for Jack and drew him tightly against her as they came together for the first time as husband and wife.

When she woke cradled in his arms hours later, there was a small wrapped box on her pillow. Outside the curtains, moonlight streamed in over them and the cold winter breeze rustled the leaves on the lemon and orange trees in the courtyard beyond their private suite.

Jack shifted them so that the pillows were behind her as he handed her the box. "You gave me your gift earlier. Now it's time for me to give you mine." When she tore at the paper, he laughed and said, "So I was right—that *is* how you open presents."

Mary lifted the top from the box and, when she saw his gift, the tears she'd barely managed to hold at bay all day finally spilled down her cheeks. Lifting the delicate Christmas ornament out of the box, she marveled at the workmanship and artistry that had gone into creating the porcelain angel.

"That day in the diner, when you called me *Angel* for the first time—" She looked up at him through the tears that clung to her eyelashes. "I was already yours."

"And I was yours."

The clock in the square struck midnight as they reached for each other again to start the first new day as husband and wife with heat, passion...and unconditional love.

A love that would last forever.

Epilogue

January

Mary laughed out loud as Jack swung her up into his strong arms on the sidewalk in front of their new home in Palo Alto, a suburb thirty minutes south of the city and five minutes to his new office building in the heart of Silicon Valley. She wound her arms around his neck and marveled, for what had to be the thousandth time, that he was really hers.

"Our new neighbors are probably looking out from behind their curtains wondering about the crazy new couple on the block."

"Crazy in love," he said, before *really* giving the neighbors something to talk about by kissing her passionately.

Breathless by the time he lifted his mouth from hers, it took her a few moments to realize he was carrying her up the front walk. He took the key from her and unlocked the door.

"Ready to move in, Mrs. Sullivan?"

Lord, how she loved him...and it thrilled her to pieces every time she realized she was now a Sullivan, too.

This time she was the one kissing him in full sight of the neighborhood before replying, "Take me home, Jack."

Her heart filled with joy as he carried her over the threshold and into the living room. Slowly, he put her down, making sure her curves slid against his hard muscles in as many places as possible.

"When are the movers coming?" she asked in a voice made husky with the need that just grew stronger every day they were together.

"In an hour."

She was already pulling his shirt up as she said, "That's plenty of time to christen our house properly."

Jack's hands got just as busy stripping off her clothes and they were both nearly naked when he remembered to lock the front door and draw the drapes. As he moved back across the room to her, yet again, Mary was struck by his incredible male beauty. Every time she saw his broad shoulders, rippling abdominal muscles and long, strong legs, she lost a little more of her self-control.

A beat before he reached her, she leaped on him, wrapping her arms and legs around him. He responded by lowering her to the soft carpet…and kissing her senseless.

An hour later, when the movers came, they were fully dressed again and giddy as two naughty children who had gotten away with sneaking into the cookie jar. Mary directed the placement of the furniture while Jack supervised the unpacking of his home office so that it very closely resembled the old garage he and his partners had worked out of for so long.

After the movers left, Mary and Jack walked hand in hand out through the French doors to the backyard. He gathered her against his chest. “One day, I’m going to build a tree house with our children in that big oak.”

She leaned her head against his shoulder as she looked up at the sky through the leaves. “And we can have Sunday lunch under the shade of the branches, just like my mother used to put on every weekend when I was a child.”

It no longer hurt to think about Italy, and Jack loved

to hear her tell stories in Italian as he became more and more fluent in her native language. But though she'd loved rediscovering her childhood town during Christmas, she knew she was exactly where she was supposed to be.

Mary Sullivan was finally home.

February

Jack had been making Valentine's Day plans for weeks. As soon as Mary woke, there would not only be dozens of roses waiting for her in every room of the house, but he'd also have a plate of piping-hot heart-shaped pancakes ready to serve to her in bed. They'd follow that up with a leisurely boat trip up the Bay into San Francisco, where they'd have dinner at a swanky restaurant and then close out the night dancing.

He was going to give her a perfect—and memorable—Valentine's Day.

Jack was wrist deep in pancake batter when the phone rang. He quickly snatched it up before it could wake Mary. Five minutes later, he was cursing as he hung up. Somehow the roses he'd ordered had been delivered to the wrong house, and the woman who'd received them had been so overjoyed that her husband had begged the delivery guy to pretend he'd brought them to the right house. The florist promised to bring Jack and Mary's roses soon…that was, if they could locate another supply of them.

A beat later, the rain that had been threatening all night long started coming down, along with a harsh wind. So much for the romantic boat ride. Neither of them would enjoy turning green around the gills.

Okay, so he'd make sure to serve her the best pancakes in the world and then he'd improvise the rest.

Fifteen minutes and a dozen inedible pancakes later—*why the heck wouldn't the darned batter cooperate?*—Mary walked into the kitchen.

Her eyes went wide at the unexpected—and enormous—mess. "Jack, if you were hungry, you could have woken me up to make you pancakes."

"I was going to surprise you with breakfast in bed for Valentine's Day." He pulled one of the awful things from the frying pan and held it up.

His wife always took his breath away, but never more than when she was gazing at him with such love in her eyes.

"Oh, Jack, they're shaped like hearts. That's so sweet."

Frustration at all of his grand plans giving way to disaster had him blurting out in full detail just how wrong the morning—and his plans for the rest of the day—had already gone.

Mary threw back her head and laughed. "What a spectacular mess."

Though he was just starting to see the humor in it himself, he needed her to know the truth. "This was supposed to be the most romantic day of your life."

Still laughing, she drew him close. "Roses and heart-shaped pancakes and boat rides are all wonderful, and I love the care and thought that you put into today, but do you want to know what I find really romantic?"

He could never think straight when she was in his arms, and it took all the focus he could muster up to answer, "Tell me, Angel."

"First, there's the way you bring me coffee in the morning."

He reminded her, "It's cold before you can even take your first sip because I can't keep my hands off you long enough to let you drink it hot."

"See what I mean? Very romantic," she said as she nuzzled closer. "And then there's the way you always give me the best seat at the movies and have them douse the popcorn with butter and salt because you know it's my favorite guilty pleasure...apart from you." She gently brushed his hair out of his eyes. "I love the way you always hold my hand when we go for a walk, and how you look at me like you can't believe I'm yours. And then there's the fact that every single day we've spent together has been the most romantic day of my life."

"I love you."

"I love you, too." She went up on her tiptoes to kiss him, and, a breath before her lips met his, she whispered, "Happy Valentine's Day."

March

Sales of the Pocket Planner had been spectacular during the Christmas holiday and had kept climbing from there. While the press was still interested in Mary and Jack's fairy-tale love story, lately they'd been even more interested in what his next brilliant invention would be.

Mary loved watching his brain work as he focused intently in his office. Despite his heavy workload, he'd been a wonderfully devoted husband. Still, in the past two months she'd learned that a little seduction could be a very valuable way to help Jack's synapses click back into gear when he got stuck on a problem.

She was nearly on his lap by the time he looked up and noticed her. For a moment, his eyes remained unfocused, then quickly turned dark and heated with desire.

"Just what I needed," he murmured as he tugged her onto his lap. "Beautiful inspiration."

Her short, silky robe slipped open as she wrapped her arms around him. He traced the swell of her breasts with his fingertip. "So pretty." He leaned in to the curve of her neck and breathed her in. "So sweet." He pressed his lips to her earlobe. "So soft."

Mary had come into his office to tempt and tease Jack for a few minutes…but within seconds, he was the one seducing her.

She'd never known husbands and wives could continue to have such naughty sex, but as Jack stripped her robe away completely, lifted her up onto his desk and entered her with one perfect thrust, she quickly—and blissfully—learned otherwise.

"Now, that," he said as he gathered her close a while later and carried her into their bedroom to continue the seduction started in his office, "is the perfect way to end a workday."

She pulled him down with her onto the bed and agreed, "Absolutely perfect."

April

The teddy bear was squashed between Jack and Max as the two men hugged. "Congratulations, Max."

After Mary congratulated Max, as well, Jack's brother said, "I can't wait for the two of you to meet my new little boy." He looked both exhausted and ecstatic as he took them back into the maternity ward.

As soon as they walked into Claudia's room, Ian immediately bounded off the bed and into Jack's arms. "I'm a big brother."

Jack gave the little boy a smacking kiss on his cute mouth. "Congratulations, Mr. Incredible."

Ian held his arms out for Mary next. "Baby Adam is little."

"Yes," Mary said as she cuddled him, "and he's perfect, just like his big brother."

Claudia was glowing with happiness. "I'm so glad you're both here. We all are."

"We wouldn't have missed it," Jack told her. When Max had called with the news that Claudia was in labor,

Allen had offered them his private jet for the flight from San Francisco to Seattle.

Claudia held out the newborn for Jack to cradle, and Adam gazed up at him with big eyes.

"He's an old soul, isn't he?"

His sister-in-law nodded as Max settled beside her on the bed and she leaned against him. "That's why we decided his middle name should be Jack."

Mary brushed a gentle fingertip across the baby's cheek, wonder in her eyes. "Adam Jack Sullivan," she whispered, "you're a very lucky boy to be born into this extraordinary family."

Ian tugged her long, dark hair to get her attention. "Me, too! I'm a lucky boy, too!"

"We all are," Jack agreed.

Ethan burst through the door with a flustered—and obviously enamored—nurse hot on his heels.

"I'm sorry, but there are too many of you in here now," she tried to protest. But when he gave her one of his lady-killer smiles and said, "Please," she simply turned beet-red and fled.

"I hear there's a new Sullivan." Ethan held up a bottle of champagne in each hand. "Time to celebrate!"

May

"Can I open my eyes yet?" Mary asked as Jack helped her out of the car. She knew they were going to be spending the weekend in Lake Tahoe, but he'd asked her to close her eyes a few minutes ago so that their final destination at the lake would be a surprise.

"Soon," he promised.

His deep voice sent the blood racing through her veins. With her eyes closed, she was deliciously aware of the feel of his palm against hers and his clean, masculine scent.

After she'd taken about twenty steps, he said, "Go ahead, open your eyes. Happy birthday, Angel."

They were standing just at the edge of the lake on a private bay full of pine trees. All of the winter snow had melted by late May and the lake was a crystal clear blue. The blue jays were chirping and the sun was making sparkles dance all across the surface of the water.

"What a beautiful spot." When she turned to give him a kiss, she noticed he had a picnic basket in his hand. The crowds of famous actors and models with whom she'd celebrated her birthdays in previous years had nothing on a quiet picnic in the Tahoe pines with her husband. "Thank you for bringing me here."

After they were settled on a soft blanket, he said, "I'm thinking we should build the cabin right in this spot."

She almost dropped the glass of wine he'd just handed her. "Build a cabin? Here?"

His beautiful grin stole her breath, even before he said, "It's ours, Mary. Every last tree and pinecone and grain of sand."

Jack knew she didn't need expensive gifts or extravagant gestures to prove how much he loved her. Just as she knew he didn't need any of that from her. But sometimes, she decided as she put down her glass, then pulled him closer for a *very* passionate thank-you kiss, extravagant—and decadent—was exactly right.

June

"I know you'll love California, Mama. Please come stay with us for a while." Jack moved behind Mary to massage her shoulders as she listened to her mother's stubborn refusal to get on an airplane for a visit to the United States. Barely holding back her sigh, Mary said, "Give Papa my love." When she hung up the phone, she let the sigh go. "I tried, but she won't leave home even for a week."

Clearly sensing her frustration, Jack pressed a kiss to the top of her head. "I loved the time we spent in Italy over the holidays. How about you show me how different your town looks in the summer?"

Hope leaped in Mary's chest even as she said, "But your workload with the new product line—"

"Can wait."

A few days later, Jack got to show off just how far his Italian language skills had come as he directed the driver from the airport to Rosciano. Six months ago, Mary had been frightened and wary during this trip. Now she couldn't wait to see everyone again.

She flew out of the cab and into her mother's arms, where she stayed for a long while. Finally, her mother drew back and took a long look at her.

"Love has made you even more beautiful, *tesoro.*"

"I'm happy, Mama." Mary instinctively reached for Jack's hand. "So happy."

"Good," her mother said, then gave a pointed glance at Mary's still-flat stomach, "but a baby will make you even happier."

That evening, after the moon had risen, the air was warm as Mary and Jack climbed hand in hand to the top of a hill high above town.

"Your mother was quite eloquent today as she explained how I can be a truly good son-in-law by providing her with many strong grandsons and beautiful granddaughters. Although," he said with a grin, "she speaks pretty quickly and my Italian still needs work, so I may have filled in the blanks with some ideas of my own."

Mary had to laugh at her mother's new focus. Now that she'd had the Christmas wedding she'd always dreamed of for her daughter, Lucia Ferrer was ready for her next big dream to come true: grandchildren. Maybe, just maybe, Mary hoped, a newborn baby would convince her mother to finally make the trip to California.

"I can't wait to hear what the two of you came up with," she said.

At which point Jack brushed the hair away from one ear and began to whisper his own incredibly naughty plans for the two of them…in perfect Italian.

July

Jack always felt like a kid again on his birthday. For weeks beforehand, whenever he talked about the big day, Mary smiled in a secretive way and zipped her lips shut with her fingers. Or, if she'd been on the phone with his mother and he'd walked into the room, she'd abruptly say goodbye and hang up.

"You're planning something for my birthday, aren't you?" he'd asked.

"Yes," she'd replied, instead of denying it, "your mother was telling me how to make your favorite cake."

He tried to get the other details out of her in the best way he knew how, but even his seductive powers of persuasion couldn't get her to spill the beans.

Finally, on the morning of his birthday, she gave him the tickets to Sears Point Raceway in Sonoma, a world-class track only ninety minutes from their house.

Most people were surprised when they found out about Jack's love of race cars but not Mary. She'd simply nodded as if the final puzzle piece was slipping into place, saying, "I always knew there was something dangerous about you."

Jack loved everything about the racetrack. The smell of fresh burning rubber in the hot summer sun. The thrill of watching the cars zip by in the blink of an eye. The amazing skill of the drivers going more than two hundred miles an hour.

He'd never thought to share his love of racing with his wife, but as soon as she'd given him the tickets, he found out she'd practically grown up at the Italian Grand Prix with her father, who had taught her to love the sport.

"Speed. Danger. The thrill of victory." She was clearly as excited as he was to get to the track. "What's not to love about it?"

He was walking proudly with his beautiful wife past the gates into the stands when Mary surprised him yet again by steering them in the opposite direction.

"You didn't think *watching* the race was going to be your birthday surprise, did you?"

Wait a minute. Mary couldn't have possibly arranged for him to—

"Mary! It's been too long."

One of racing's greats, Alvin Rusker, gave Mary a kiss on each cheek.

"I'd like to introduce my husband, Jack Sullivan. Jack, this is Alvin."

"Ah," Alvin said as they shook hands, "so you're the lucky man who managed to steal Mary's heart." He grinned at Jack. "Ready to get behind the wheel?"

"Surprise!" Mary said, clearly thrilled with herself for having managed to keep him in the dark about her amazing gift.

Jack barely stopped himself from jumping up and

down like a little boy. But before he gave Alvin his answer, Jack had to pull his wife into his arms to kiss her breathless.

Finally, he turned back to Alvin. "Now I'm ready."

The track was fast, the car even faster. Every last one of Jack's boyhood dreams came true as he took lap after lap in one of Alvin's race cars.

It was the best birthday he'd ever had. One full of speed. Danger.

And the thrill of being in love with the most incredible woman he'd ever known.

August

Mary handed Yvette, Susan and Janeen thick towels to wrap up in during their break out on the beach in San Francisco. "You are doing a fantastic job today. I'm very proud of all of you."

The girls beamed at her. "Thanks, Mary. And thanks for thinking of us for this commercial." Janeen was the most excited of all of them as she said, "I can't believe I'm going to be on TV!"

Georgina called Mary over to take a look at some of the film they'd shot. "How's this look, boss?"

Mary grinned after she looked the film over. "Fantastic, as always."

"Well, the way you directed the girls a few minutes ago in the surf was great. This is going to be a top-notch commercial. I take it you're enjoying consulting with the ad agency?"

"It's been a really nice challenge," Mary told her friend. "At first I wondered if I was in over my head, but Jack kept reminding me of the times when I was hired to model and the ad agencies ended up using my conceptual ideas instead of sticking to the storyboards."

"You definitely married the right guy," Georgina said. Her eyes lit up as she spotted something over Mary's shoulders. "He's not too hard on the eyes, either."

Mary turned, surprised to see Jack walking across the sand toward them. After the secrecy of their courtship, Mary loved the way he always kissed her hello now, no matter where they were or who they were with.

Her knees were weak by the time he turned to smile at Georgina.

The director gave him a mock glare. "You're not here to distract my advertising genius, are you, Jack?"

He grinned unrepentantly but promised, "If you let me stay on set, I'll sit in the background and won't cause any trouble."

Of course, when Yvette, Susan and Janeen saw him, they all gathered around for hugs and to pepper him with their recent dating and career news. Mary loved how he'd become so much of a father figure to them.

"Nothing but trouble," Georgina muttered as she tried to hide her grin, clearly as deep under his spell as the rest of them. "Back to work, everyone, before we lose the light. And you," she said, pointing at Jack, "sit over there and be good. Or else."

After dragging Mary against him for one more kiss, he left the commercial set they'd constructed on the beach that morning.

It took her a few moments for her synapses to start firing properly again. "I'm ready whenever you are," she said to Georgina.

But, instead of getting right back to business, her friend put a hand on her arm. "I'm happy for you, Mary."

Mary could still feel Jack's kiss tingling on her lips and his loving gaze on her as she told Georgina, "I am, too. Happier than I ever thought I could be."

September

"Do you ever think about what would have happened if we hadn't met each other last December?"

They were taking a late-evening stroll on the paths through the marshlands near their home. While Jack greatly enjoyed the surprises they gave each other and the many exciting moments they shared together, it was everyday moments like this that he loved best.

Her hand was in his and the sun was still quite high in the summer night sky as he replied, "No, I've never wondered that."

Mary turned to him in obvious surprise. "You haven't?"

He smiled at his wife, thinking how amazing it was that she grew more beautiful by the day. Love, more than one of their friends had remarked in the past nine months, had given her an even brighter glow than she'd already possessed.

"We were meant to be together. And whether we had met last Christmas or ten years from now, I would have still loved you. Truthfully," he added as he tugged her into his arms, "the only thing I'm wondering is how long it will take us to get back home and get you into bed."

"Did you know I was the fastest girl on my track team?" She gave him a quick kiss before taking off, running in the direction of their house at a quick clip.

Jack chased after her, laughing—and loving her more and more—every step of the way.

October

Mary and Jack stood at the top of a hill in Napa Valley and looked out over the rolling vineyards. The crush was just starting and the air was perfumed with the scent of grapes.

"Growing up in Italy, the local winery owners would let us in to crush grapes with our feet in barrels. And then they'd pour the juice into cups for us to drink afterward." She laughed as she looked down at her feet and added, "Unfortunately, I'm not sure how many of us thought to wash our feet before getting into the barrels."

Jack loved hearing her speak about her childhood. Rosciano was in the heart of the Abruzzo wine region of Italy, and when a friend of his who owned a winery in Napa suggested they come up for the weekend to be a part of the crush celebrations, Jack had known Mary would love it.

"What do you think about chucking it all in and opening up Sullivan Winery?"

"Maybe one day," she said as they headed down the hill toward the winery buildings. "But for now I'm rather partial to our life just the way it is."

His friend David waved them over when they got to the stone-walled barn. "Up for crushing some grapes?" He pointed to a barrel full of grapes. "If you are, hop in."

Jack grinned at Mary. "What do you say you show me how it's done?"

She was clearly thrilled with the plan as she kicked off her heels. After she took off her stockings and he rolled up his pants and both of them quickly washed their feet, they got into the barrel, laughing as the grapes squashed beneath their toes. They were quickly covered in juice, not just their feet but their legs and clothes, as well.

He would never get enough of the sound of her laughter or the taste of her kiss. And later, as they sat out under the night sky and sipped the juice they'd made together, followed by one of his friend's vintages, Jack made a wish on the stars above.

His wish was that the children he and Mary would have together one day would also find a love this deep and true for themselves.

November

The Sullivans had agreed to gather together at Mary and Jack's house for Thanksgiving. Max and Claudia arrived first with Ian and Adam, and Mary was amazed by how much both boys had grown. Ian immediately ran into the backyard to play, and Mary scooped up Adam into her arms, where he happily settled while Jack poured his brother and sister-in-law drinks.

Mary was holding the baby on one hip when she answered the door to find Ethan on the doorstep.

"Hey, beautiful," he said in his typical flirtatious way. "You look good with the kid. When are you and Jack going to start popping them out?"

Mary was laughing as she gave him a kiss hello. "You sound just like my mother. No wonder she adored you so much when she met you at our wedding."

"All those pretty Italian girls," he said with a wistful look. "I really should get back to Rosciano soon."

"Let me know when you're done flirting with my wife," Jack called out to Ethan, "and I'll get you a drink."

Mary was about to close the door when a shiny black limousine pulled up. Finally, she was going to meet William Sullivan. Every time she and Jack made plans to see him, his trips to San Francisco had been rerouted to other cities at the last second. Mary sympathized, as her travel schedule had once been just as hectic.

As he emerged from the vehicle, she noted that he was just as good-looking as his brothers, but unlike Jack, Max and Ethan, she couldn't read William's expression. She knew he was an artist, a very talented one, but even Jack seemed to find his brother a bit of a mystery.

"You must be Mary."

She held out her hand. "It's lovely to finally meet you."

His gaze softened as he stroked a hand over Adam's soft, dark hair and Mary finally saw there was more than a physical resemblance between William and his three brothers.

Howie, Larry and Layla arrived a few minutes later and helped fill the house with laughter and love. And when they all sat down a short while later to the huge spread of food, Mary wished both her parents and Jack's could have been with them, too.

Hands down, it was the best Thanksgiving she'd ever had.

Mary had so much to be thankful for. Jack's love. A relationship with her parents that was better than ever.

Being a part of the amazing Sullivan family. Her flourishing career.

And, just maybe, if her suspicions were correct, she and Jack would soon have even more to be thankful for....

December

"Happy anniversary, Angel."

Jack and his brothers had finished building the Lake Tahoe cabin a few weeks earlier, and tonight Mary and Jack were lying tangled around each other on the soft rug in front of their new river-rock fireplace.

Mary felt so warm and safe with her head cradled against Jack's chest listening to his heart beating steady and strong. Normally, she would have stayed right where she was. But she had a surprise for Jack that she just couldn't wait another moment to give him.

When she got up, his heated gaze followed her every step as she took something from the bags they'd dropped just inside the front door and then returned to kneel in front of him.

She held out a small wrapped package, but instead of opening it, he stroked his hand over her cheek.

"I love you."

"I love you, too."

A moment later, he pulled back the red-and-green wrapping paper and uncovered the beautiful ornament inside. It was a handcrafted clay Christmas tree, with Mary's and Jack's names together at the top. Off the edge of each of the branches along each side of the miniature tree was room for additional names to be added.

"If our first child is a boy, I'd like to name him Marcus after my father. And if it's a girl—"

Jack interrupted before she could finish speaking. "Are you pregnant?"

"We're going to have a baby, Jack."

"I thought last Christmas was the best I'd ever have," he said in a reverent voice as he pulled her close and laid one hand over her stomach, "but you've made every day better than the one that came before it."

Together they rose to hang the new ornament on the tree next to the angel he'd given her last year on their first Christmas together.

One year ago, both Mary and Jack had been looking for a Christmas miracle, but they'd given each other so much more than either of them could ever have dreamed of having.

"Look," he said as he pointed up to the ceiling. "Mistletoe."

And as Mary and Jack Sullivan kissed beneath the sprig of mistletoe, both of them knew there were many more miracles to come....

Present Day

Glancing down, with tears in her eyes, Mary looked at the two Christmas ornaments sitting in her lap, which were more precious to her than anything else she owned.

From that first Sullivan Christmas through all the Sullivan Christmases that followed, these two small ornaments represented the deep and true love between her and Jack. She felt so incredibly blessed by the exciting life she'd led, the children who made every single day a delight...and most of all, loving, and being loved by, Jack Sullivan.

The sounds of happy voices coming up the walk brought Mary from her memories. Wiping her damp eyes with her fingertips, she stood up and carefully placed the two ornaments on the tree.

Looking up, she whispered, "I love you, Jack."

When she opened the door, her family was standing in the fresh snow smiling at her. Marcus and Nicola were standing on the front steps with Chase and Chloe. Gabe, Megan and Summer were coming up the path laden down with brightly wrapped gifts.

"Merry Christmas," they all said as they kissed and hugged her, and then began to pile into the cabin.

It was time for another Sullivan Christmas to begin.

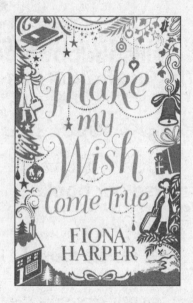